"You have a prob... Miss Rutledge,"

Cam said. "Why didn't you defend yourself?"

She faced him squarely. "I did."

"Really?" he drawled. "So what would you have done if I hadn't stepped in to save you?"

She eyed him. "Save me? I had everything under control."

"Lady, you've got a lot to learn. A friendly piece of advice, Miss Rutledge—protect and fight for your territorial rights all the time or these test pilots are going to eat you up alive."

Shaken, Molly replied, "Captain, you obviously want me to be just as arrogant and aggressive as the guys in my class. Well, I won't. I'm a woman and I respect my ability to handle situations in a different way. With tact, diplomacy and care."

An incredible urge to reach out and thread his fingers through her silky hair struck him. The feeling caught him off guard, and he snapped, "Then don't expect me to come to your rescue next time. Good night, Ensign Rutledge."

Dear Reader,

Welcome to Silhouette **Special Edition**...welcome to romance. Each month, Silhouette **Special Edition** publishes six novels with you in mind—stories of love and life, tales that you can identify with—romance with that little ''something special'' added in.

And this month is no exception to the rule—June 1991 brings *The Gauntlet* by Lindsay McKenna—the next thrilling WOMEN OF GLORY tale. Don't miss this story, or *Under Fire,* coming in July.

And to round out June, stories by Marie Ferrarella, Elizabeth Bevarly, Gina Ferris, Pat Warren and Sarah Temple are coming your way.

In each Silhouette **Special Edition,** we're dedicated to bringing you the romances that you dream about—the type of stories that delight as well as bring a tear to the eye. And that's what Silhouette **Special Edition** is all about—special books by special authors for special readers!

I hope that you enjoy this book and all the stories to come.

Sincerely,

Tara Gavin
Senior Editor

LINDSAY McKENNA
The Gauntlet

Silhouette Special Edition

Published by Silhouette Books New York

America's Publisher of Contemporary Romance

To Robert Langford,
internationally known sculptor and carver;
Ursula Langford, his wonderful wife;
Donna Jo Wagner, a dear friend;
Anne Parsons, my editor; and Leslie Kazanjian.
I count all of you as friends and
thank you for your help, guidance and love.

SILHOUETTE BOOKS
300 East 42nd St., New York, N.Y. 10017

THE GAUNTLET

Copyright © 1991 by Lindsay McKenna

ISBN: 0-373-09673-9

First Silhouette Books printing June 1991

Books by Lindsay McKenna

LINDSAY McKENNA

spent three years serving her country as a meteorologist in the U.S. Navy, so much of her knowledge about the military people and practices featured in her novels comes from direct experience. In addition, she spends a great deal of time researching each book, whether it be at the Pentagon or at military bases, extensively interviewing key personnel. She views the military as her second family and hopes that her novels will help dispel the "unfeeling-machine" image that haunts it, allowing readers glimpses of the flesh-and-blood people who comprise the services.

Lindsay is also a pilot. She and her husband of fifteen years, both avid rock hounds and hikers, live in Ohio.

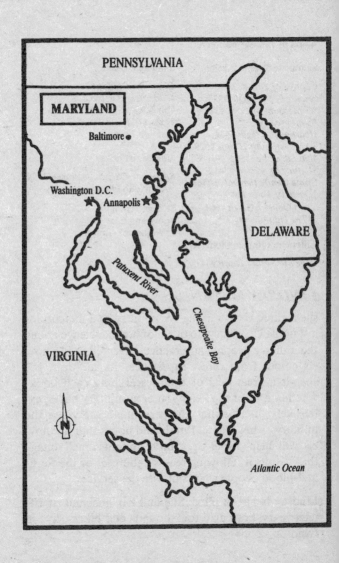

Chapter One

"How could you do this to me, Molly?" Jason Rutledge demanded. "My only daughter fails Navy flight school!"

Molly stood uncertainly before her father in the den of her parent's spacious, richly appointed, New York City penthouse. She felt heat flame up her neck into her cheeks, and inwardly chastised herself for blushing. At twenty-three, she wished she'd outgrown such girlish reactions.

Her father, standing rigidly behind his desk, was a lean, spare sixty-year-old with steel-gray hair and steel-rimmed glasses. Scott, her brother, sitting nearby in his motorized wheelchair, was a younger, much less harsh version of the older man. Molly's stomach knotted as her parent glared at her, his blue eyes narrowed. "Father—"

Jason gestured irritably to the left. "You graduated from Annapolis with honors, Molly, and won the right to go to Navy flight school. So few are chosen for it. Foreign countries send their best and brightest to train there. And you failed, Molly. You failed. What about Scott? You've let your brother down, too. You promised both of us you'd do your best to win your wings.''

Molly opened her mouth, then shut it. Having just driven to New York from Whiting Field near Pensacola, Florida, she was physically and emotionally exhausted. For six weeks she'd trained at Whiting, trying to make the grade at the toughest flight school in the world. She hadn't attained the level of flight skills necessary to receive her wings. All the way home, she'd tried to prepare herself for this confrontation; but to no avail. Since her mother's death thirteen years ago, her father had run their family with an ironclad hand. Molly longed to see some sign of softening in her father's set, demanding features, but found none. Scott was hanging his head, staring disinterestedly at his hands clasped in his lap.

Pacing back and forth behind his huge maple desk, neatly stacked with files, Jason shook his head. ''All my—I mean, our—hopes were pinned on you. I was an ace in the Navy during Korea! Your grandfather was in the Navy during World War II, and was also an ace. He even earned the Navy Cross.''

''I know that.'' Unable to hold her father's incisive glare, Molly stared down at her simple leather shoes.

''If Scott hadn't had the accident he'd have gone on to Annapolis instead of you. He would have gotten his wings.''

Hurt, more than anger, stirred in Molly's heart. Licking her lips, she whispered, ''Father, I did the best I could for both of you. I'm sorry, truly I am. I gave it all I had.'' She shrugged, her voice softening. ''I just don't have what it takes in the cockpit. My instructor said I'd make an excellent commercial pilot, but not a fighter pilot."

With a snort, Jason crossed to the bar and poured himself a Scotch on the rocks. "We supported you all the way through Annapolis. Weekly letters from Scott. Phone calls from both of us. My God, short of flying for you, Molly, we couldn't have done more. We couldn't get the wings *for* you!" He took a hefty gulp of the Scotch and shook his head.

The hurt in Molly's chest widened. She had dreaded coming home for her thirty-day leave before her next assignment. Lifting her chin, she tried to smile but failed terribly.

"I've been assigned to the Navy test pilot facility at Patuxent River, Maryland, to train to become a flight engineer. Do you know how many Annapolis graduates want that plum? Maggie and Dana both agree that working on testing planes is just as respectable a vocation as being a pilot." Her best friends, whom she'd met at and gone through Annapolis with, were still at Whiting Field, finishing flight school.

"Good God, Molly! Hasn't four years at Annapolis done anything for you? Navy pilots are recognized as the best in the world. Being a flight engineer is like being the bridesmaid."

Frowning, Molly held her father's gaze. "I disagree with you. My grades were excellent, Father. Not everyone gets a shot at testing. I think I can do it."

"You thought you could get your wings, too," Jason pointed out angrily. He set his glass on the desk with a sharp bang. "What makes you think test-pilot school is going to be any easier, Molly?"

"Well, I don't—"

"Damn right, it won't be. It will be ten times harder! Everybody and their brother wants to test planes, to be a 'Golden Arm.' Out of all those jet jocks, only a handful make it to that level of skill. If you thought flight school was tough, believe me, young lady, think again about Patuxent River. They wash out nearly everyone—only ten percent graduate."

Molly glanced over at Scott, who was watching her silently, accusation in his green eyes. She sighed. "All I can do is try, Father."

"Besides," Jason went on as if he hadn't heard her, "the test pilots are the stars. Flight engineers never get the glory."

"It's my understanding that the flight engineer *is* the test," Molly gritted out. "The flight engineer makes up the program that the pilot uses to test the aircraft. No engineer—no test. I think that's pretty important."

"But the world only recognizes test pilots—not the shadows behind the scenes!"

"Besides," Scott added dejectedly, "my friends don't know anything about flight engineers. They all know about test pilots."

"Then," Molly said with forced lightness, "I guess you'll learn a lot about what I do in the letters I write to you, Scott, and educate your friends in the process."

Glumly Scott muttered, "I guess.... But it's not the same, Molly."

An ache threaded through Molly, so deep that she could only stand in the thick silence as both men studied her. She tried to remember what Maggie had told her: do the best you can, with no apologies. There is no failure if you try. Still, Molly couldn't help but say, "I'm sorry I disappointed both of you. I promise I'll do better at Patuxent River."

Jason Rutledge sat down, holding his Scotch between his hands. "Retrieve our honor, Molly. My associates at the stock-brokerage firm couldn't believe you were washed out of flight training. You don't realize the embarrassment it caused me to admit that my daughter didn't make the grade. At least let me give them good news that you're making it as a test-flight engineer at your new station."

Molly knew suddenly that she would never endure thirty days at home with her father and brother. "If it's all right with you, Father, I'm going to leave in about a week for Lexington Park. It's a town right outside the gates of Patuxent River. I'll have to find an apartment and get moved in."

"Fine." He glanced over at her. "Do you need money?"

"No, sir."

"Are you sure?"

"Very sure."

With a sour face Jason muttered, "I'm a millionaire twenty times over, but money can't buy me the one thing I wanted most for this family: an heir to carry on our Navy-pilot tradition."

Knowing that every emotion registered on her face, Molly turned away, drained. No amount of "I'm sorrys" would make her father let go of his disappointment at her failure to get her wings. She left the den as quietly as she had come, and climbed the stairs to the second floor of the penthouse.

At the top of the steps, Molly hesitated, peeking into Scott's room. Her father had had an elevator installed to make it easy for him to move from floor to floor by wheelchair. *Top Gun* posters hung on the walls. So did posters of the F-14 Tomcat, the Navy's premier fighter.

The F/A-18 Hornet, another Navy fighter, was promi-
nently displayed on the wall above Scott's bed. Plastic
models of all the modern-day airplanes cluttered his
bookshelves. Molly felt sorry for their housekeeper,
Emma Sanders, having to dust and pick up everything
her brother left littered about the room.

Molly opened the door to her bedroom. Once inside,
she stopped, feeling an immediate sense of comfort and
security. The walls were papered with pale-pink and white
flowers. Moving to her bed, she picked up her doll,
Amanda. When her mother, Corrine May Rutledge—
daughter of a very rich banking family—had died of
cancer, Molly had spent hours on her bed, crying for her
loss. Only Amanda, a rag doll whose painted face was
nearly worn off from years of loving, had offered any
solace.

Smiling gently, Molly barely touched Amanda's gold
yarn hair. "How many of my tears did you soak up over
the years, Mandy?" When Molly was nine years old, her
mother had bought Amanda for her as a birthday gift
because the doll had blond hair and green eyes like
Molly's.

Life had become harsh and demanding after her
mother's death. Her father, who had always run his
stock-brokerage house like a military machine, had
brought that strict, cold order home. Molly remembered
sobbing alone at night, longing for her mother's warming embrace, kisses and gentleness.

Who would have thought that Molly Rutledge would
turn out to be an Annapolis graduate? It still surprised
Molly to think about it. She shook her head and placed
Amanda back against the bed pillows.

Turning around in the middle of the room, she
breathed in the past she'd left behind four-and-a-half

years ago. It was a soft room in comparison to the harsh conditions she'd endured at Annapolis. Her china tea set was arranged on one shelf; several other dolls that shared the loneliness of this huge penthouse with her sat on another. Everything in the room shouted femininity, not militarism.

With a slight quirk of her lips, Molly pulled her suitcase up on the bed and began to unpack. In the eyes of her family, she was an utter failure. The only way to redeem herself was to become a test-flight engineer. Had she jumped from the frying pan of flight school into the fire of test school?

Her hands shook slightly as she slid her folded lingerie into a dresser drawer. Somehow she had to make her father and Scott proud of her again. After stowing the empty suitcase under her bed, Molly took a shower. Changing into a pair of dark gray slacks and a light peach-colored sweater afterward, she was ready to face her family for dinner.

Just as she reached for the doorknob, a knock sounded. The door swung open to reveal Scott sitting in the hallway.

"Dinner's on, Molly."

"Thanks, Scott." She picked up a hand-painted silk floral scarf and tied it into a loose knot around her neck.

Scott's hands rested on the wheels of his chair. "Father's really upset. No one feels like eating."

"Life goes on, Scott. I've already apologized. If this funereal atmosphere is going to continue for the next week, I'll leave sooner."

"Oh . . . no. You promised to tell me all about Whiting Field. Your letters are one thing, but hearing the stories in person is best." Scott forced a smile. "Come on, you can go down in the elevator with me."

Molly nodded and waited patiently while Scott turned his wheelchair around on the hardwood floor and headed toward the elevator at the other end. "At twenty-five, I'd think you'd have other things to occupy you than waiting for my stories," she told him dryly.

Moving his wheelchair into the spacious elevator, Scott shrugged. "Father has given up on me becoming a stockbroker. It just isn't for me."

Molly pressed the button that closed the brass and glass door, and laughed for the first time since her arrival home. It felt good to discuss something other than her failure as a pilot. "Knowing Father, he doesn't want to turn his company over to us or anyone. Not that I'd want it. I'm not cut out for the barracuda halls of stockbrokering."

"Roger that."

Molly smiled. For as long as she could remember, Scott had wanted to fly and become a Navy pilot—a life plan preordained by her father since Scott's birth. Scott would go to Annapolis, graduate and become a pilot like the other men of the Rutledge family. An auto wreck two weeks before he was to leave for Maryland had paralyzed him from the waist down. As an afterthought, Jason Rutledge had pushed Molly into the appointment. She'd gone willingly, wanting to uphold the family honor.

The doors whooshed open to the first-floor hallway, and Molly followed Scott out of the elevator. As always, the highly polished oak floors and the expensive oil paintings lining the walls, made the place look more like a museum than a home.

"Scott, haven't you found anything that interests you yet?"

"Your continuing saga in the Navy is what interests me, Molly. I really enjoy your letters. You're a great chronicler. I read and reread them, and then I call my friends and relay your stories."

Molly winced. She ached for Scott, who still felt guilty over having driven that fateful night. The accident wouldn't have happened if Scott hadn't been drunk. Luckily, he was the only one who'd been hurt.

She patted her brother on the shoulder and said, "I still think you ought to get interested in something other than my less-than-glorious naval career," she teased.

"Naw. You're the highlight of my life, Molly. You know that."

Molly's fingers tightened momentarily on Scott's shoulder. Her thoughts moved ahead, to entering the test-pilot school's doors, in spite of her apprehension at potentially failing her family again. But Molly dreaded her stay with her family. Her new training program couldn't come a moment too soon.

Dressed in his olive-green flight suit—his favorite uniform because it was loose and comfortable—Captain Cameron Sinclair sat at his desk muddling through the stack of mandatory paperwork that always materialized when a new class of students started TPS. He glanced out the window of his office.

The June morning was beautiful at 0800. Cam had been at work for two hours already. Frowning, he laid down his pen and thought of his wife, Jeanne, and their son, Sean. Even now, he remembered the exact number of days, hours and minutes since they'd died. One year. Twelve of the worst months of his life. Picking up the pen, he ran his fingers absently along its smooth lines.

Depression had become a familiar friend. He knew fellow instructors called him "the Glacier" behind his back. But why should he smile and joke when it was the last thing he felt like doing? They had loved ones to go home to every night, while his apartment was huge and empty. As empty as his heart felt.

The parking lot was to the left of his office, and Cam noticed a tall, slender woman getting out of a gray station wagon. She was wearing a light blue Navy summer-uniform skirt and blouse. He lifted his chin, interested, the pressure on his heart lessening slightly. It had to be their woman student, Ensign Molly Rutledge.

Cam watched her leave the parking lot and make her way up the sidewalk to the doors of TPS. His office sat just to the left of the doors, so he had an unobstructed view of her progress.

The sun filtered through her loose blond hair, which glinted with gold highlights. She was decidedly feminine, Cam thought. She wore her garrison cap at an angle, her bangs pushed to one side to allow it to sit on her brow. Cam was struck by the serenity of her face, and unexpectedly, the cabin in the Smoky Mountains where he used to spend time with his family came to mind.

Her eyes were green, like the light of the sun shining through the leaves of trees along the trails they used to hike. Or were they gold and blue, reminding him of the sun high in the sky? Cam couldn't be sure. He'd have to get a much closer look. One thing, he thought, taking a deep breath, Molly Rutledge was pretty in a clean-cut sense. Her face was smooth and nearly symmetrical. Her blond brows were slightly arched, emphasizing her wide, alert eyes. Her nose was small and straight.

Cam shook himself. As a test pilot, he was used to making minute observations. Now he was taking Molly apart with the same sort of appraisal, but he wasn't retaining his usual objectivity. He hadn't felt anything since his family's death, so why was his heart thundering in his chest? As she drew closer, Cam saw that despite her regulation low black heels, Molly's legs looked slender. His eyes narrowed in appreciation.

When his gaze settled on her mouth, he felt himself tighten in physical reaction. Her lips were delicately shaped, as if by a master artist. Cam found himself wanting to reach out and touch that soft, gentle mouth to see if it was real or just a figment of his fevered imagination.

Whenever a new class arrived at TPS, Cam secretly labeled each student with a name that embodied that person in his mind. And using that intuition, he was usually correct about who would and who would not graduate. Molly was tall, like a reed giving and bending in the wind. She was all grace and femininity. None of those attributes would serve her well at TPS, he thought sadly. What was needed was bullheadedness, strength, endurance and plenty of machismo.

Unable to tear his gaze away, Cam shook his head as she approached the door, her black purse hanging from her left shoulder and her records in her right hand. "You're a gossamer angel ready to enter hell," he muttered. "This place chews men up and destroys them on a regular basis."

His words sank into the silence of his office as he watched Molly disappear inside the doors. A part of him wanted to jump up and go meet her in the foyer. She'd be looking for the commandant's office, and he could point it out to her. Suddenly the need to meet Molly Rutledge ate at him, and, startled, Cam digested the unexpected feelings. Was he alive, after all?

The discovery was pulverizing to Cam, and he sat there, absorbing the fact of his reawakening emotions. He heard voices in the hall beside his office. *Her* voice.

It was muted, so he couldn't make out the exact conversation. Stymied, he shook his head. Cam was a test-pilot instructor; Molly would be assigned to First Lieutenant Vic Norton, the flight-engineer instructor.

"Lucky bastard," Cam said to no one in particular, and looked back down at the work on his desk.

So what name would he give *her?* "Angel" was certainly appropriate: soft, gentle and serene. Molly floated, she didn't walk; there was such grace in her movements. Muttering to himself, Cam grimaced. How had she stolen into his work? Okay, so he'd call her Angel. She'd never know it, and certainly no one else would.

Cam sighed. A sad smile shadowed his features. Angels wouldn't make the grade at TPS. It would be a mere matter of weeks before pretty Molly Rutledge would be politely asked to leave. As Cam forced himself to mind his own business, his heart still twinged at the thought of the brutal demands that would be placed upon his angel.

Chapter Two

"So, you're the woman we've all heard about."

Molly turned on her heel at the grate of words flung in her direction. She stared up into the dark features of a tall Navy officer, his sandy hair cut short. Molly stepped back from his overpowering presence. He stood glaring down at her, his hands resting imperiously on his hips while he sized her up. In his flight uniform adorned with patches from his F-14 Tomcat fighter squadron, he was all warrior.

"Yes, I'm Molly Rutledge."

"*Ensign* Rutledge," he sneered, not offering his hand. "The name's Martin. *Lieutenant* Chuck Martin. I'm a TPS candidate. When I got here yesterday and they told me a broad was going to try and make it through as a flight-test engineer, I thought they were joking." His brows dipped. "Are you serious about this? A man could've had your slot."

Molly stood in the hall, her books in hand. She'd just finished seeing the commandant and was on her way to the women's locker room at the other end of the building. Martin was hovering over her like a furious eagle who'd had his territory threatened. She smiled coolly.

"I didn't 'take' any man's slot, Lieutenant. I earned it."

With a snort, Martin said, "I wonder how."

Molly had heard this kind of comment often enough to know he meant that she had slept her way to TPS. Her lips thinned. "Mr. Martin, I resent the implication."

"What implication?" He grinned suddenly, feigning ignorance. Then his smile disappeared. "Let's get one thing straight between us, Rutledge. I've got to fly with flight-engineer students. If I have to fly with you, my grades will be lower because you're a woman. There's no way in hell I'm getting kicked out of TPS because I have to fly with a woman."

Bridling, Molly kept her voice low and neutral. "You're out of line, Mr. Martin."

"No, the Navy is—for allowing a woman here in the first place."

Molly saw an office door on her left quietly open. A tall, lean pilot emerged, resting his shoulder against the doorjamb and idly watching them. Who was he? An instructor? Another student? Her attention was divided between Martin and the other pilot. The other man's pale blue eyes held her captive—probing, merciless eyes that made Molly feel as if he saw within her to her most secret parts. Shifting her gaze back to Martin, she said, "My right to be here will be decided by how I conduct myself as a student. Grades will tell the full story, Mr. Martin."

"Just stay out of my way, Ensign. You'd better hope like hell we don't get assigned to work together. I don't want my grades brought down because of you."

"I'm responsible for my grades, not yours," Molly shot back. Her gaze darted to the officer in the doorway. Why was he eavesdropping on their embarrassing conversation? Molly was sickened. TPS was going to be like Whiting Field all over again: she'd have to prove herself through hard work and long hours of study.

Martin grimaced, allowing his hands to drop from his hips. He settled the garrison cap on his head. "Later, Rutledge. Just stay away from me in class and hope you and I don't get assigned to each other."

Molly watched Martin swagger past her and out the doors of the building. When she turned around, the door to the office was closed, the officer gone. Disgruntled, feeling the pressure tripled within her, Molly continued down the hall toward the women's locker room. Who was the mystery man in the office doorway?

She couldn't shake the memory of his eyes: light blue with huge black pupils that seemed able to pierce her heart and look directly into her soul. Dark brown brows lay slightly arched across his assessing, critical eyes. His square-jawed face was spare looking, and had been emotionless. Martin's attack hadn't rattled her half as much as that officer's sudden and unexpected appearance had.

In the locker room, Molly stowed her helmet and oxygen mask above the gray metal cabinet. She hung one of her olive-green flight uniforms and her flight boots in the locker itself—soon she would be flying at least once a week. Her equipment stored, she knew she had until 0900, when the candidates would meet to be briefed on what would be expected from them. Her hands damp, her heart beating in fear, Molly forced herself to leave the safety of the small locker room and head directly to the classroom on the second floor where the meeting was scheduled to take place.

Molly knew from long practice to walk in on an all-male class as if she owned the place. She was grateful for the four years of experience Annapolis had provided, because as she opened the door, fourteen male stares met her. A blond-haired lieutenant nearest her smiled and thrust out his hand.

"You've gotta be Molly Rutledge. I'm Leland Bard, hoping to become a flight engineer, too."

Bard's infectious smile was just what she needed, and Molly shifted her load of books to her left arm to shake his hand. "Hi, Leland."

"My friends call me Lee."

"Great. Call me Molly."

He gestured toward two desks. "Have a seat. I guess the festivities will be getting underway shortly."

Relief was sweet for Molly. She had a friend already, and it helped break the ice. Before, Dana and Maggie had been like bookends, protecting her. There was something to be said for the Sisterhood, if only for providing companionship in very exclusive all-male surroundings.

Lee sat down, stretching out his short legs in front of him. "You weren't what I expected."

Molly slid into the desk next to him and neatly stacked her books under it. "Oh?" She opened her notebook, her pen ready. Soon the commandant and instructors would file in and be introduced. Then the students would be assigned to them.

"I was expecting some hard-charging, gung-ho ring knocker to make an entrance."

She grinned, noticing the volume of conversation in the room was getting back to what it had been before she entered. She saw Martin on the other side of the room with a small, tightly knit group of what she was sure were pilots. His scowl had deepened upon her arrival. Devoting her attention to Bard, who appeared to be in his late twenties, Molly said, "I'm hard on myself, not others."

"In this place, that'll count. I understand there are eight flight-engineer students and eight test-pilot candidates. You realize only four from each group will make the grade?"

"Makes me nervous."

With a sigh, Lee nodded. "I got here a couple of days ago. My wife found an apartment in Lexington Park for me and our two kids. Housing's at a premium around here."

Molly agreed. Without her considerable monthly allowance from her father, she couldn't have afforded the apartment she'd rented. "It's rough."

"Gonna get rougher." Lee leaned toward her, his head cocked but his gaze roving around the bantering student groups. "I think we're lucky."

"Why?"

"There's a Marine Corps captain here by the name of Cam Sinclair—a TPS instructor. They call him 'the Glacier.' I guess he's been here two years and is a hard-nosed bastard, failing sixty-five percent of the pilots he instructs."

"Sounds like Lieutenant Griff Turcotte," Molly said, thinking of Dana's flight instructor at Whiting Field. She explained her comment to Lee.

"Well—" Lee chuckled after hearing about Turcotte "—we can thank our lucky stars we don't have Sinclair. They say his face is made of granite. He never smiles, cracks a joke or does much of anything except stare you down. Ice in his veins in the cockpit and ice on the ground. Guess that's why he's a Marine—they drain the blood out of them during their swearing-in ceremony. Then they inject them with Marine Corps juice or something. At least, that's what I've heard," he said with a smile.

Molly smiled in return, and the image of the officer leaning against his doorjamb came to mind. His face had been utterly devoid of expression. Even Griff Turcotte, as much of a bastard as he'd been to Dana, was human, his feelings readable on his face. "I'm finding in this business that jet jocks hide a lot under that mask they wear."

"Yeah, but Sinclair's reputation is awesome. I mean, what happened to the guy to make him like that? Frankly, I'm glad we don't have to interface with him much." Lee grinned. "We just have to contend with these jet jocks who think they're the greatest."

"From what I hear," Molly said, "we're the power behind the scenes. The tests we design are the ones that make or break the whole thing. All those jocks do is drive the bus."

Tittering, Lee replied, "Don't let those boys overhear that comment, Molly.... Heads up—here come the instructors. Time to get this dog-and-pony show on the road."

The small groups of students quickly took seats, and silence fell over the room as six officers dressed in flight suits filed in, somber expressions on their faces. In the second row, Molly was close enough to read the black leather patches sewn above the left breast pocket of each flight suit. Each instructor's name was stenciled there in gold lettering.

The last man to enter was the one she recognized from earlier. There was a tight, coiled explosiveness to the way the officer walked; an internal tension was reflected in each of his brisk movements. Curiosity ate at Molly, and she quickly scanned the instructors' name tags.

Her heart thudded once, underscoring her intuition. The last pilot was Cameron Sinclair, "the Glacier." Those ruthless, roving, light blue eyes looked over the crop of students almost with disdain, she thought. Lee was right: the instructor's face was absolutely expressionless.

But she would rely on her own internal radar, a special intuitive ability she'd had since birth, to make her final decision about Sinclair. She thought of Maggie's contention that all women had this ability—something special passed on to them in their genes. If Molly ignored the obvious and allowed herself to experience the energy that surrounded Sinclair, she felt no fear of him, only compassion. Why? Her left brain, that portion of her that used only logic, was stymied.

The instructors sat down in chairs facing the students. As the commandant got up to speak at the podium and introduce each instructor, Molly zeroed in on Sinclair. Once he'd perused the group, his eyes became unfocused, looking above the group at the wall behind them, as if he had mentally checked out, wasn't really here at all, Molly noted. She sensed sadness around him. It wasn't anything more specific than that. His eyes were opaque, hiding any feelings he might be experiencing. His generous mouth was flexed into a tight line, the corners drawn in, as if he were in pain.

Pain? Confused, Molly knew Sinclair had to be in top physical shape or he'd never be here at TPS. It couldn't be physical pain. Her heartbeat suspended itself when

Sinclair slowly turned his head and pinned his gaze directly on her. Heat swept up Molly's face, and she quickly averted her eyes, nervous as she'd never been before. Had he sensed her perusal of him? He must have! Sinclair might be stone-faced, but his own intuition was very much up and functioning to feel her inspection of him so immediately.

Cam scowled, his focus remaining fixed on Molly Rutledge. Somehow he'd felt her gaze on him. When he'd shifted his eyes from the wall to where she sat, a sweet ribbon of discovery had flowed through him when he realized she had the most beautiful green eyes he'd ever seen. They were distinctly green and gold, like summer leaves kissed by sunlight. How intelligent and compassionate she appeared to be, he reflected, as her eyes widened when he caught her staring.

Disgruntled by his own thoughts, Cam wondered how he could really "know" that about Molly. Molly... Now he was calling her by her first name. Snorting softly, Cam pulled his gaze away from her. She had looked down quickly to avoid his stare, and Cam couldn't resist looking at her one more time. Her cheeks were stained a flaming pink, her delicious mouth was compressed. There was such softness and openness to Molly that Cam continued to stare at her like a starving man. What the hell had gotten into him? Other women officers worked at TPS in various billets. He didn't stare at them like a slavering wolf on the prowl.

When she licked her lower lip with her tongue, Cam groaned inwardly. It was such a sensual motion. Did she do it on purpose, knowing somehow that he was still watching her? No, Cam decided sourly; Molly Rutledge didn't possess that kind of guile. Besides, Martin's accusation that she'd slept her way into TPS was sheer stupidity on the student's part. No one got to TPS without damn good grades and top qualifications.

Molly wasn't the "type" to be at TPS, Cam decided finally. He knew that someday a woman would succeed at the male-dominated bastion that was TPS. Brutally honest with himself, as he'd always been, he admitted he'd expected a more assertive type of woman to beat down the door, not this angel face. How Molly would survive here was beyond Cam. And the way she'd handled the confrontation with Martin had been all wrong. She should have nailed him right between the running lights with equally harsh words, so Martin would respect her and back off. As it was, Molly was inviting another attack.

Well, she would have to learn to protect herself. Flight testing was a world that involved brash egos, keen intelligence and plenty of macho hustle. If she indeed had what it took, then that soft exterior was either a lie hiding a shark beneath it, or a facade to throw everyone off about her true strengths. Still, as Cam sat there waiting to be introduced and give his five-minute spiel, he wondered what Molly Rutledge really was made of. It wouldn't take long to find out—TPS began in earnest tomorrow morning. From that point on, every student was in a life-or-death struggle to come out on top of the stack. Second place would never do.

Refusing to look up at the instructors, Molly could feel Sinclair's cool, continuous appraisal of her. He was the last to speak, and she felt it safe to lift her chin and look at him then. His carriage was proud, his spine ramrod straight, his shoulders thrown back, shouting a justifiable self-confidence. As he wrapped his long fingers around the lectern and shifted his weight to one booted foot, Molly had her first opportunity to fearlessly study Sinclair.

She didn't listen to his words as much as their inflection, the emotion behind them. There wasn't much of that, she admitted. As Lee had said, he appeared to be a machine with no heart. Molly didn't want to believe that about anyone. Still, Sinclair never cracked a joke, as the other instructors had, to put the students at ease. Nor did he smile. He was the only Marine Corps pilot up there; the rest were U.S. Navy personnel. Maybe it had something to do with interservice rivalry among the branches. The Marine Corps was a branch of the Navy and paid by the Navy. Molly smiled. No self-respecting Marine wanted to admit it; they were far too independent and arrogant to acknowledge that fact.

After the welcome-aboard speeches, it was time to meet her instructor. Molly liked First Lieutenant Vic Norton. One of two flight-engineer instructors, he was short and compact, with curly black hair and a round face that was sober looking, yet friendly.

As Molly prepared to leave the room after a round of introductions with her fellow flight-engineer students, she felt an odd sensation. Turning her head, she saw Sinclair's blue gaze locked on her, even though he was standing with a group of aspiring test pilots clear across the room. Sudden heat threaded through her, shakiness following in its wake. No man had ever had such a powerful effect on her.

Turning, she bumped into Lee. Her books went flying. All conversation in the room halted. Molly died inwardly.

"I'm sorry," she whispered to Lee, and crouched down to retrieve her books. When feeling particularly vulnerable, Molly had a terrible tendency to become clumsy.

She flushed with embarrassment as Lee bent over to help. "My fault, Molly."

"No, it was me," she murmured. All eyes were on her, and Molly tried to blot them out. What must Sinclair think of her? Did she realize how much he'd shaken her up? He probably thought she was a brainless idiot. And why did she care what he thought anyway?

Lee restacked the books into her arms and Molly quietly thanked him. Gradually the noise level in the room returned to normal, and she retreated as quickly as possible. The library was on the second floor, and that was where she wanted to be—alone. Lieutenant Norton had given them a huge reading assignment to prepare them for tomorrow morning's class, and she wanted to take advantage of the extra time. The library would be a perfect place to read. At least there, she could escape Sinclair's scathing blue gaze.

"Hey, Cam, take a look at this." Vic Norton handed him a thick file marked Rutledge, M.

Cam took the folder, gesturing for Vic to have a seat in his office. The flight engineer shut the door. "What's this?"

"The lady's file. Man, it knocked my socks off. Now I know why she got assigned to TPS. Take a look."

It was normal procedure for Cam to acquaint himself with all the students' files. He tried to tell himself he hadn't particularly been looking forward to reading up on Molly. Opening the file, he quickly scanned the important data. His brows rose.

"She got washed out of flight school?"

"Yeah. Hung in for six weeks and then got deep-sixed. Still, the IP's evaluation shows she's got good aptitude, if she wanted to leave the service and go for a commercial pilot's license. I think I've got a pretty good prospect in her."

Frowning, Cam continued to page through her file. "You really think so?"

"Yeah, why?"

"She's a cream puff, Vic."

"Oh?"

"Look at her face."

"Good-looking as hell."

Cam glanced over at his friend. "Is that all you swabbies have on the brain—sex?"

Grinning, Vic shrugged. "Hey, I'm happily married, but that doesn't mean I don't still appreciate women. And Rutledge is definitely worth appreciating."

Cam read some of her bio. "Comes from a well-to-do background."

"More like a silver spoon, I'd say. Her father owns one of the hottest brokerage firms in the Big Apple. She's got his genes. I'll bet beneath that sweet face of hers is a real hustler. Those jet jocks think she's soft, too, but my money's on her to fool every last one of them."

"She's had it easy," Cam remarked, handing the folder back to Vic. He wanted to hold on to it, but it would have appeared unusual. "It's my experience that people who've had it easy don't make it when the chips are down. I don't think that face is skin-deep. She's soft."

"Naw, I think you're wrong." Vic grinned and tapped the folder against his knee. "I overheard one of your students bitching about her."

"Martin, by any chance?"

"Yeah. He's already bad-mouthing her to the other pilots."

Frowning, Cam rubbed his jaw. "I saw him nail her in the hall. I'm his instructor."

"He's going to have to learn to keep his mouth shut, and if he's got a problem, go to you."

"Hmm." Martin was one of those jet jocks who contended women were worthless—except in bed.

"Glad he's your problem and not mine," Vic said airily, rising. "Eat your heart out, Sinclair. I think Rutledge is gonna make the grade."

Cam shook his head. "Never." After all, his just looking at her in the classroom had made her drop her books, he thought. After Vic left, Cam sighed. For some damned reason, he couldn't get enough of looking at Molly Rutledge. Why was he so drawn to her? Looking at his watch, he saw it was 1700. Time to eat. He wasn't really hungry—he'd lost twenty pounds after the death of his family. The paperwork on his desk begged to be done. He'd go over to the restaurant on the base, get a take-out order and go to the TPS library. That was his place to hide. No phone to answer, no people dropping in unexpectedly to disrupt him. He could finally get his work done.

Molly's stomach growled ominously. The library, small and intimate, was empty. She'd gotten interested in one of her textbooks on software programming, and time had gotten away from her. Looking at her watch, she realized it was 1730. Her back was to the library entrance, and she heard the door open and close. Her scalp prickled and she twisted around in her chair to see who had come in.

Her heart dropped hard in her chest. It was Cameron Sinclair. He stood, a scowl working its way across his broad brow. In one hand he held a sack of food, in the other an armful of files.

"You."

Molly blinked at the whispered word. Said as a curse? Searching his hard, unyielding face, she wasn't sure. His pale eyes pinned her, and she felt like quarry.

"I . . . uh, is the library off-limits after 1700, Captain?" She'd already screwed up, judging by the dark look on his features. Maybe at night the library was for instructors' use only. She rose suddenly, her thigh brushing the desk, and two of its four legs jerked off the carpeted floor.

Her books went flying, sailing gracefully across the aisle to thud like small explosions into the row of library shelves.

Cam watched the unfolding events in disbelief. Molly had jumped up, almost toppling over the desk. Her hands flew to her cheeks as she stood watching her books fly. To compound the error, she stepped back, almost falling over her chair, which didn't slide well against the carpeted floor. His own hands full, Cam was helpless to do anything but watch. Molly caught her balance, but the chair tipped over backward, crashing to the floor. Cam's heart wrenched in his chest as he saw her eyes fill with utter embarrassment.

"Klutz," she said apologetically, kneeling down in front of the shelves. "I've always been a klutz, Captain. I'm sorry. Libraries are supposed to be quiet."

Cam sensed something sad in Molly's apology. He set his sack and files on another desk. Her gold hair swung effortlessly, like a curtain, hiding her bright-red features, and Cam found himself wanting to reassure her that her very human reaction to him wasn't bad or wrong.

"You don't need to apologize." God, he sounded hard and unforgiving. The thought was validated when she twisted a look up at him, her blond bangs thick and barely touching her brows, a panicked look on her face. Groaning to himself, Cam felt pulled into the shadowed worry of her now dark green eyes.

"My father always says when I get nervous I'm like an elephant in a china shop," Molly offered breathlessly, reclaiming her books and stacking them back on her desk. As she leaned down to retrieve her pen and notebook, her hip caught the desk's corner.

"Ouch!" Molly bit back the rest of her retort, dolefully rubbing her aching hip, sure a bruise would appear shortly.

Tucking her lower lip between her teeth, she avoided Sinclair's searching gaze. Before she could bend down again, he was there, picking up her pen and notebook. Molly stared at his hand. His knuckles were large, the fingers long. Pilot's hands. Strong, guiding hands. Forcing herself to look up, she expected accusation from him and tried to prepare herself emotionally for his censure.

"Here, take these before you do any more damage to yourself."

Oddly, his eyes weren't hard-looking any longer. Molly reached out, her fingers brushing his. The sensation of contact was sharp and warm. "I— Thanks, Captain."

"First days are always nerve-racking." Cam suddenly felt nervous, almost shy, about being in her presence. How could that be? He had more questions about his unexpected reaction to Molly Rutledge than he'd ever had about any woman in his life.

Gripping the notebook, Molly nodded and managed a slight smile. "The last couple of months have been all of that and more," she admitted wryly.

"You always drop things when you're in a clinch?"

His voice was hard again. Molly nodded. "I thought
when I grew up, I'd leave the bumping and running into
things behind. I guess I'm a born klutz."

Her honesty unstrung him. Cam stared down at Molly,
noticing every nuance. Her blond hair was fine, reminding him of spun sunlight. The lashes framing her eyes
were long and curly. She wore no makeup, yet her lovely
sculptured lips were cherry red. Her skin was flawless and
velvety. The urge to reach out and brush her fiery-colored
cheek was very real. Cam ruthlessly squashed the idiotic
yearning.

Abruptly he turned away. "I've got work to do," he
informed her gruffly. "And to answer your question, the
library is open to everyone. It's not considered off-limits
to students at any time." Molly Rutledge was, indeed, a
cream puff. And—God help him—he felt protective of
her. What would happen when Martin or another of the
test-pilot students blamed her for his poor grades? How
could she possibly stand up to the withering cross fire that
took place in a flight debriefing?

Feeling as if she'd proved to Sinclair that she was a
loser, Molly turned and went back to her desk. As quietly
as possible, she packed her books into her huge black
leather briefcase and prepared to leave. Sinclair seemed
to want to be alone, she thought. She felt like an in-
truder in his space, his territory. Dejectedly, Molly
walked to the door.

"Good night, Captain Sinclair," she said softly.

Cam looked up, her contralto voice moving through
him like a warm memory of happier times, of times he
knew would never again come into his life. "Good night,
Ensign Rutledge."

With a small sigh, Molly left. Outside in the hall, she
stopped and took a deep breath. She'd felt eviscerated by

his opaque gaze. She *was* a klutz, incapable of being calm and in control during a critical situation. Would Sinclair talk about her to the other instructors? Would they get a good laugh out of her clownlike antics in the classroom and library? Turning, she walked down the empty hall, no longer hungry, just sorely disappointed with herself.

Chapter Three

Molly was in the computer room, working on her very first flight test at one of the many terminals. Lieutenant Norton wasted no time getting his students busy programming. The large room had a tile floor, blue walls and overhead fluorescent lights that bothered Molly's eyes. Every chance she got, she took the ream of papers spewed out by the printer into the library and worked on her budding flight test there, instead.

Without fail, TPS closed at 2100 every night. Only the instructors had keys to the massive facility. Once students left, they couldn't reenter the building until 0600 the next morning when the instructor on duty reopened it. A number of other flight-engineering students shared the computer room with Molly, working laboriously at their terminals until 1700, chow time.

Left alone, Molly worked through dinner, time slipping away from her. It was Thursday, and she knew that test-pilot students would be assigned to them. Molly only hoped Chuck Martin wouldn't be assigned to her. Obviously he hated her with a passion. Every time he saw her in the hall or in an adjacent classroom, he'd glare ominously. Not wanting to feed the flames of animosity, Molly refused to react at all.

The glass door to the computer room opened and closed. Molly sat at the terminal desk, calculator in hand, rerunning her mathematical figures to compute with the variable of the F-14 Tomcat fighter, which would be utilized in her particular test. It was a simple test in her estimation, getting her used to folding in knowledge of aerodynamics with edge-of-the-envelope testing on this particular aircraft. All Norton wanted from her was a series of high-altitude climbs, leveling off the plane and utilizing degrees of climb.

"Rutledge?"

Molly cringed inwardly. She'd recognize Martin's grating voice anywhere. Lifting her head, she saw his angry features shadowed under the harsh lighting. He stood imperiously, hands on his hips, while he glared down at her.

"Yes, Lieutenant Martin?"

"You see the pair-up list?"

Molly hesitated. "You mean who we fly with?"

"Hell, yes. *That* list, Rutledge!"

"Lieutenant, there's no need to shout. Obviously, you're upset about something."

His nostrils flaring, Martin jabbed his finger in her direction. "Damn straight, I am. You're assigned to *me* for the first test flight on Wednesday."

Molly saw the door open, and Cam Sinclair silently enter the room. Her lips parted, and she looked between the two men. Cam stood just inside the door, poised and listening. Evidently, Martin hadn't noticed his entrance. "I don't make up the schedule, Lieutenant Martin," Molly said without rancor.

"You're the last person I want to fly with, Rutledge. You're a woman. You can't possibly have a handle on testing." He gestured violently toward the printout sheets surrounding her. "Paper chase, that's all you're playing, and at my expense. Within a month, you'll be out of here. You aren't qualified to be a flight engineer in any way, shape or form. The whole damn thing's a sham, and I'm gonna pay for it!"

Cam's eyes narrowed as he heard the anger in Martin's lowered voice. His glance flicked to Molly. All week, he'd tried avoiding her. It had been nearly impossible. Curious how she would handle Martin's second attack, Cam stood quietly, his arms folded across his chest. Molly knew he was there. Would she alert Martin? If she were smart, she wouldn't. Let Martin tip his hand. Still, Molly ought to be standing up and defending herself better. Sitting at the desk, her blond hair in mild disarray, she looked like a college ingenue, not an engineer.

"Lieutenant, I'm sorry you feel that way," Molly stated quietly.

"My *career* hinges on you!" Martin exploded in exasperation. "You don't get it, do you? Hell, you can get knocked up, have a kid and get out. Me, I've gotta stick around. Flying is my whole life. You see this as some kind of game that can be played while it's easy, knowing you can walk away from it any time you damn well please."

Molly saw Sinclair's face remain passive. Wasn't he going to interfere? And then she realized he wasn't, because this was her fight. "I can assure you, Lieutenant, the Navy is my career, too," Molly said determinedly. "I just survived four years at Annapolis on my own merits. And as for getting pregnant and asking for a medical discharge, that's not in my plans. I'm here because I want to be a good flight engineer. Why can't we throw down the red flag and be friends? We're bound to work together sooner or later.''

''Yeah, well, I guess it's sooner. Someone at TPS has got it in for me. I suppose you went to your 'significant other' and complained, and that's why I got it in the neck with this flight assignment.''

Molly refused to get angry. ''I don't have a 'significant other' here at TPS, Lieutenant,'' she said coolly. ''Now, if you'll excuse me, I've got work to do—and so do you.''

Martin cursed and his hand snaked out. He gripped her shoulder.

Molly flinched, feeling his fingers dig deeply into her. She opened her mouth to protest, but out of the corner of her eye, she saw Sinclair react instantly.

''Martin,'' Cam whispered tautly, coming up behind him, ''I suggest you get your hand off Ensign Rutledge. *Right now.*'' What was the idiot going to do? Take a swing at her? Cam took a step back and tensed, almost expecting Martin to turn and punch him. The pilot's face was livid when he whirled around. When he saw who it was, he looked startled.

''Captain Sinclair...''

''What were you going to do, Martin?''

''Er, nothing, sir.'' Martin backed away and shrugged weakly. ''We...uh, were just talking.''

His tone lethal, Cam said, ''Let's get a couple of things ironed out here and now, Martin. Ensign Rutledge has the finest academic record of *all* the students in this class, pilot or engineer. Got that?''

Martin jerked his head in a nod.

"Second, she has a degree in aeronautical engineering. Do you?"

"No, sir—"

"Third, the commandant makes out the flight schedule weekly. You will be flying with every test engineer a number of times, including Ensign Rutledge. Now, I suggest that if you've got a problem with the assignment, you talk to him directly."

Martin took another step back, pale. "Yes, sir."

"Dismissed, Martin."

Molly cringed at the iciness of Sinclair's voice. A chill worked its way up her spine. He'd positioned himself near her chair, facing off with Martin.

"Yes, sir!" Martin spun on his heel and left promptly.

Molly released a breath of air, giving Cam a grateful look. "Thank you, Captain."

Cam stared at her. He saw the turmoil in her huge green eyes. Yet her voice was unruffled—soft, without any indication of how troubled she was by Martin's attack. And an attack was what it had been. "You have a problem, Miss Rutledge."

Molly blinked belatedly. "Problem?"

"Why didn't you defend yourself?"

Sinclair was pulverizingly male in a way that shook her. Molly turned around in her chair, facing him squarely. "I did."

Cam shook his head. "That's twice Martin's attacked you."

"He's upset, that's all."

"And you weren't?"

"Of course, but—"

"What's it take to get you to raise your voice and really defend yourself?"

Shocked, Molly stared at him for a long, painful minute. "Captain, just because I'm not one of 'the boys' and don't choose to act in an aggressive manner doesn't mean I can't defend myself."

"Really?" Cam drawled. "What were you going to do when Martin grabbed you by the shoulder? Sweetly ask him to let go?"

"I suppose you think my retaliation should have been a fist in his face?"

Cam nearly smiled. Nearly. So, she had some spunk, after all. "That would have been against regulations."

"I'm glad one of you macho jet jocks thought of that."

His mouth twitched. For the first time, Cam felt like laughing. It was a breathless discovery. Molly Rutledge sat there with that spun-gold hair, in her rumpled olive-green flight uniform and black boots, looking positively beautiful and defiant.

"So, what would you have done if I hadn't stepped in to save you?"

Molly eyed him. "Save me? I had everything under control, Captain. Sooner or later, Lieutenant Martin would have eased off the throttle. I wasn't giving him a reason for further aggression."

Cam shook his head. "Lady, you've got a lot to learn here at TPS. Don't you understand that flight engineers have to defend themselves at all times? You're responsible for the test that's flown. A pilot can make your test look good or bad. And many times it's hard to prove who's at fault. Believe me, in the debriefing room after the flight, I see the test-pilot students trying to blame the engineer's flight program for their poor performances."

"I know pilots don't always fly well, Captain. They have bad days, too."

"A friendly piece of advice, Miss Rutledge—protect and fight for your territorial rights at all times, or these student test-pilots will eat you alive. You'll get blamed for flight failures whether they're your fault or not, and your grades will drop."

Shaken, Molly pursed her lips. "Captain, you obviously want me to get a good dose of male hormones into my bloodstream so I can be just as arrogant and aggressive as the guys I'm in class with. Well, I won't. I'm a woman, and I respect my ability to handle situations in a different way."

"I'm not saying you've got to turn into a man. Just speak up for yourself—get feisty. You're capable of that, aren't you?"

He was taunting her now. Molly hated the feeling Sinclair was invoking. "I will not turn to cursing or pushy and aggressive tactics to win my point. I'll use logic and diplomacy."

If nothing else, Cam thought as he watched her, she was stubborn. "Logic and diplomacy get blown to hell in those debriefings, Ensign. For your sake, you'd better get a little spunk and assertiveness, if you're hoping to stand the heat in that kitchen with those jocks."

Smarting beneath his assessment of her, Molly turned around in her chair. "Excuse me, Captain, but I've got work to do. Thank you for your advice, but I feel strongly about handling situations with tact, diplomacy and care."

An incredible urge to reach out and thread his fingers through her loose, silky hair struck Cam. He shook his head, wondering what had come over him. The feeling caught him off guard, and he snapped at her. "Then don't expect me to come to your rescue next time. Good night, Ensign Rutledge."

"Good night." Unhappily, Molly watched Cam turn away, leaving her alone in the huge computer facility. She fought the awful feeling of failure. She'd felt this way after washing out of flight school. Wasn't there anything she could do right? Pressing her hand to her brow, she closed her eyes, the sting of tears behind her lids.

Cam hesitated at the glass door, watching Molly press her hand against her eyes. Feeling like a first-class heel, he almost went back in to comfort her. No, he couldn't do that. Still, his conscience gnawed at him. He shouldn't have been so hard on her. Martin had done enough damage without Cam hitting her broadside with another salvo from another direction.

Dammit! He stood, torn, watching as she sat at the terminal, her hands covering her face. Was she crying? She had every right to do so. Troubled, Cam put his hand on the door handle. As an instructor, he played a dual role with the students. First, he had to terrorize them enough to wring out their best, whatever that was. Second, he had to be a support system for them, to encourage them to surpass what they thought was their best. But he'd just gone in there and terrorized her.

Irritated, Cam let his hand slip off the handle. How had Molly gotten through four years at Annapolis? Surely she'd handled far more harassment and pressure than this. He watched as she lifted her head and rubbed her forehead. Her face was pale, but he didn't see any tears on her cheeks. What kind of woman was she? Molly was a genuine enigma to him. Still, Cam knew without a doubt that they'd shred her in debriefing if she didn't stand up for her programs—logic and diplomacy were the first to go in those heated exchanges.

Muttering to himself, Cam turned away, not wanting her to discover him still standing there. It would be the ultimate embarrassment to her if she spotted him. A huge part of him wanted to stay. Stay and do what? As he shuffled down the hall toward his office, Cam shook his head. Molly interested him. Maybe the word was *fascinated*. She was unlike any woman in the military he'd met or worked with.

"Too soft," he said under his breath. "She's too soft to stand the attacks she's going to have to go through."

Molly tried to dismiss the entire crisis that had taken place, but she couldn't. Her stomach growled, but she wasn't hungry. Glancing at her watch, she saw it was 2100. Time to go home and get some sleep. Unsettled, she logged her software program into the files of the computer and shut down the terminal.

Placing the yards of computer printout in her briefcase, she left the room. As she headed from the elevator to the main doors, she saw Captain Sinclair's office door open, light spilling out into the semidarkened hallway. Hesitating, Molly felt the urge to stop and speak with him. About what? To defend her way of handling situations? He'd made himself perfectly clear about how he thought she should handle them.

It was obvious Sinclair didn't think much of her, either. Leaving TPS, Molly decided to try to call her friends at Whiting Field. She desperately missed Dana and Maggie. Perhaps they could shed some light on her most recent problems.

"I think you should've decked Martin," Maggie Donovan told her, anger in her voice. "That kind of jock only understands one thing, Molly, and that's aggression equal to his own. What he puts out, he gets back."

"I don't agree," Dana Coulter's voice countered from the other phone. "You said Captain Sinclair broke it up?"

"Yes," Molly admitted unhappily. She sat on her couch, her legs folded beneath her, the receiver resting against her hand and shoulder.

"He defended you," Maggie said.

"No, he didn't," Molly countered. "I've already told you his view of the situation. Martin ripped me open, and he just added salt to my wounds."

"I think he was trying to get you to see how you need to change your behavior to fit the circumstances," Dana pointed out. "The fact that he came to your rescue means he's on your side."

"He sure didn't look it. Gosh, gals, Sinclair is like ice all the way through. He could put holes in you with those eyes of his. You should have seen Martin back down. The guy was tripping all over himself, backpedaling."

"Of course." Maggie chuckled. "Martin isn't going to take on his instructor. Martin's smart for gigging you when you were alone. He's trying to make you fail, Molly, before you even get a chance."

"He's a male chauvinist, that's all."

"No," Dana argued passionately. "Martin's more than that, Molly. He's really dangerous to your career. You've got to show more backbone. Maggie's right. That kind of guy only respects an equal response to whatever he throws at you. Sinclair was doing you a favor by telling you how to arm yourself against Martin."

"Well, if that bastard Martin keeps it up," Maggie shot back, "I'd hang a sexual harassment suit on him."

"Sinclair was right there. He heard Martin chewing me out. If there were grounds for it, don't you think he'd do something about it?"

"There is no man alive who's going to stand in your corner on a sexual harassment charge unless you bring it to him in writing," Maggie said vehemently. "Damn, Molly, you can't be laid-back about this. At Annapolis, Dana and I were there to help defend you against goons like Martin. But we aren't there anymore, as much as I wish we were. You *have* to start developing that backbone we both know you have."

"Molly," Dana begged gently, "Maggie's upset at Martin, not you. We know you believe diplomacy and a more passive response can win the day, but sometimes it can't. Take Sinclair's advice. He wasn't out to rub salt in your wounds—only to help bind them in the best way he knew how."

Glumly, Molly nodded. "I don't know what I'm going to do. If my father hears about this, I'll just get another chewing-out. I don't need a third one."

"Hang tough," Dana urged. "Sinclair could be your ace in the hole. If things get bad, go to him. Talk to him. I think he's on your side."

"And if that doesn't work," Maggie added, "deck Martin and tell Sinclair to take a flying leap."

Laughing, Molly thanked her friends. She hung up and remained on the couch, thinking, the afghan tucked around her legs. Her friends *had* protected her at Annapolis, to a large degree. Maggie's fierce confidence made her a guard dog of sorts. And Dana was at her shoulder to back up whatever Maggie put into motion. Between her two friends, no upper or lower classman at Annapolis had wanted to put her at risk.

Picking up her cup of tea, Molly sipped the hot liquid pensively. Dana and Maggie had been her buffer zone against the aggressive male world of the military, it was true. Yet she knew she couldn't handle it the way Maggie did, with equal assertiveness—which was exactly what Sinclair had suggested. And she didn't possess Dana's deadly calm voice and bristling defenses that no man dared test.

Looking around her quiet apartment and seeing the clock on the wall tell her it was midnight, Molly sighed. Tomorrow a letter would arrive from Scott, and he would want to know every detail of her week. On Saturday would come the dreaded phone call from her father, who would wring every nuance of the week's events from her with endless, probing questions. Rubbing her brow, Molly wondered how she was going to tell them about Martin. It was beyond her to think of lying. Perhaps she could avoid telling them.

With a grimace, Molly removed the purple and pink afghan and sat up. Every time she'd tried the ploy of avoiding a topic with her father, he'd ferreted out whatever fact she was trying to hide and made his verbal berating doubly harsh. Molly stood and took the partially filled cup of tea into her modern kitchen. She rinsed out the cup and set it in the dish drainer. How much she missed Dana and Maggie! They'd been such a happy threesome at Whiting Field, their apartment ringing with kidding, laughter and good times, despite the pressures on them.

Looking around, Molly left the kitchen and headed to the huge bathroom to soak in a tub of hot water. To her dismay, her thoughts revolved back to Cam Sinclair. God, but he looked forbidding, yet she was powerfully drawn to him. Why? How? Molly didn't think Dana was right about Sinclair. He seemed to hate her as much as Martin did. So why was she so drawn to him as a man? What chemistry was at work? It was totally illogical.

* * *

Cam tossed restlessly in his bed, the sheet tangled between his long legs. Light from the street invaded the bedroom, filtering through the pale yellow sheers. He glowered at the clock on the monkeypod nightstand. It was midnight. Why the hell did Molly Rutledge's vulnerable face hang in front of his eyes every time he shut them?

His guilt over how he'd handled her earlier had made his whole evening miserable. Miracle, his black Labrador, lifted her head from the braided rug that sat parallel to the bed. Her huge brown eyes glimmered with question. Cam waved his arm in her direction.

"Go back to sleep," he muttered to the dog and turned over, his back toward her. Punching the pillow into the right shape, he lay there, his gaze shifting to the nightstand on the opposite side of the king-size bed. On it were two photos. One was Jeanne dressed in a beautiful orchid gown. The photo had been taken about a year ago, a month before the airliner had crashed, taking her life. Cam stared at it, wanting to feel something . . . anything. Only numbness followed. Since the day of the crash, his feelings had been destroyed.

The other photo was of his five-year-old son, Sean. He had Cam's black hair and his mother's dark brown eyes. Gone. They were both gone. Cam felt Miracle's paw on the edge of his bed.

"Go lie down," he ordered the dog. When Jeanne was alive, they'd go to bed and Miracle would jump up and play with them, bouncing crazily from bed to floor and back. Since Jeanne's death, Cam hadn't allowed the Lab up on the bed.

Miracle whined, pawing impatiently at the mattress.

Cam turned over. His anger melted away. The dog's head was tilted, her eyes lifted to look up into his. Reaching out, he patted Miracle's sleek ebony coat.

"Go lie down, girl. She's gone. Forever." He gently removed Miracle's paw from the bed. "Go on...."

The dog whined softly, wagging her tail in a friendly fashion. Incredible sadness deluged Cam. "There's no more play, pup. No more...."

Miracle lowered her head and turned away, her paws clacking against the hardwood floor as she made her way over to her braided-rug bed. She plunked down, resting her head on her paws, her eyes never leaving his.

Cam grimaced and turned away, unable to stand the grief he saw in the dog's sad gaze. In her own way, Miracle missed Jeanne and Sean as much as he did. Playtime had been every night—a free-for-all of fun, laughter and crazy-kid antics. A soft smile tugged at Cam's mouth as he closed his eyes. Jeanne had been such a child at heart, so spontaneous and filled with life. She saw all that was good in life, while Cam saw the reality of it. Still, he'd looked forward to their playtime, letting Miracle up on the bed. It was silly and childish, but he didn't care. Jeanne had brought out the child in him—his laughter and hope. Now all that was destroyed.

The only thing left of what they'd shared was four-year-old Miracle. Cam knew the dog remembered Jeanne and Sean, remembered better times. She'd loved Sean dearly, had always been watchful of him, always there as a wonderful and protective companion.

But as Cam closed his eyes again, it wasn't Jeanne's or Sean's face that hovered before him. It was Molly Rutledge's serious features, her green eyes mirroring genuine hurt, her mouth pursed to hold back the pain he was sure she'd felt from Martin and his own scathing attack.

This was crazy! He didn't even know her! And yet, as he lay there, Molly haunted him. Just what the hell was it about her that was triggering this ridiculous response? Cam tried to hide from the memory of his urge to go back into the computer room and hold Molly after he'd laced into her. It was her mouth, so delicate and wonderfully shaped, that beckoned to him. And to look into her serene green eyes laced with gold, was to know peace. Peace! Something he'd not felt in the year since his family had been brutally ripped out of his life.

To stare at those sculpted lips was also to acknowledge the heat building almost painfully in his lower body, a strictly carnal hunger that wanted satiation through Molly and no one else. With a groan, Cam pulled the pillow over his head and tried to escape his rampantly wild thoughts and needs. God, he worked with women every day. None of them affected him. Why her? Why soft, slender Molly? She was such a graceful creature among a group of hard, harsh men. Yet, on one level, Cam admired her stubbornness to stick to her guns and be herself, not allowing the situation she lived in to change her convictions. He admired that quiet gutsiness.

The rest of the night held only bits and snatches of light sleep. When dawn came, Cam got up in a foul humor. Miracle, as if sensing his ogreish mood, remained on her braided rug and simply watched him come and go from the master bathroom as he shaved, climbed into his flight suit and then returned to the bed to shut off the clock radio.

Cam went in to the facility early and proceeded directly to the student file drawer that held information on the current students. Locating Molly's file, he tucked it under his arm and walked down the long, empty hall to the coffee room. After starting the coffee, he sat on a plastic chair at one of the tables and opened the file. Maybe by absorbing every bit of information on Molly Rutledge, he'd finally get over whatever was eating him, and he could enjoy a decent night's sleep again.

While the coffeemaker gurgled away, Cam riffled through the file. He started at the back, at the beginning of her naval career. The folder was at least two inches thick, containing her Annapolis years and Whiting Field experience. He dug for something in particular, like Miracle tracking a scent. Every prospective Annapolis student had to fill out a biography: why they wanted to attend the elite school.

"Finally..." he muttered. Frowning, Cam began to read her beautiful handwriting with its feminine flourish. Time slipped away as he continued to read page after page, discovering Molly. There was a four-and-a-half-year-old picture of her, taken at high-school graduation. Cam touched the color photo. Molly's hair had been very long and loose, flowing across her dark blue graduation gown in carefree abandon. She looked hopeful and joyous, her smile warming him even now.

Cam scowled, looking down at Reason For Entering Annapolis. Her brother had originally been scheduled for the academy and had been unexpectedly injured beforehand. Shaking his head, Cam read on. Molly was taking Scott's place? He looked up. The coffee was ready. So, she had volunteered to step into her brother's boots and take his place at the academy.

As he got to his feet, Cam's mind whirled with questions. Did Molly really want to be in the military at all? Had her family forced her into going? Yet, looking at her grades, she was a brilliant aeronautical engineering graduate. She had a nice balance of understanding of

math and mechanics, but hadn't lost her decidedly
feminine side in the process.

"Enigma," he muttered, retrieving a cup of steaming
coffee and sitting back down. He glanced at his watch. It
was 0530. In half an hour, the instructor on duty for the
day would officially open TPS. Running his fingers down
the thickness of her file, Cam decided he'd better read in
a hurry to cram as much information as possible about
Molly into his memory before that happened. He wanted
no one, especially Molly, to know what he'd done. It
wasn't against regs, but it was unusual.

She's an unusual case, he told himself and sipped the
coffee gratefully. Very unusual. And interesting. God,
but she fascinated him! At the same time, Cam worried
for Molly. It was obvious she wasn't cut out for the dog-
eat-dog atmosphere of the military. Here she was at TPS,
one of the toughest, most demanding military schools in
the world. How the hell was she going to survive in this
environment?

Chapter Four

"Well, how did your first flight test go?" Scott wanted to know.

Molly gripped the phone hard, pacing back and forth in front of her couch in the large living room. She'd just gotten home at 1700 when the phone rang. "It went," she said, refusing to lie. If Scott wanted details, he was going to have to ask the questions to drag it out of her.

"What kind of a grade did you get?"

Wincing, Molly sat down and shakily began to unlace her black flight boots. "I got a seventy-five percent."

"Is that good?"

"It wasn't failing."

"What'd the other flight engineers get?"

"The grades went all the way from seventy-five to ninety-five, Scott."

"Jeez, were you at the bottom of the barrel, Molly?"

Pushing the boots to one side, Molly unzipped the lower legs of her suit and tugged the thick white cotton socks from her feet. "Yes, I was last on the list." She tried to laugh. "Look at it this way, Scott—I've got nowhere to go but up."

"Well, did they give you the hardest of the flight tests? Is that why you almost flunked?"

Molly felt a cry deep within her. "Look, Scott, I'm really tired. You're calling me a day early. I need to get supper and then I'm going to hit the books. I've got a lot of studying to do."

"Oh…yeah. Well, I was just real excited, Molly. You said the test was Friday, and I couldn't wait until Saturday to find out how you did."

"Do me a favor?"

"What?"

"Don't tell Dad about my grade just yet, okay? He'll be calling tomorrow, and I'll tell him then."

"Sure, Molly."

"Gotta run, Scott. I love you, and I'll see you later. Bye." Molly hung up the phone as if it were burning her hand. She stared blackly down at it, almost wanting to unplug it from the wall. The thought was tempting, especially under the circumstances. Right now, all Molly wanted was someplace where there wasn't a phone or anyone who wanted a piece of her.

She walked to her bedroom and shed her flight suit to get a quick, hot shower. Lee Bard had told her about the rolling beach at the air station that few people ever utilized—mostly because it was part of the naval facility and off-limits to tourists and locals.

Dressing in a pair of comfortable white cotton slacks and a pale pink tank top, Molly picked up her lavender windbreaker as she headed out the door of her apartment. The sun was still bright in the sky for the Friday evening. Under her left arm were a couple of textbooks and a notepad. Maybe the beach would be an ideal place to relax, read a little and just "chill out," as Scott would say.

Getting directions at the gate from the Marine Corps guard on duty, Molly drove her station wagon to what appeared to be one of many parking areas for the point. As she got out, the salt air filled her lungs, and she inhaled it deeply. Some of the tension she'd carried since flying with Chuck Martin at midday sloughed off.

The beach was a golden color—picture perfect, in her estimation. For as far as she could see in either direction, the beach was empty, dotted with plenty of sand dunes shaped and created by the winds that sprang up off Chesapeake Bay. It was June, and the storms for the year had passed into history.

Molly allowed the tranquillity of the beach and the glassy-smooth cobalt water to soak into her. She muddled through the grasping sand in her tennis shoes. With a slight laugh, she stopped and took them off, then carried them in her left hand. It felt good to dig her toes into the grainy texture of the sand as she wove in and around the many dunes.

Nearly a mile from the parking lot, Molly found her spot. It was a cul-de-sac nestled between two fairly large hills laden with salt grass. In front of her, as she spread out her well-used purple beach blanket, was an unobstructed view of the bay. Although the sun's rays were sliding across the eastern expanse of the bay, she could barely make out white sails of yachts dipping up and down on the surface. More tension flowed from her as she shrugged out of her backpack which contained a sack dinner and her textbooks.

Her legs crossed, her elbows resting on her knees as she munched on a tuna sandwich, Molly thought about Cam Sinclair. Funny, all week, at every turn, she'd seemed to run into him. And always he was a gentleman, nodding deferentially in her direction, opening doors for her or whatever, but never offering a smile or any indication of emotion in the depths of his haunting pale blue eyes or his continually pursed mouth.

Did Cam ever smile? Molly wondered, munching on the sandwich. What would his face look like if he did? She closed her eyes, trying to imagine just that. And then, when a keening sea gull flew low, she reopened them. With a laugh, Molly tossed a bit of her sandwich up in the air. The gull dived, catching the choice morsel with grace and quickly gobbling it down.

In no time, Molly had a plethora of gulls circling above her between the two dunes. She gave her potato chips to the beggars, and time spun to a halt. The slight breeze, the salt air, the warmth of the sun's rays, plus the dozens of gulls who cautiously edged toward her towel or flew around her head, made it a magical time for Molly.

Finally out of food, she shrugged her shoulders at the birds. All she had left was an apple, and Molly used her small pocketknife to cut off bits of it to toss to the gulls who stayed around her blanket, begging. Test-pilot school was forgotten. Chuck Martin no longer existed. Her laughter was full and lilting, absorbed by the inconstant breeze and pleading cries of the seabirds.

The flock of gulls suddenly took wing as a unit. Molly saw the black shape of a dog hurtle up and across a nearby dune. Before she could move, she saw a sleek black Labrador bounding toward her, its pink tongue lolling out of its mouth.

Startled but pleased, Molly stood.

"Hi there, fella." As the dog came up to her, she saw the Lab was female. Extending her hand, Molly smiled as the dog fearlessly approached, wagging her thick tail furiously. She was wet, with water glistening on her ebony coat.

"Excuse me. I mean girl. Hi. How are you? And who do you belong to?" Molly leaned down. The dog wore a leather collar with a rabies tag, as well as another tag. Looking closer, Molly smiled.

"So, you're Miracle. I wonder what you did to earn a name like that?" She petted the dog's sleek, damp head, taken by the animal's affectionate nature.

Molly had crouched down, her arm around the dog's neck as she patted her, when she saw the outline of a man appear on the crest of the same dune. The sunlight was behind him, and she narrowed her eyes to try to make out who it might be. Obviously, the dog's owner.

"Miracle! Heel!"

Molly straightened, her heart racing. No, it couldn't be! The voice was excruciatingly familiar. Yes, the man dressed in jeans and a polo shirt certainly might be Cam Sinclair. The sunlight was blinding, and Molly lifted her hand to shade her eyes as Miracle scooted away, obeying her master's sharp command. Halfway down the dune, the Lab met the man and dutifully sat, her tail thumping hard on the sand.

"Hi," Molly greeted him uncertainly. It was Cam Sinclair, all right. As he looked at her, she felt herself go all shaky inside—a response that was new and startling.

"I didn't expect to see anyone out here at this time of day," Cam replied. Miracle whined, looking eagerly toward Molly. He stood, his hands shoved into the pockets of his jeans. "Sorry if she mauled you. Miracle's still a puppy at heart."

Smiling, Molly walked to the bottom of the dune. How handsome and relaxed Cam looked now. Almost human! "That's okay. I love animals."

"She was after all those gulls she saw flying around these two dunes."

"I was feeding them my dinner."

Cam watched as the breeze blew a number of strands of Molly's hair across her shoulder. She looked pretty in her civilian clothes, her bare feet giving her a decidedly childlike appearance. "Oh."

Without warning, Miracle turned and bounded back down the dune, leaping up on Molly, her black paws landing on Molly's chest. Cam yelled at the Lab but she didn't listen. He came down the dune and reached for the dog's collar, to jerk her away from Molly.

"No...it's okay." Molly laughed breathlessly, affectionately roughing up Miracle. She played with her, and the dog leapt and bounded around her in high spirits.

Embarrassed by Miracle's inexplicable antics, Cam stood helplessly by and watched her and Molly play with each other. They were like children. The light in Miracle's eyes was alive as she dodged and leapt playfully, avoiding Molly's hand. It was Molly's laughter that sent a sharp shaft of longing through Cam's heart, through his entire body.

Suddenly Molly wasn't the Annapolis grad or the TPS student. She was simply a woman. A beautiful one, who melted into the texture of the sand dunes, the peaceful lap of the bay water and turquoise sky laced with sunset colors of pale pink, lavender and gold. Cam didn't have the heart to scold Miracle for not minding him. How long had it been since he'd really, honestly played with the Lab? A year, he admitted.

Finally, Molly fell to the blanket, giggling. Miracle collapsed beside her, panting heavily. Placing her arm around the dog's shoulders Molly looked up at Cam. There was a dark scowl on his face, as if he totally disapproved of what she'd done. Feeling too good from the unexpected romp and exercise with the dog, Molly gasped, "She's great for aerobics, isn't she?"

Cam edged a bit closer to the blanket, his hands still deep in the pockets of his jeans. "Yeah, she was—I mean, is."

"How did Miracle get her name?" Molly shifted her gaze back to the dog, who responded by licking Molly's hand.

"Four years ago I wanted to get a dog. I went to the dog pound over in Lexington Park. They were going to put her to sleep the next day, so I took her because I didn't want to see her killed. That's why I decided to call her Miracle."

Molly sized him up. "I like someone with a kind heart," she whispered.

Flushing, Cam negligently dug the toe of his tennis shoe into the sand. "I don't know about a kind heart. I felt the dog was worth saving."

Smiling, Molly ruffled Miracle's head between her hands. "Soft heart or not, you did a good thing. She's wonderful! I'll bet you get your share of exercise when you walk her."

"I do. I come down here a couple of times a week to run her. She gets cooped up in my apartment, and I can't let a big dog sit for too long."

Molly liked Cam's thoughtful nature. "They say animals mirror their owners. Does she?"

Cam grimaced. "I don't think so."

He was so serious. And there was such sadness in his eyes and around his mouth. Something in her wanted to alleviate it, but Molly didn't know how. "When I was growing up, I had a dog. She was a purebred, because my father said they were the only kind to have, but it really didn't make any difference to me. Pooky, that was her name, was a Border collie. Father wanted to get me a German shepherd or a Doberman pinscher, but my mom wouldn't allow it, saying they were too temperamental and moody to trust around a child.

"So I ended up with Pooky." Molly looked past Cam, the memories coming back deep and strong. "She loved me so much, and my whole life revolved around her. My brother was the firstborn, and he was always the center of attention. Pooky and I stayed in my bedroom where I served her tea, shared my dolls with her and read her fairy tales." Molly smiled shyly down at Miracle, who had her head cocked to one side, as if listening intently to each word.

"Pooky died a month after my mother did. I never felt so alone."

Cam frowned. "How old were you when your mother died?"

"Ten." Molly rallied, petting Miracle fondly. "Father wanted to get me another dog, but I just couldn't do it. Pooky was one of a kind. And even at that age, I knew nothing or no one could ever replace her."

Pain widened in Cam's chest—not only for himself, but for Molly. What had her mother's passing when Molly was at such a young age done to her? He tried to ferret out the damage, but found none. Surely it had scarred her. Jeanne's passing and the loss of Sean had certainly scarred him for life. "Did you love your mother?" The instant the words were out of his mouth, he regretted the stupid question.

"Very much. We were close. Father's a workaholic, and it was Mom who kept things going at home for Scott and me. Yes, I loved her more than life." Molly stroked Miracle's neck and shoulders. "This is wonderful, getting to meet a dog like yours. She reminds me so much of Pooky—loyal and loving. I'm really glad I ran into you here on the beach, even if it was an accident." Molly smiled, meaning it.

Uncomfortable with Molly's openness, Cam called Miracle to his side. The black Lab hesitated, licked Molly's hand one more time, then slowly rose and trudged hesitantly to his side. Cam felt like a heel. He wasn't able to give Miracle the kind of open, loving warmth Jeanne had bestowed on her. Now Molly was offering what Miracle so missed. He wondered hotly what it would be like to be stroked by Molly's small, graceful hand. For a moment, he envied Miracle.

"I've got to get going," Cam stumbled. "I'll see you at school on Monday."

"Sure..." Molly tried to smile, but it was impossible. She'd totally embarrassed herself in front of Captain Sinclair, who was obviously uncomfortable in her presence. Miracle hesitated at the top of the dune, turned toward her and barked. Then she spun around, disappearing down the other side with her master.

Packing up her items, Molly thought she'd never felt as alive as she had in those few minutes with Cam and his dog. At least he hadn't been icy with her, as he was at school. There had been a change in him, although it was subtle. Why was he so unhappy? As Molly shrugged into her knapsack and folded her towel, she cringed at the thought of going home. The weekend stretched in front of her. On Saturday her father would call, demanding a detailed verbal report of her week's activities.

Slowly, Molly walked through the sand. The sun hovered on the horizon, the sky a pale pink tinged with lavender. Its setting was going to be spectacular, and the beauty momentarily raised her plummeting spirits. How she longed for the kind of freedom Miracle had.

Cam's face swam in front of her. All her worry lifted, and a ribbon of warmth spread through Molly. What kind of magic did he hold over her to lift her unaccountably from her own private hell? Whatever it was, Molly thanked the Fates for bringing them together this evening. That had been a miracle in itself.

"Stop whining." Standing in the living-room doorway, Cam scowled. Miracle stood at the front door, as if waiting to be let out. Cam knew the dog was thinking of Molly. Wasn't he, too?

Running his hand through his hair, he entered the living room, sat down on the overstuffed couch and picked up a newspaper. The six o'clock news was on TV, and Cam watched it with disinterest. Miracle came over to sit primly near his feet. She whined again.

"Stop," Cam pleaded, putting the newspaper aside and patting the Lab. "I know you liked her a lot. And yes, she played with you." Cam frowned. "I'm sorry, I should play more with you. Maybe I'll try from here on out. Okay?"

Miracle thumped her tail on the hardwood floor.

With a shake of his head, Cam sat back. "You like her, don't you? I can tell by the look in your eyes. Of course, what's there not to like?" Cam stopped. "God, I must be going crazy, talking to a dog like it understands me."

Miracle whined and licked his hand.

"Sorry, pup. I didn't mean it." Cam stroked her velvet ears absently. "Who knows? Maybe we'll run into Molly on the beach again sometime." *Did she go there often?* Cam wondered. Cam wasn't sure he wanted to meet her again on a less-than-military basis. She invited investigation. Molly was personal and unafraid to reveal her private side. *Was she that way with everyone? My God, if she was, she was asking for trouble.*

"Seventy-five percent! Molly, that's almost failing!"

"Father, it wasn't bad for a first test flight."

"But everyone else got higher grades. How do you think you'll stay in the thick of the competition when you come in dead last?"

Biting her lower lip, Molly tried to control her rampant feelings of hurt and frustration. "I'll do better next time. I have nowhere to go but up." She wasn't going to tell her father that Chuck Martin had continually harassed her in the cockpit, making her extremely nervous. So nervous that she'd blown the timing in two out of the four test ascents, which had contributed to her poor first showing.

"That's what you told me when you went to Whiting Field to earn your pilot's wings, Molly. You used those exact same words, young lady."

"Father, I don't have anything else to tell you. I gave it my best shot. I am trying."

"Scott's disappointed in you."

What's new? Molly almost asked. Instead she said, "I gathered that." He hadn't wanted to talk to her today. She supposed it was his way of punishing her for doing so badly.

"Molly, he's not eaten since talking to you on the phone yesterday."

"Father, I'm sorry! What do you want me to do? Slit my wrists?"

"Molly, don't you dare take that tone with me. Your mother wouldn't approve."

"My mother's been dead fourteen years!" A sob caught in her throat.

"I think we should terminate this phone call. You're obviously upset, and so are we. I hope, for all our sakes, that you'll have better news for us next Saturday."

"I'm sure I will, Father," Molly whispered.

"Don't forget to write Scott his weekly letter. You know how much he looks forward to them."

"Yes, Father."

"Goodbye."

Molly heard the phone click, and the line went dead. Dully, she placed the receiver back in the cradle. It hurt to feel for a long moment afterward. Molly hated it when he referred to her mother. He always threw her death in Molly's face, and she reacted as if she'd been physically slapped. Rubbing her hands against her long thighs, Molly forced herself to get up. Time to study, time to bury herself in the books—in another world. A world not as harsh as the one she lived in with her family, she reflected glumly.

As she went to her office, Molly thought fondly of Cam and Miracle. The dog loved effortlessly and was so uninhibited about showing her love. Why couldn't human beings be the same way? Why did they have to be so complex? Sitting down at her desk, Molly pulled the textbook on software programming toward her. Next week would be spent preparing for a Friday test flight. Who would be assigned to her? God, not Chuck Martin!

* * *

"Psst, Molly!" Lee Bard leaned over toward her desk and slipped her a piece of paper. "Read it and weep. What black cloud do you have over your head?"

Molly glanced at the paper. It was the test assignments. Her eyes narrowed.

"Martin? I've got Martin *again*?"

"Shh, keep your voice down. Bad luck, Molly. I'm really sorry. Martin's a tail wringer."

Molly sat in shock as the rest of the students filed in for the Wednesday class in aerodynamic theory. Her hand tightened around the paper. Panic filled her. If she flew with Martin again, she would lose her confidence—what little she had left. Internally, Molly tried to gird herself. The debriefing session on Friday would be a son of a bitch if she flew with Martin. Yet, she had no recourse. Was the commandant plotting to get rid of her?

A huge part of her wanted to talk to Cam Sinclair about this, but Molly was afraid that if she did, it would be seen as favoritism—or worse: that she was crying because TPS was too hard on her. No. Somehow she had to find the grit and utilize it. What would Friday bring? She was confident of her latest test program. How would Martin fly it?

Cam sat at one end of the debriefing table, notebook in hand. Next to him was Vic Norton. His four pilots had been paired up with Vic's flight engineers. The eight students sat around the long rectangular table, their faces sober and serious. Cam kept glancing at Molly, who sat diagonally across from him. She was pale, her green eyes a dark green. Chuck Martin sat across from her, flushed

and tapping his pencil angrily against the polished table-
top.

The atmosphere in the room was always tense, Cam
noted. They sailed through the first three flight debriefs.
The last one was Molly and Martin's. Cam tried to hide
his interest in her flight.

"Report, Mr. Martin," Cam ordered.

"Two of my three tests were blown by Ms. Rutledge's
lousy program."

Cam looked up to see the effect of Martin's scathing
comment on her. Molly sat, grimly unresponsive. "Oh?"

"Yes, sir. She had a series of rolls and chandelles for
me to fly. The degree of roll was too much, and I had one
hell of a time making the bird fit the demands of what she
wanted. I busted the first roll. On the second try, I fit the
bird in the parameters." Martin glared at Molly. "The
chandelles were a complete loss. They were too tight for
me to execute properly."

Molly clenched her hands in her lap beneath the table,
so no one could see her do it. She waited impatiently for
Vic Norton to ask her questions.

"Molly?" Vic asked. "What happened out there?"

In a smooth, unruffled voice, Molly gave her assessment of the flight tests. "And as for Mr. Martin's inabil-
ity to fit the F-14 into the roll configuration, it was a
matter of his flying skills blowing the test—not my program."

"Bullshit!" Martin cried, jumping up. "Honey, I came
off carrier duty in the Med, and believe me, we get our
share of bogey flights in that area. I've got the best flight
record in the Tomcat for landings and takeoffs."

Molly stared at him. "That has nothing to do with
anything. My program wasn't flawed."

Cam watched them argue back and forth. Molly's voice remained soft and quiet. At every opportunity, Martin scathingly attacked her program. He wondered if Norton was going to intervene on Molly's behalf. When he didn't, Cam knew he couldn't either. It would be seen as favoritism. Maybe her program had been inadequate. Martin *was* a qualified Tomcat pilot with plenty of carrier duty over the past four years.

Finally the room quieted. Norton glanced over at Cam. He scribbled some figures on his board and handed it to him. Cam read the grade for Molly: seventy percent.

"Are you going to cross-check her program against the video?" Cam asked. He looked pointedly at Molly, hoping she would jump in and demand the video be played. She stared back at him, hurt mirrored in her eyes. Not a word came from her.

"I don't think it's necessary."

Molly's heart stopped as Cam passed the board across the table to her. Both instructors had to grade and sign off each student's flight. She saw an eighty-five percent next to Martin's name. Her heart dropped when she saw the seventy next to hers. With a shaking hand, she signed the board and handed it to Martin. The pilot grinned triumphantly.

Everyone was dismissed. Blindly, Molly shouldered past several students and dived out into the hall. She was breathing hard, feeling the panic and the pain. Martin had screwed up her flight. She hadn't! But they didn't believe her. Norton wouldn't even view the videotape to confirm what she'd said! They were all against her! All of them!

Fighting back the real need to cry, Molly quickly left TPS. She didn't want to go back to the apartment for fear of a Friday-night call from Scott. Right now she just needed to be alone to sort out what was happening and what she could do about it. The beach was the only answer. Dana had always gone swimming when things got bad. Well, she wasn't much of a swimmer, but at least the beach would be deserted and she'd be alone.

As she got into her station wagon and drove off, Molly felt a terrible need for a friend. If only Dana and Maggie were here! They'd know what to do. Her safety net was gone, and she felt helpless and vulnerable as never before—almost as bad as when her mother had died. Fighting tears, Molly guided her car out to one of the many parking lots at the beach. At least, being alone, she could cry.

Cam stood at the window of his office, his hands on his hips. He watched Molly drive out of the parking lot. Damn! Why hadn't she stood up for herself? This was the second time that Martin had blasted her and she'd taken it broadside. He shouldn't care; but dammit, he did. With a snarl, he whirled around on the heel of his boot and grabbed his garrison cap. Settling it on his head, he walked quickly down the hall toward the parking lot located at the rear of the facility. Something told him she was heading for the beach.

As Cam climbed into his sporty car, he wondered how he knew that. The pain in his chest was widening by the second. It wasn't for himself; it was for Molly. Something just wasn't making sense, and he was going to get to the bottom of it—one way or another.

Chapter Five

Molly strode blindly past the dunes and went directly to the solid sand near the water. Tears spilled down her cheeks as she walked fast, trying to burn off the anger and injustice she felt. Once her father and Scott found out about her grade, they'd hit the roof. And why had Lieutenant Norton not looked at the video of Martin's flying? If he had, she knew that somehow her flight-test program would have been vindicated.

Damn them all! Molly couldn't pay attention to the circling gulls who cried to her, floating near and then arcing out over the bay. She barely felt the warming June breeze that had sprung up to caress her hot, damp face or noticed the sun slanting across the water, making the light look like dancing diamonds on the surface. Her total concentration focused on her hurt and disappointment in herself.

How long she walked, wandering aimlessly among the dunes, Molly didn't know. Finally sitting down beside one of them, she brought her legs up and rested her face against her knees. Crying had helped because she felt cleaner and more calm. The edge of panic wasn't quite so near, and that was good.

"You're damned hard to find when you don't want to be found."

Molly gasped, her head snapping up and to the left. Cam Sinclair stood a few feet away, hands resting on his hips, his eyes narrowed on her.

"Wh-what do you want?" she croaked.

Cam came forward, fighting himself. Molly's face was flushed with spent tears, her green eyes huge and luminous with those yet to be shed. Her blond hair was in disarray, her garrison cap clenched in her hand. A huge part of him wanted simply to crouch down, put his arms around her and rock her. With Molly, his protective mechanism was working overtime.

Halting a foot away, Cam hunkered down in front of her, placing himself at her level. "I want to talk to you."

Sniffing, Molly avoided his stare.

"Look at me when I'm talking to you," he ordered tightly. Cursing himself for his harsh tone, Cam added, "Lesson number one—you stare your enemy in his face. Don't ever lose eye contact. It's called a bluff. Whoever blinks first, loses."

Molly forced herself to hold his gaze. "Are you my enemy?"

"No."

"Really? Then why are you here? To rub salt in my wounds like you did the last time?"

Cam scowled. "When was that?" When had he hurt her?

With a muffled sound, Molly said, "You sided with Lieutenant Norton just now in the debrief room without ever seeing the video."

Recalling the conversation, Cam shook his head. "Hey, I didn't mean to hurt your feelings in there. I was giving you an opportunity to defend yourself by suggesting that Norton watch the video of your flight."

Her eyes rounded. "It sure didn't sound like it."

"Did it ever occur to you that it was your job to fight hard enough and long enough to force Norton to look at your video, not mine?"

"I will not raise my voice and act like a three-year-old child to get my way, Captain Sinclair."

The anger in her eyes was real, but it didn't transfer to her voice. What had stoved Molly up so badly that her anger was short-circuited against herself? "So you played martyr instead, and took the fall whether it belonged to you or not."

Molly's mouth dropped open. "How dare you!" She leaped to her feet. She wasn't fast enough. Cam unwound like a tightly coiled spring, straightening and reaching out, his fingers wrapping around her arm.

"Running—again?" he taunted close to her ear.

"Let me go!"

"Or what?" Her flesh was firm and supple, and Cam longed to open his arms and give her the safety she needed. But to do so would weaken her, not help her.

Glaring up at him, Molly whispered, "Or nothing. Please let me go."

"Will you stay and talk, not run?"

His fingers felt like a hot brand against her arm. Impatiently she said, "Yes, I'll stay!"

"Good."

The gentleness of just that one word shook Molly. His face was still hard, but his voice had turned warm and coaxing. She stared up at him, not knowing what to make of him.

"Now, come on. Let's sit down and talk."

"About what?" Molly demanded petulantly, sitting cross-legged on the sand. Cam positioned himself a foot away, opposite her.

"You."

"Look, if you're going to sit there and rip me up—"

"Ensign Rutledge—" Oh, to hell with it. "Molly, give me a chance. You're behaving like I've got a report card or something to deliver. I don't," he said softly.

When he whispered her name, Molly sat very still. She tried to wrestle with her fear that he was going to expertly dissect her performance today. Her entire life since leaving home had been exactly that: a report card. She was held accountable for every minute of her life. She feared that he'd point to her mistakes just as her father and Scott did.

"Look, I can't take a dressing-down right now. I've had about all I can take."

"I understand." Cam didn't, but he was going to try. Opening his hands in a gesture of peace, he urged, "Tell me about your father. I know your mother died when you were ten. What's he like?"

Completely taken off guard by his questions, Molly hesitated.

"I know this is personal, but what we share stays with me. I won't use it against you, Molly. I promise."

Although Sinclair was still in his flight uniform and looked very much the warrior, Molly responded to the softened grate of his voice. The sensation was almost tangible, as if a cat were licking her with its roughened tongue. Needing to confide in someone, she nodded.

"I miss my friends, Dana and Maggie. I used to be able to talk to them when things got tough. They're still at Whiting Field and—"

"You're up here all alone without any friends or family?" Cam guessed, trying to keep his voice low and warm. He saw his effort work a minor miracle with Molly. She placed her hands on her knees and opened up to him.

"I'm so lonely without a friend here. The last two weeks have been pure hell. Martin's trying to sink me before I even get a chance to prove myself and—"

"Whoa! Slow down, gal." Cam held up his hand. "Let's backtrack. I want to know about your father. What's he like?"

With a sigh, Molly told him. At one point, she thought she saw his eyes soften for just an instant. Or had it been her imagination? Maybe it was the evening light, the way the sun was slanting across the bay. She talked about her father for a good ten minutes.

"So, to sum it up, you report in to your father *and* your brother on a weekly basis?" Cam asked. He struggled mightily to keep the disbelief out of his voice.

"Yes, sir."

"When we're alone like this, let's drop the military formality, okay? Call me Cam, and I'll call you Molly. Fair enough?" Cam wondered where that had come from. Well, it was too late to take it back. Molly's face lit up with such gratefulness that it didn't matter.

"Okay...Cam. Scott, my older brother, hangs on my every word. It really makes his week to get my letters and phone call."

"Doesn't he have his own life? A job?"

Molly shrugged, making geometric designs in the sand in front of her crossed legs. "No."

"Tell me about your friends, Dana and Maggie."

Eagerly Molly filled him in on the two women, who were really more like sisters to her. Cam's face remained stoic and without expression. She hesitated halfway through her explanation.

"Why am I telling you all of this?"

"Because I want to know."

"Why?"

"I care what happens to you, Molly." God help him, he shouldn't, but he did. Cam felt himself falling apart inwardly when he saw her eyes fill with tears. Gruffly, because he knew he couldn't stand to see Molly cry without taking her into his arms, he told her, "I care enough to help you learn how to help yourself. What else did Maggie and Dana do for you?"

The harsh edge in his voice halted her tears. Molly blinked them away and continued with her story of how they'd met and become the closest of friends at Annapolis. By the time she'd finished, the sun had set and the sky was a bold apricot laced with the pink trim of the clouds that hung over the bay.

Cam said nothing for a long time, digesting her story and trying to put the pieces together. Molly looked so alone sitting there in front of him. He was amazed that she genuinely trusted him with all this personal information. Yet, without it, he'd be helpless to understand her actions and reactions at TPS.

"When you're angry or upset, do you always retreat?"

Molly stiffened. "I don't retreat."

"I sat in that debrief room this afternoon and watched you crawl deep inside yourself, Molly."

"Martin had no business verbally abusing me the way he did!"

"He was defending his territory. What were you doing?"

"What? What territory? That test was supposed to be us working as a team."

"Every test pilot maps out his territory, and then he defends it, Molly. Do you think Martin is going to say 'Yeah, I screwed up the flight'?"

"I expect him to be honest!"

"Because you are?"

"Of course."

"Who taught you that?"

She glared at him. "My mother."

"Test pilots by nature are self-protective, Molly. They've got egos as big as the Chesapeake Bay. Martin's record is impeccable. He's a hotshot jet jock and knows it."

"I don't care if he thinks he's God. He's not! He made mistakes up there in the air today, Cam. I was there. I saw it happen!"

"Prove it to me," he goaded her softly.

"I tried today."

"By acting like a cream puff in debrief? Give me a break, Molly. Why didn't you demand that Norton view the video? I haven't seen it, either, and it may or may not prove a thing, but at least it would put Martin on notice that you're going to start protecting *your* territory."

Molly scrambled to her feet. "I will not play these little-boy games, Cam! We're supposed to be mature adults."

"Martin was a six-year-old squalling like a scalded cat in there this afternoon," Cam drawled, holding her furious gaze. "Who do you think won that battle in your personal war with him? Who did Norton believe? Who got the better grade?''

"You gave him an eighty-five!" Molly flung heatedly. "I didn't!"

"You didn't give me a choice."

"I what?"

"Come on, sit back down. We're not done talking."

Breathing hard, Molly sank back to the sand, her fists clenched in her lap. "I wasn't aware I had anything to do with Martin's grade. You do."

"You're wrong. I assess my student in three areas. First, how he presents his report of the flight. Second, through the video analysis. Third," Cam drilled her, "the flight engineer's report. You think Martin's the only one who's going to try and make you look bad when he blows a test? Every man in there will do it, Molly. And if you don't want to get washed out in the first month, you'd better start defending yourself."

Molly felt at a loss. Hanging her head, she mulled over Cam's suggestions. "I won't become like them," she said finally. "I refuse to lower myself to their level of infantile behavior to get some notice or a better grade."

Without meaning to, Cam reached out, his hand settling on hers. "Who taught you not to fight for yourself, Molly?"

His hand was firm yet comforting on hers. A lump formed in her throat. "My mother never raised her voice to my father."

"You don't have to be exactly like her." Cam ached to lean closer, frame her face and kiss her pursed lips. Her face was filled with such pain that he felt tears come to his eyes. Tears! He hadn't cried in nearly six months. Reluctantly, Cam removed his hand, realizing he was becoming too involved with Molly. If he was going to help her, he had to remain distant and objective. There was danger in allowing her to affect him.

With a shrug, Molly whispered, "You think I'm a wimp."

"No. I don't think your family gave you the support or the tools for learning to stand up for yourself." His voice became lined with emotion. "Molly, if you really want to make the grade at TPS, you're going to have to start defending yourself."

"I'm not going to yell or curse to achieve it."

"You don't have to."

Lifting her chin, Molly looked at him miserably. "Isn't this sad? Why can't the world get along without all this ridiculous drama and clash of egos? Why can't everyone behave like well-mannered adults?"

"Just because you can, doesn't mean everyone else does."

"You never raise your voice. At least, not that I've heard."

Cam's mouth curved into a slight smile. "Wait and see. Some of these jet jocks have to be brought down a peg or two when they start trying to run over the flight engineers."

His smile sent a sheet of warmth and hope straight to her injured heart. The entire shape of his face changed, and Molly's breath snagged. How handsome, how approachable Cam looked when he smiled, even if it was just a sliver of a smile tugging at one corner of his well-shaped mouth. Her trust in him doubled. "I thought you said flight engineers had to stand on their own two feet."

"They do. Once that's done, and I view the video and put it all together, I may end up dressing down one of my students in private for trying to blame the engineer instead of owning up to pilot error. But I can't do that unless the engineer has the confidence and belief in his program in the first place. If you don't have faith in it, how can I?''

"I see your point. I'll admit you've got a scary reputation here at TPS.''

Cam's smile broadened. "Yeah?''

"Do you know what they call you?''

"Probably a lot of unkind expletives that you'd never repeat because you're too sweet and kind, Molly Rutledge.''

It was her turn to smile. She wanted to reach out and touch his hand, to thank him, but she stopped herself. He was an instructor; she, a student. "I don't know about 'sweet and kind,' but you're right, cursing's for the birds. When I arrived at TPS, I found out they called you 'the Glacier.'''

Cam nodded, familiar with the nickname. His smile faded, and his face became implacable once again. "I earned it'' was all he'd say. When Molly tilted her head and gave him that probing look, Cam moved uncomfortably. Dusk was upon them, and more than anything in the world, he wanted to stay here with Molly and talk. Simply talk. He was starved to find out everything he could about her. That realization startled him, haunted him. He got to his feet, brushing the sand off his uniform.

"I've got to get going.''

"Sure...'' Molly stood uncertainly. She hadn't realized how tall Cam Sinclair was until he stood only inches away from her. The need, the desire to turn and walk into his arms was there. How could that be? It dawned on Molly that she knew absolutely nothing about this enigma of a pilot. He knew everything about her. Everything! Could she really trust him?

"I never expected this."

"What?" Cam wanted to reach over and tame several strands of her hair wafting against her flushed cheek. He throttled the urge.

"Your helping me." She studied him in the dusk, his face shadowed and harsh looking. "You didn't have to come out here."

Cam thrust his hands on his hips. "Yes, I did."

"Why?"

"Because I'm a sucker for the underdog, that's why."

"For a loser."

"No." He shook his head. "Molly, you've never been a loser. But you're no longer in an academic environment. You're out in the big, cold, cruel world of life. Things are different out here. You need to learn to adjust." He managed a tight smile. "My money's on you to do just that. I think beneath that cream-puff face and those soft words is a backbone of steel."

She shoved the sand around with the toe of her polished boot. "I've never met a cream puff with a spine."

"Well, I have. Come on, chin up. Get through this weekend and start Monday on a new note. Let those guys, and in particular, your instructor, know you're going to defend your territory."

She smiled tentatively. "Thanks, Cam. For everything."

He found himself wanting to kiss her. When Molly's lips parted as she lifted her head to meet and hold his gaze, it nearly unstrung him. Cam took a step back, digesting the urge. Since his wife had died, he'd not felt anything. With Molly around, he suddenly was feeling so much, so fast, that it created havoc within him.

"I haven't done anything. Come on. Let's get back. I've got things to do tonight." That was a bald-faced lie.

All he had to do was bring Miracle down to the beach for her run and then spend another quiet, lonely night at home with only the television for company.

Molly nodded and fell into step next to Cam. Of course he had a girlfriend, people to see and places to go. After all, it was Friday night, and that was party time. There was no ring on Cam's left hand, and she felt a bit of envy. Whoever the lucky woman was, Molly hoped she appreciated Cam's sincerity and sensitivity. She'd never met a man willing to sit and listen for nearly two hours without interrupting her as Cam had just done. His few questions had been incisive and clear.

Hope built within her with each step she took at Cam's side. The bay was afire with red-orange color, mirroring the horizon. By the time they reached the parking lot, Molly felt an incredible surge of self-confidence. Yes, she had to take her father and Scott's call tomorrow, but she would do it with new firmness and commitment.

At their cars, Cam turned and threw her a mock salute. "I'll see you Monday, Molly."

She smiled. "Monday."

Cam was in the coffee room at 0600, getting his first cup for the day, when someone entered the room. It was Monday, and most students and instructors didn't start arriving until 0700. He turned.

Molly stood hesitantly at the door. "I didn't know you were here."

Cam managed a crooked grin and took a sip of the coffee. "I work here, too."

Molly rolled her eyes. "Sorry. I just didn't expect you."

She looked like hell, he thought. Her eyes were dark, with shadows in their lovely depths. Although her hair was neatly brushed and her uniform as unwrinkled as a flight suit could be, Cam sensed a terrible trauma in Molly.

"Come on over and get some coffee. Did you think about what I said to you Friday night?" He stepped aside, giving her plenty of space.

Molly nodded and looked for her cup among the others. It was pale pink with flowers painted on its side. "Yes, I did."

Cam leaned against the wall. "So, what's your game plan?" What the hell was eating her? He saw her hand shake as she poured coffee into the mug.

"I—I got sidetracked over the weekend, Captain—"

"Cam. We're alone."

Taking a shaky breath, Molly turned toward him, the mug gripped in both hands. "Okay."

"You look unhappy. What happened?"

Molly refused to say anything.

"Your father?" Cam guessed grimly, moving to one of the many chairs placed around the small room and sitting down.

"Yes."

"Get a royal chewing-out?"

Molly stared at him. "How did you know?" Cam looked more relaxed than she'd ever seen him. And if her eyes weren't deceiving her, his face was softer, less hard-looking. Maybe it was her overactive imagination. Since the blistering call from her father on Saturday, all she'd wanted to do was to call Cam and talk about it. Molly didn't want to abuse his kindness, though, and their conversation had kept her sleepless most of the weekend.

"Lucky guess." Cam shrugged. Molly was nothing but lines of tension. "Want to talk about it?"

"You don't want to hear any more of my sordid family affairs, Cam."

"Try me."

Exhaling sharply, Molly began to pace the length of the room. "Why are you doing this for me?"

"Because I happen to think you're worth the time and trouble to develop as a flight engineer," Cam said quietly. It wasn't a lie, but it wasn't the total truth. He wondered if dark shadows showed under his eyes as they did under Molly's. Sleep had eluded him all weekend, and Cam felt like a wild man inside. Only in Molly's presence did that edgy, hungry feeling chafing at him disappear. She brought him a sense of serenity he'd never experienced before.

Molly stopped, considering his explanation. "I wish . . . I wish . . ."

"What?" Cam asked softly.

"Never mind."

"No, what is it?"

She managed a wry laugh. "Don't mind me. I'm finding I'm such an idealist and a romantic about life."

"There's nothing wrong with that, Molly."

She looked down. "I wish you were my friend instead of an instructor interested in helping a wayward student, that's all," she admitted, her voice barely audible.

Cam sat very still. "I've never had a woman as a friend."

"I gathered as much."

"Now you're insulting me."

She smiled sadly. "No. Just wishful thinking, that's all."

"You'd be more comfortable talking about your problems if I were your friend, is that it?"

"Honestly, yes."

"Okay. Can I be your friend?" Cam watched her eyes widen beautifully, hope coming back to them. It made him feel good and clean inside where nothing but a vacuum had existed before.

"You aren't just saying that to make me feel better about telling you my personal problems?"

"No." He thrust out his hand. "Let's shake on it."

"This is crazy."

"No, it's not."

"It won't work, Cam."

"Why?"

"Because I'm a student and you're an instructor. That's a conflict of interest."

"It would be if you were a test-pilot student, but you aren't. We're on safe ground. Don't worry." Cam held her uncertain gaze and groaned to himself when she tucked her lower lip between her teeth, thinking about his offer. Molly had the most beautiful mouth he'd ever seen. What would it be like to touch it with his? What would she taste like? Sunlight? Laughter? Those things and more, he was sure.

Reaching out, Molly slid her hand into his. "Okay. Friends."

"Deal." He grinned broadly, holding her hand firmly. "Don't look like I just slit your throat."

"I've never had a friend who was a man, either."

"So, we're both doing something new—together." Trying to control his rampant feelings, Cam released her hand. "Sit down. Let's talk about your Saturday phone call."

Grimacing she said, "I'd rather not."

Cam spread out his long legs before him, actually enjoying her company in ways he'd never fathomed. "Want me to take an educated guess?"

"No. It boils down to Father being upset with my seventy-percent grade."

"And?"

Molly set the cup on her thigh. She really didn't feel like a cup of coffee. "He...uh...he started yelling at me. Father's been upset before, but he's always controlled himself. This time—" Molly shrugged painfully " —I told him everything."

"Why?" Cam asked gently.

"Because I believe in being honest."

"Withholding certain information isn't being dishonest, Molly. Why give your father fuel to fry you with?"

"I don't know."

There was such hopelessness in Molly's voice and in her eyes. Cam throttled his anger toward her unfeeling, selfish father. It wouldn't do any good at this stage of their burgeoning friendship to tell Molly that her father was wrong and she should be strong enough to run her own life, instead of letting him run it for her.

"Next time, omit certain details. Just try it."

Rolling her eyes, Molly whispered, "I've just got to get a better grade this Friday, Cam. I've got to!"

Reacting strongly to her desperation, he nodded. "So, what kind of game plan have you come up with to guarantee it?"

Molly sat there a long time, thinking. Somehow, with Cam around, it was easier to separate her chaotic and injured emotions from her work at TPS. "I thought— well, I thought I might ask Lieutenant Norton if I could use the same flight program that Martin knocked on another pilot. The pilot wouldn't know it, though. Only Norton—and you—would."

Cam raised his brows. "You're a pretty sharp cookie," he congratulated her. "By using the identical test with another pilot, you can prove to Norton that it was pilot error.''

"Yes, I hope to. That is, if the pilot I'm assigned doesn't blow it, too. I know I haven't pushed the F-14 out of its envelope, Cam. I know the test can be flown. I think these guys figure that because we're just learning how to do this, we aren't as demanding or sure of ourselves. I've got a degree in aeronautical engineering, and I know airplanes as well as they do, from another direction. I might have gotten kicked out of flight school, but that doesn't take away my expertise."

"I like your thinking. And you're right—no one can take away what you know." Cam grinned, liking the way she was applying her knowledge to support her argument for her program.

Molly colored fiercely beneath his praise. "Do you think Lieutenant Norton will go along with my idea?"

Cam shrugged and sipped his coffee. "I don't know. Give him a gung-ho presentation. We'll just have to see." Chuckling to himself, Cam thought how much he would enjoy seeing Martin's face when that same test program was flown to perfection by another pilot. There were a lot of ifs in Molly's plan, but it was feasible. A good feeling threaded through him at the feisty quality he saw in Molly's green eyes. He hadn't seen it there before, and it pleased him to think maybe he'd had something to do with putting it there. For the first time in a long time, Cam felt happy. Truly happy.

Chapter Six

"Cam, you got a minute?"

"Yeah, what is it, Vic?" Cam stopped at the instructor's office.

"Come in and shut the door."

Doing as he was asked, he saw the troubled expression on his friend's triangular face. "Problems?" It was only 1000 on Monday morning. Cam wondered if Molly had seen Vic about her plan.

"Look at this request from Ensign Rutledge."

Cam feigned no prior knowledge and read the neatly typed flight-report suggestion. "Looks fine to me."

"It's the same one she used last week."

Cam handed it back to him. "So?"

"It was blown last Friday."

"By her or Martin?"

Vic scowled. "What do you mean?"

"Are you so sure Martin followed the parameters of her flight test?"

"Well...no. But Rutledge just sat like a bump on a log in debrief. What was I to think? Martin's a veteran pilot. She's fresh out of the academy. He's got more air experience, and I believed him."

"But she's got a degree in aeronautical engineering."

"I suppose..." He tapped the desk with his long fingers. "This is really an unusual request, Cam."

"But not an illegal one. Look at it this way, Vic. If Dalton, who's assigned to Rutledge this Friday, flies this test well, then it turns the heat on to Martin, not her. Right?"

"Yes, it would." Vic got up, shaking his head. "What's she trying to prove, then? If her test was good, why the hell didn't she stand up for it in debrief? She acted as if she didn't care one way or another if I viewed the video. And Martin was hotter than a Fourth-of-July firecracker."

Cam sat down. "Maybe we're just too used to a man's way of doing things, Vic."

"Say that again."

"Women, at least in my experience, aren't hard-nosed and challenging, like men. They're more tactful and diplomatic. Maybe this is Rutledge's way of trying to set the record straight. What would it hurt? If Dalton flies that test perfectly, then you have some reassessing of her capabilities to do, that's all. And it would also shed some light on Martin and his tactics, which would become my responsibility to contend with."

Rubbing his jaw, Vic nodded. "I like her, Cam, but she's too soft. Too laid-back. Martin took her head off in there last Friday."

Cam said nothing. If Molly had been his student, he'd have handled the scenario differently, but that was water under the bridge. Besides, he had no business trying to tell Vic how to instruct. "Well, I say give the lady a second chance. Won't hurt anything, will it?"

"No," Vic groused. "Except she won't be learning anything new this week."

"Have her work on another test flight, then, for the coming week," Cam suggested.

Brightening, Vic smiled. "Thanks for the input. It's hell being an instructor here. I'm glad you've got a couple of years of experience or I'd be lost sometimes."

Easing out of the chair, Cam nodded. "Don't worry about it. I don't think you'll be disappointed with Rutledge. She's adjusting to a lot of variables."

"I've got the patience, Cam, but there's no time for anyone here. It's a pressure cooker from day one."

"Amen to that," he muttered. "Well, I've got a flight with a student. See you later, Vic."

"Yeah. And thanks."

Molly's hands were damp. She kept them hidden beneath the debrief table, clutching her flight-program file. Next to her sat Phillip Dalton. Barely able to sit still, she shifted her gaze to Cam, who sat at the other end with her instructor, Vic Norton. Next to Cam was Chuck Martin, looking smug and confident as usual. The expression on Cam's face didn't change, but Molly could detect a glint in his eyes. It made her feel a little calmer.

Vic nodded in Molly's direction. "Well, how'd the flight go today?"

Molly deferred to Phil Dalton.

"Piece of cake," Dalton assured them in his Missouri twang. "We executed two barrel rolls precisely on the money called for by the test, and two chandelles."

Martin scowled. "Wait a minute, that was the same test I flew last Friday." He swung his gaze to Vic Norton. "What gives here, sir?"

Vic ignored Martin and focused all his attention on Dalton. "Did you have any trouble with the requirements of the test?"

"No, sir." Dalton grinned affably. "We was happy as a hog in a mud wallow up there. Matter of fact, I did so well, I went and did it twice."

"No problems?" Vic pressed.

"Nope." Phil looked over at Molly and winked. "The lady knows how to call 'em."

"Bull!" Martin exploded.

"Sit down, Mr. Martin," Cam growled, nailing him with a lethal glare.

"But, that's not fair! Dalton flew the same test I did! Since when does a flight-engineer student get to repeat a test? If they screw up the first time, you mean they get a second chance?"

Vic's mouth tightened.

"Martin," Phil drawled, "if brains was dynamite, you wouldn't have 'nuf to blow through your nose. Read between the lines, buddy. Molly's test was a good one. Of course, she had the best damn test-pilot student here to fly it with her."

Cam sat back, hiding a smile. Martin was flushed and angry. Molly was looking at Dalton as if he'd said the most beautiful words she'd ever heard spoken. He shifted his glance back to Vic, who was grim.

"This isn't fair!" Martin protested violently, remaining seated.

"That's enough, Lieutenant," Vic ordered tightly.

"I was set up."

Phil laughed outright. "Come on, Martin! You'd complain if you was hanged with a new rope, wouldn't you? From the way I see it, you got a good grade flying this exact test last Friday. What are you bellyachin' about?"

Molly tried hard not to smile. Phil Dalton, in her opinion, was a knight in shining armor in the debrief room. His soft Missouri drawl effectively shattered the tension every time Martin tried to escalate the situation. She risked a glance at Cam. His eyes were shining with laughter. Bowing her head because she was afraid she was going to laugh outright, Molly busily took the test out of the folder, placed it on the table and read it out loud.

When the debrief was completed, Molly got a chance to look at her score. Norton had awarded her an eighty percent. She grinned broadly, passing the board to Phil, who had been given a ninety-eight percent. The good-looking pilot gave her a loose grin and then winked.

"Nice going, Molly."

"Ditto, Phil."

She could hardly wait to get out of debrief. Somehow, Molly wanted to pull Cam aside and thank him. Yet, if she did it here, at TPS, it might give the wrong impression. Would Cam walk Miracle on the beach this evening?

Molly stood on the beach, shifting from one foot to the other. She had gone home, changed into a pair of comfortable tan shorts and a white blouse. Her pale yellow beach towel contained a sack dinner, a couple of textbooks and a notepad. It was 1900; the sun was low on the horizon. Where were Cam and Miracle? Going back to her towel, Molly sat down and decided to eat.

She tried to still her excitement. As she sat cross-legged eating her first sandwich, she heard the bark of a dog. Was it Miracle? Before Molly could get up, the black Lab burst between the sand dunes, galloping eagerly toward her.

Laughing, Molly got up just in time. The Lab wagged her tail furiously and nuzzled Molly's hand. Molly's heart accelerated as she lifted her head. Cam Sinclair looked devastatingly handsome in a pair of well-worn cutoffs, his feet bare, a green polo shirt revealing the powerful breadth of his chest and shoulders.

"Hi," she ventured, patting Miracle's head.

Cam nodded and walked toward her. The happiness in Molly's eyes made his heart hammer hard in his chest. She looked joyous, her hair pulled back into a loose ponytail, tendrils at each temple. Out of the baggy flight uniform, Cam decided, Molly looked tempting as hell. She was tall and slender—like a willow, perhaps.

"Miracle knew you were here," he said, coming to a halt a few feet from her beach towel. Cam noted the textbooks she'd brought along.

"Oh?"

"She must have picked up your scent the minute I let her out of the car. She took off from the parking lot half a mile from here and made a beeline in this direction. I figured she'd spotted a snipe or a gull."

Molly laughed, fondly rubbing Miracle's silky ears. "Call me Big Bird."

A smile barely touched his mouth. "You came out here to meet us?"

"Yes." Molly felt heat in her face as she held his penetrating gaze. "I just wanted to thank you properly for all your help, Cam. I didn't think it would be wise to go into your office after debrief and do that. Martin was really upset.''

"He lives to be upset," Cam said dryly. "You're right, though. If he'd seen you in my office, all hell would have broken loose."

Molly gestured to her towel. "Come and sit down. I was in the middle of finishing my supper. I've got another roast-beef sandwich left. Want it?"

"No...thanks."

Miracle promptly went over and sat next to Molly.

"I even brought Miracle a doggy bone." She dug in her knapsack, holding up the plastic bag that contained several small dog treats. "May I?"

"Sure. She'll be your friend for life." Touched by her thoughtfulness, Cam sauntered over and sat down on the other end of the towel. It would be poor manners to remain standing, and even poorer manners to refuse the dog bones for Miracle. Just being around Molly on a one-to-one basis made Cam yearn to be with her.

"I didn't know another way to meet and thank you," Molly explained, feeding Miracle one small bone after another until they'd disappeared.

Cam brought his legs up, wrapping his arms around them. Molly sat with Miracle stretched out beside her. "I like your creative tactics," he congratulated. He was happy to see the contented look on her face. "It's Friday night. I thought a single, good-looking lady would be out with her 'significant other.' ''

Rolling her eyes, Molly said, "I don't have time for a significant other."

For some reason that pleased Cam. Actually, he felt a huge flood of relief flow through him. "Yeah, you've got a lot of other pressures on you right now."

"Just TPS."

"What about your family?"

She shrugged. "I never looked at it that way."

Cam wished she would. "Well, at least when your father calls this Saturday, you'll have good news for him. Vic gave you a good grade, but you deserved it."

"Thanks." Molly flushed and avoided his eyes. She was glad Miracle was there to pat; otherwise she wouldn't know what to do with her hands. A sweet kind of nervousness always sizzled through her when she was with Cam. The bay breeze had mussed his short black hair, making a few strands fall over his brow. He looked approachable, almost human right now.

"This afternoon, I felt like jumping up and down for joy." She grinned. "Strictly a kid's reaction. But when Phil came to my defense and cut Martin down to size, I thought it was wonderful. I shouldn't take such pleasure in Martin getting his just deserts."

"I would. I thought you were going to smile in there."

"I ducked my head and put my hand over my mouth so Martin couldn't see me do it."

Chuckling, Cam nodded. "Yeah, I noticed."

"You don't miss much, do you?"

"Not usually."

Molly turned toward him, the dusky light softening the lines of his face. There were crow's feet at the outer corners of his eyes, and they deepened when he laughed. "After our conversation the other night, I walked away realizing I know absolutely nothing about you, Cam."

"Not much to tell."

"Where were you born?"

"Billings, Montana. I was a city kid. My dad is a printer and typesetter. He owns his own business in the downtown area."

"And your mother?"

"She raised three of us. I've got two younger sisters. One is married and has a baby. Carrie, the youngest, is seriously thinking of a career in the military."

"You wouldn't object?"

Cam shrugged. "No. She's got the personality for it."

"Oh?"

"She's a strong, confident girl."

"Not a cream puff?"

Cam shrugged. "I said you were a cream puff with a steel backbone. You just have to discover it, that's all."

"So, where do cream puffs fit into life's big picture?" Molly wondered aloud, interested in how he saw her.

"They make great mothers," he said, and then realized his gaffe. "That was not a chauvinistic comment, Molly, so get that look off your face. It's just that—" he stumbled "—a woman like you has such warmth and sincerity about her, it seems wasted in the military, which doesn't value those things and thrives on their exact opposite."

She digested his comment. "I think you can be low-key, diplomatic and 'soft,' to use your word, and still work effectively in the military."

"Not without a lot of personal heartache and injury, Molly."

"Things are looking up for me at TPS. I'm excited about my next flight test. I'm sure I'm over the hump. Lieutenant Norton seems more interested in what I'm doing, now that I proved my other flight program wasn't a dud."

Cam didn't have the heart to break the hope he saw in her eyes and heard in her voice. God, what he'd give to simply lean over and capture that mouth of hers beneath his. Every time he was around her, she stirred the fires within him he thought had died so long ago.

"Well," he said, rising, "you've got nowhere to go but up. I've got work to do for class next Monday, so I'd better get going." He hoped it didn't sound like a lie, because it wasn't. It was a poor excuse, though, for leaving Molly's company. To be honest, Cam wanted to stay; but if he did, talk would quickly be replaced by touching, kissing and then— He called Miracle to his side. The Lab bounded up and wagged her tail.

"I'm glad we got to talk," Molly told him. How ruggedly built Cam was, his lean frame tight with muscle, his posture expressing the confidence that emanated from him like sunlight.

"Me, too. See you next Monday."

After Cam and Miracle disappeared over the dune, Molly reluctantly returned to her books. He was so shy and hesitant with her. Why? The information she'd dragged out of him had been just that—dragged. Closing the book, Molly looked out at the calm waters of the bay. Gulls floated effortlessly above it, and a few paddled on the surface. There was something touchingly vulnerable about Cam, despite his fierce looks and hard expression. This evening, he'd smiled more readily. He'd even laughed, and the sound had gone through her like a song. Cam Sinclair was an enigma, Molly decided.

"Enough daydreaming," she told herself sternly, opening the textbook. At least she didn't have to dread this weekend. Her father would be pleased with her grade.

"Only an eighty, Molly? That isn't going to raise your average by much."

Frustrated, Molly changed position on the couch, the phone against her shoulder. "Father, it's very good! I'm going to be able to turn things around."

"I think you're getting overly optimistic."

"An eighty is better than my last two grades. Besides, Cam was the one who gave me support on my idea to re-run the same test with a different pilot."

"Who's this Cam fellow?"

"He's a test-pilot instructor here at the facility."

"But you're a flight-test engineer. Aren't you supposed to be working with your assigned instructor? He certainly can't be it."

"Father, he's been here for two years and is savvy about how the school runs. His support means a lot to me."

"Well, don't put all your eggs in one basket, Molly. He could turn on you."

Molly laughed. "Not Cam. No, he's as steady as the sun rising and setting."

"Your idealism about people scares me. Particularly the way you see men. At least twice at Annapolis you had your heart broken by some boy."

"They were men, Father, not boys. And I'm not a little girl anymore, either. Each of the men I met gave me something good, and I learned something about myself from the experience. I don't consider it bad just because we broke up."

"Just stick to the business at hand, Molly. You can't afford to get romantically involved with anyone at TPS. It's going to take everything you've got to make it through. A relationship would pull your focus."

"Father, there's no man in my life, okay?"

"What about this Cam?"

"I told you. He's a friend, that's all."

"Well, Scott wants to talk to you now. I'm sure he's going to enjoy hearing how you turned the tables on Martin. And, Molly, I expect an even higher grade next week."

Molly nodded. "I'll try my best, Father." She was eager for Monday to come. A new happiness bubbled within her as her father handed the phone over to Scott. Although she talked to her brother, her heart centered on Cam. Did he realize how much he'd done to help her? She didn't think so. An idea came to mind, and Molly smiled. Monday, she would have a pleasant surprise for everyone at TPS. In reality it was her way of thanking Cam, but no one would realize it.

"What's this?" Vic Norton grinned broadly at the huge plate of cookies next to the coffee urn Monday morning.

Cam had just entered the room along with Phil Dalton. "Hey, what have you got there?"

"Look at this, Cam. Chocolate-chip cookies. My favorite."

"Mmm, Lordy! Those look scrumptious," Dalton said, grabbing a handful.

"Wonder who brought them?"

"Somebody with a heart and soul." Dalton sighed, munching contentedly.

Cam politely took two, leaving enough for everyone else. Norton and Dalton were sitting around the cookies like two big guard dogs, with looks on their faces that dared anyone else to try and reach for one. "Well, if you gentlemen will excuse me, I've got work to do. Don't get a bellyache."

Norton tittered. "Wouldn't think of it, Sinclair."

Cam made his way down the hall, now active with students coming in for the first class, and ducked into his office. The door was open already, which was normal. What wasn't normal was the small plate of cookies wrapped in plastic on his desk. He closed the door and set his mug down. Coming around behind the desk, Cam spotted a small envelope with his name flourished across it.

The chair squeaked in protest as he sat down and leaned back, the pristine white envelope in hand. He opened it and read the note, which said: "Thank you. Molly." Cam raised his eyebrows, looking at the plate of cookies.

"You're something else, Molly Rutledge. Something else..." He grabbed the plate. So, she was the one who'd baked those cookies for everyone. Cam smiled. The warmth in his chest expanded as he lifted the wrap, the odor of the cookies filling his nostrils. God, how he'd missed home cooking. Judging from her cookies, Cam would bet his right arm that Molly was one fine cook.

As he sat munching a cookie, savoring it, Cam reflected back on the past year. In some way, Molly's appearance had awakened him from the deep freeze his emotions had been stuck in. Meeting her on the beach Friday night had been a surprise. An endearing surprise. On Sunday, when he'd taken Miracle for a walk, he'd looked for Molly, but she hadn't been there. A terrible kind of loneliness had stalked him the rest of the day, and he'd been unable to shake it off.

He took another bite of cookie. "You truly are an angel from heaven, Molly."

Cam entered a filling classroom several hours later to give his lecture and overheard Martin speaking.

"Hey, Bard, who made these cookies?"

Lee was stretched out, books open on his desk. "Molly made them."

Cam was standing at the lectern, arranging his notes, when Martin got up and threw the cookie he'd been holding into the wastebasket at the front of the class.

"You got a problem, Martin?"

"I just got rid of it."

Cam held Martin's narrowed gray gaze. The pilot's chin was solid, his teeth clenched. "See me in my office after lunch."

"Yes, sir."

Though angry, Cam made sure his face and voice didn't relay his personal feelings. Martin might dislike Molly, but to openly show that kind of disrespect, not to mention wasting a homemade cookie, was unforgivable. Especially in front of twenty other students. He was glad Molly hadn't arrived in time to see Martin's reaction.

Martin showed up at Cam's office at exactly 1300. Cam invited the pilot in, ordering him to shut the door.

Martin came to parade rest in front of Cam's desk. Cam held the pilot's fixed gaze.

"What's your problem with Ensign Rutledge?"

"She's a woman, sir. An incapable, bumbling woman."

"Oh?" The word came out silkily, with a lethal edge to it.

"On both flights she's been assigned to me, she drops the damn pencil, the knee pad and God knows what else before a test. I've never seen anything like it."

"She's not incapable." Cam recalled the library incident with Molly. When nervous, she dropped things and ran into things. He was sure she'd be very nervous flying with Martin, who obviously disliked her.

"We disagree, sir."

"Look, Martin, you're going to have to put aside your personal prejudice and try to get along. Surely this isn't the first time you've run into a situation involving working with a person you didn't like. You have to make it work."

"Is this little talk all because I threw her damn cookie into the wastebasket?"

Cam shook his head. "Just the straw that broke the camel's back, Mr. Martin. What has you so set against a woman in our business?"

"Where I come from down in Texas, women are good for one thing, and that's flat on their back."

"Real redneck, aren't you?"

"Yes, sir. I am. And I don't make no bones about it. Usually, I can keep my personal opinions out of my career because there are very few broads involved with it. I can't help it if Rutledge managed to get here on her back."

Cam's hand tightened on the arm of his leather chair. He stood slowly. "Martin, let me make it real clear to you—back off and start treating Ensign Rutledge with respect. I will not tolerate your attitude, nor will the commandant, if this gets to his attention. Do you read me loud and clear?"

His eyes flashing, Martin came to attention. "Yes, sir."

"Dismissed," Cam growled. He stood there, breathing hard after Martin had left, anger boiling through him. The stupid bastard really believed what he said. Should he alert the commandant to the deteriorating situation? Or would this talk with Martin force the pilot to cool off and back down?

A pile of paperwork stared back at Cam. It was the last thing he wanted to do. He hadn't seen Molly all day, except once, in a hall, when they were going in opposite directions. He wanted to thank her for her thoughtfulness. Everyone except Martin had gradually found out that Molly had baked the cookies. She hadn't told anyone, but Lee had seen her bring them in early. Cam surmised that Molly would rather have had no one know it was her. Martin probably thought she was bringing cookies to butter up her instructor, Vic Norton.

Disgruntled and restless about Martin, Cam finally sat down. His office door was open, and he heard Molly's lilting laughter floating down the hall. Pen poised in hand, he hoped she was coming this way. He wasn't disappointed.

"Hi." Molly smiled and poked her head around the corner.

"Hi. Come on in." Cam looked at his watch. "You've got ten minutes before the next class starts." She looked breathless and excruciatingly beautiful. She shifted the load of books against her hip.

"Okay."

"Shut the door."

Molly's heart beat a little harder as she quietly closed the office door. Turning around, she melted beneath Cam's blue gaze. The harshness that was normally there was gone. It stunned her. It excited her. "What's going on?"

"Nothing," Cam said lazily, leaning back in his chair. He grinned and opened the side drawer of his desk. "I just wanted to thank you personally for making the cookies. As you can see, I've got them hidden where no one can get their grubby mitts on them.''

Smiling, Molly looked into the drawer. ''Yep, they're all there. I bet you've got them counted.''

''How'd you know?''

''Give me a break. What man isn't a little boy underneath that macho facade? Really, I don't think you realized how much you helped me last week, Cam. I tried to think of a way to show my thanks.''

He liked the flushed quality of Molly's cheeks and the sparkling green and gold of her eyes. ''You cook as good as you bake?''

''Sure do.''

Cam groaned. ''Listen, you don't know what the smell of those cookies did for me this morning.''

Softly she asked, ''What?''

''It just brought back a lot of good, warm memories. Bread baking in the kitchen, lemon tea smelling fragrant and filling the air... Little things.'' Cam roused himself from his thoughts, seeing sadness in Molly's eyes. ''It was a nice gift, Molly. Thanks.''

''From the sounds of it, maybe what you need is a good home-cooked meal.''

''Is that an offer?'' Cam couldn't stop himself. By regulations, he shouldn't be fraternizing with Molly.

''Sure is. How about this Saturday I cook for you? Come over about 1700?''

The offer of a real home-cooked meal was too big a temptation. An even larger one was spending time alone with Molly. ''You got a deal, Miss Molly Rutledge.''

''Great! It'll feel good to cook for someone other than myself. Dana, Maggie and I took turns cooking at Whiting Field until I got washed out. We had great dinners every night.''

"I'd settle for one great dinner," Cam said fervently, meaning it.

"You've got it." Molly glanced at her wristwatch. "Oh, I've got to run! See you later, Cam—I mean, Captain Sinclair." Molly turned and bumped into the edge of the desk. Her books went flying.

Cam got up and quickly retrieved them for her. She looked terribly embarrassed.

"I'm such a klutz. I'm sorry—"

"No," he told her in a low voice filled with emotion. "Don't you *ever* dare apologize for the way you are, Molly." He put the books in her waiting arms, holding her shocked gaze. "I like you just the way you are. Understand?"

Chapter Seven

The doorbell of Molly's apartment rang. She gave a flustered moan, wiped her hands on a towel and hurried out of the kitchen. Glancing over at the formal dining room, the glass-topped bamboo table set to perfection, she moved to the living room. She had spent all day Saturday cleaning and cooking in preparation for Cam's arrival.

Breathless, Molly hesitated at the door, looking down at herself. Was she dressed too casually? Should she have gotten her nails manicured? There hadn't been time! Quickly touching her nearly shoulder-length blond hair, she answered the door.

Cam smiled tentatively as the door opened. His smile widened in appreciation as Molly appeared before him, looking a bit bedraggled. His heart beat heavily in response to the pristine simplicity of her beauty. She wore no makeup, yet her emerald eyes and the natural ripe

color of her lips were emphasized by the pink flush on her
cheeks. As always, her hair was pleasantly mussed—the
kind of hair a man could find such great pleasure in tun-
neling his hands through.

"Hi...I know I'm a little early."

"No, that's okay. Come in." Molly's stomach clenched
with nervousness at the shadow in his blue eyes as he
looked her over. She should have brushed her hair before answering the door. Touching the throat of her ruby-
colored blouse, Molly said by way of apology, "You
couldn't tell I came from a home where Miss Manners
was born and raised."

Cam held out a bottle of wine to her. "Where I come
from, we didn't know who Miss Manners was. Here...I
hope this is a suitable wine for the fabulous-smelling
dinner you're cooking." The pleasure on her face made
Cam feel damn good about himself as she cradled the
wine in her hands.

"Wonderful! A red Grenache! It will be perfect with
the meal." She shut the door. Cam was wearing comfortable clothes, which made her feel better about her
choice of a blouse and white slacks. The July evening was
warm without being humid, and Molly had opened the
huge living-room and dining-room windows to the saltily
fragrant breezes of the Chesapeake.

She stood uncertainly, gawking at Cam. How terribly
handsome he was—even better looking, she thought, in
civilian clothes. His ivory-colored chamois shirt was open
and revealed the powerful column of his neck and a bit
of dark hair showing above the white T-shirt he wore beneath it. His sleeves were neatly rolled up and cuffed at
his elbows. She liked the pale blue slacks that matched the
color of his eyes. They outlined the male perfection of his
narrow hips. Normally Cam had a five o'clock beard at

this time of day. It was obvious he'd shaved before he'd come over.

"Please, come in."

"Need any help in the kitchen?" Cam saw how nervous she was, as her hands restlessly cradled the bottle of wine. Was she going to start bumping into things and dropping things? She had such a touching vulnerability woven into her insecurity.

"Well . . ."

"Back home in Montana, Ma always had us in the kitchen helping. As soon as I was tall enough to reach the sink, I was trained for kitchen duty."

Smiling, Molly relaxed because Cam was relaxed. She found herself beginning to enjoy his presence as never before. "If you've got that kind of training, I'd better take advantage of it. You can open the wine and pour it for us. All I have to do is get the bread out of the oven, and we'll be ready to eat."

"Sounds great." Cam inhaled deeply. "Whatever you're cooking, it smells like heaven."

She colored fiercely beneath his praise. "I don't know about heaven. We're going to have standing-rib roast of beef, cranberry ported apples and choux-paste fritters. And," Molly added with a soft smile, "bread made with my own hands. For dessert, I've made a cherry filbert sundae pie." The hardness usually present in Cam's face was miraculously absent. Molly saw his eyes dancing with life for the first time. Could home-cooked food mean *that* much to him? No, that was impossible. Later, she would ask him about his past. Perhaps he was divorced and missed home life. So many pilots' marriages fell apart because they were gone to sea for three to six months at a time. Cam could be another casualty of the "unfeeling" military mission. And so could his ex-wife and, possibly, his children.

Touching his stomach, Cam shook his head. "Molly Rutledge, you're an angel placed in my path. The dinner sounds like heaven, believe me." He saw her eyes grow lustrous beneath his heartfelt compliment. The apartment mirrored Molly completely, Cam thought, looking around as they headed for the kitchen. He was struck by the fact that her decor was Far Eastern. The Oriental motif added an aura of serenity that made Cam feel utterly contented; the tension that normally gripped his shoulders melted away.

"I'm no angel, believe me," Molly was saying, gesturing toward herself. "My hair needs combing, I should have manicured my nails—"

Cam reached out unthinkingly, cupping her small shoulders with his large hands. "I like you just the way you are. In my eyes, you look perfect. Okay?" He held her shy gaze. Giving her a gentle shake, he finally got her to smile.

"Okay, okay. Thank you. I'll stop worrying about my appearance."

"Good," he praised, not wanting to release her, yet knowing he must. The ruby blouse was made of pure silk, sliding sensuously against her skin, and Molly's cheeks matched its rosiness. He'd lived for this day—this time with her without the demands of school dictating what was or was not appropriate between them.

Shaken by the intensity of his touch and voice, Molly turned away. The kitchen was ultramodern, with the bar in the middle of the room. She handed Cam the opener and brought down two fine crystal wineglasses. Her hands shook as she opened the oven and brought out a golden loaf of perfectly baked bread. Setting it on the countertop, she brushed it with melted butter.

"You've gone to a lot of trouble for me," Cam commented, pouring the wine. He recorked the bottle and set it in the refrigerator.

"You're worth it."

"Music to my ears." Cam walked over and placed her glass of wine on the counter near her. Then, leaning against the bar, he took a sip of his own.

"There's no secret to you, Cam." She laughed, taking the loaf out of the pan and placing it on a breadboard to slice it. "You sound like a male chauvinist."

He shrugged. "There's a little of that in me."

"It's not a sin to enjoy good food. I love to cook. Dana and Maggie always jumped for joy when it was my turn in the kitchen."

"I'll bet they made things like beans and wieners."

"Worse—frozen dinners." Molly made a face, quickly slicing the fragrant-smelling bread. "It was terrible. Both of them are terrible cooks. Dana has an excuse, but Maggie didn't. Her mother is a fabulous cook."

"It never rubbed off on her, eh?" Cam watched as she placed the sliced bread in a red-and-white checked towel already folded into an oval-shaped bamboo basket.

"No, not on Maggie. She's a twenty-first-century woman."

"You seem to be a throwback to the nineteenth century."

Molly looked up, held gently by his gaze. There was such strength to Cam, and yet, as she was discovering, an incredible facet of sensitivity. "Now, why would you say that?" She set the bread in front of him. "Here, go put this on the table."

He picked up the basket. "You're old-fashioned."

"Pooh." Taking the standing-rib roast out of the oven, Molly transferred the succulent meat to a large oval platter. When Cam returned, she put him to work. "Here, start carving. Is that a nineteenth-century woman talking?"

He grinned and thoughtfully began to carve the steaming roast. "Saying you're old-fashioned isn't an insult. It's a compliment."

"Apology accepted, Captain Sinclair," she teased. The Caesar salad had been made minutes earlier, and Molly carried it to the table. The apartment was filled with a delightful concoction of fragrances that she loved. Right now, the place seemed like a home, not a lonely box where she lived. It was Cam's larger-than-life presence that completed the space for Molly, and she absorbed every moment with him like a flower starved for sunlight.

Cam brought in the platter and set it in the center of the table. Molly gestured for him to sit down. The bamboo chairs were on casters and had upholstered seats in a muted green and maroon fabric. The table looked as if it had come out of *Good Housekeeping* or some other magazine that exhorted the feminine arts of cooking and decorating. Cam appreciated every little nuance Molly had thoughtfully added to the atmosphere.

"Do you always cook like this?" Cam wanted to know, seating her at the table first.

"When it was my turn, I did." She laughed. "After Maggie and Dana's two weeks of frozen dinners, take-out and pizzas, I was starved for good, sound food."

Hungry on so many levels, Cam insisted she fill her plate first, passing her each entrée. Frowning when he saw how little she took, he asked, "Are you trying to lose weight or something?"

"No. Why?"

"There's not enough on your plate to feed a bird."

Laughing, Molly spread the maroon linen napkin across her lap. "I always eat like this."

"That's starvation fare," Cam muttered and heaped a huge portion of everything onto his plate without apology. The classical music playing in the background was pleasant and unobtrusive. Cam occasionally heard the lonely cry of a sea gull in the distance. His gaze kept returning to Molly, who was obviously schooled to the hilt in manners. He was less so, but it didn't matter to him. The food was delicious and a welcome relief after a year of his own cooking—mostly frozen dinners.

Molly tried not to stare openly at Cam as he ate. The food on his plate disappeared like vapor, and he went for seconds of everything. He ate as if he hadn't eaten in years! And in her opinion, the pleasure wreathing his features was something to behold. Never had she seen a man so enjoy food. He seemed almost reverent about every bite he took. Nearly half the loaf of homemade bread disappeared, Molly having eaten one slice. Where was Cam tucking it all away?

The wine bottle was empty. Molly smiled over at Cam, who had leaned back, his hands across his stomach. "I think you're going to burst any second, Cameron Sinclair. You ate enough for three starving men."

"I made a pig of myself."

"With no apologies."

He grinned, sated. "No, ma'am. No apologies." He reached out, overwhelmed by the need to touch her. Capturing her hand beneath his, he gave it a small squeeze. "Just unending compliments and thank-yous for the beautiful woman who took the time and care to create such a meal."

"It was just a meal," Molly protested, her heart leaping wildly at his brief touch.

"Food cooked with love is always the best kind," Cam said.

"Come on, let's get away from the table. We can sit in the living room and let it settle. I don't think you'll be ready for dessert for at least an hour."

With a groan, Cam slowly got to his feet, a sheepish grin on his features. "An hour sounds fine."

Shaking her head, Molly remarked, "Cam, I don't see how you can even think about having dessert. Look how much you ate!"

He glanced across the table. "I did demolish a lot of it, didn't I?"

"There won't be many leftovers, that's for sure." She moved to the living room, her wineglass in hand. A beautiful flower garden and well-kept lawn were visible just outside her first-floor window, and Molly had the bamboo sofa turned so that she could sit and enjoy the view. Walking over to the couch, she sat down, taking off her low-heeled shoes and tucking her legs beneath her. Cam sat at the other end of the couch. Molly didn't know whether to be disappointed or not. She soon found out why he'd chosen that position.

"Mind if I stretch out a little?" Cam nudged his loafers off.

Smiling, Molly shook her head and patted the sofa. "This couch invites lying down. No, go ahead."

With a groan, Cam did exactly that. His feet almost brushed Molly's thigh. "This is what a good meal does to me. It makes me sleepy afterward."

"You're more like a cougar that overate and has to go sleep it off."

"You don't mind?"

"No. Why should I?"

Cam felt an incredible sense of peace stealing over him. He searched Molly's serene face. Her fingers, long and graceful, curved around the stem of the wineglass. Everything was so perfect...so perfect. "Well, some ladies might get insulted if I dropped off to sleep after a meal."

"You're here as a friend, Cam. No expectations, no demands. Okay?"

He smiled tiredly, his eyelids drooping. "I knew you'd understand."

Molly's heart went out to Cam as he closed his eyes, his fingers laced across his belly. He was hauntingly human right now, and she was being given access to the real man hidden beneath that hard mask he usually wore. The difference was shocking, warming. As she sat there, the music flowing across the apartment, the dusk light softly invading the living room through the open window, Molly felt a peacefulness she never knew existed.

Glancing over at Cam, who had promptly fallen asleep, she knew the feeling was directly linked to him. Yes, he'd loved her cooking, but it was far more than that. He gave her a sense of confidence in herself. It was as if he instinctively knew when she was feeling insecure about herself or a situation, and was able to step in and say or do the right thing to help her achieve the balance she needed. What kind of magic spun between them? Whatever it was, Molly mused as she sipped her blush wine, it was powerful and wonderful. The evening was perfect in every way.

Later, Molly rose from the couch and went to clear the table as quietly as possible and put the dishes into the dishwasher. Sometimes, when she halted at the kitchen door to check on Cam, she could hear a soft, broken snore coming from the direction of the living room. Her heart turned somersaults in her chest. Everything was right. So right.

The phone rang, jerking Cam out of a deep, healing sleep. He sat up, disoriented. Molly came racing into the room, an apologetic look on her face as she reached for the phone, which he realized was on the lamp table at the other end of the couch.

"I'm sorry," she said. "I thought I'd turned off the ringer."

Cam eased into a sitting position as Molly came around and sat down on the couch. "That's okay," he muttered, rubbing his face.

"Hello?"

"Molly?"

Molly's heart sank. It was her father. She slid a look in Cam's direction. His hair was mussed, and his features sleep-ridden. He sat forward, his elbows resting on his long, powerful thighs, his eyes still drowsy.

"Father." How could she have forgotten that her family always called on Saturday evening? She should have scheduled the dinner with Cam on Sunday. She felt as if she were dying inside—she didn't want him to hear the conversation. "Uhh . . . could I call you back later?"

"I'm afraid not, Molly," her father answered brusquely. "I'm scheduled to fly to L.A. shortly, and I want to hear about your week."

Cam lifted his head at the pain he heard in Molly's contralto voice. He saw her hand clenched tightly in her lap, saw the anxiety in her beautiful green eyes. Not wanting to make her feel uncomfortable, he got up and went into the kitchen. But something told him to listen to her phone conversation, even if it was wrong. He stopped at the kitchen doorway, where he could see Molly sitting on the couch, her back to him. She wouldn't know he was there unless she turned around.

The phone call lasted twenty minutes. The first ten minutes she talked with her father, then she talked with her brother Scott, for another ten minutes. Cam scowled and wrapped his arms against his chest as he listened. Molly turned slightly, her profile visible. The serenity in her face had disappeared, and she was chewing distractedly on a fingernail, obviously nervous as she answered question after question. When she finally hung up Cam saw her bow her head and press a hand against her closed eyes.

He approached her quietly in his stocking feet. The distraught sound of her voice toward the end of the conversation made him reach out and place his hand on her shoulder as he came up behind her.

"You weren't kidding when you said your family called and grilled you every week."

Molly felt Cam's fingers gently massage her shoulders. His touch was at once relaxing and supportive. Miserable, she looked up into his shadowed features. She expected to find censure in his face, but instead, his eyes were turbulent with care.

"I forgot all about Father's and Scott's call." Molly got up suddenly. With a weak shrug, she turned and faced Cam. "I should have scheduled the dinner for Sunday instead."

Cam felt her pain. "No, I'm glad I was here today."

"You heard everything?"

Cam couldn't lie to her. "Yes."

"Oh, dear..."

Molly looked like a doe caught in the glare of oncoming headlights. Cam couldn't stand the despair in her voice or the haunted look in her eyes. He moved around the couch and put his hands on her shoulders.

"There's nothing to apologize for, Molly."

"Yes, there is. I would hate to subject anyone to my family's phone calls."

His hands tightened on her shoulders. "We've got some serious talking to do, Molly. Come on, sit down." He allowed his hands to slide down her arms, then captured one hand and led her back toward the sofa. Her fingers felt damp and cold.

"I'm so ashamed."

"I'm angry."

She gave him a startled look as she sat down. Cam refused to let go of her hand. He sat right next to her, their thighs brushing. "Why?" Her voice sounded shaky.

"Because no one has the right to grill you like that, Molly. Does your father call *every* Saturday wanting to know what the hell kind of grade you got at the end of the week?"

Molly winced, refusing to meet his narrowed eyes. "Yes."

"Why?"

His hand fed her stability. Molly leaned forward, and pressed her hand against her eyes. "I disappointed my father so badly when I got washed out at Whiting. He's afraid I'm going to fail here at TPS, too."

"For someone who supposedly is concerned," Cam ground out, "he didn't seem very happy over the fact that you got an eighty-two percent on your last test. He should be jumping for joy."

Lifting her head, Molly whispered, "You don't understand, Cam."

"Try me."

"My average for the first month places me in the bottom third of the class."

"That's what he was hammering you about?" Anger spiraled quickly through Cam.

"Yes."

He bit back an expletive. "So what? Every week your grade percentile is improving. You've got a long way to go before school ends. He ought to be looking at *that*, not the average. What's wrong with him?"

Molly shrugged. "You heard me on the phone. I tried to explain it to him."

Absently Cam rubbed the back of her hand. "Is he always this kind to you?"

"What do you mean?"

"Doesn't he ever compliment you on what you do right?"

"Father is one of those people who see the glass as half empty, instead of half full the way I do."

Cam shook his head. "And he pulled this same crap on you at Whiting?"

"And at Annapolis," she said timidly.

"Jesus!" Cam got up, unable to sit still any longer. He paced the living room, wrestling with his anger, saying nothing for several minutes. He knew any words that came out of his mouth would be ugly, probably upsetting Molly even more. Finally he stopped pacing and came to crouch in front of her. Taking her hands in his, he held her gaze, seeing shame clearly written in her eyes.

"Do you realize what he's doing to you?" Cam demanded.

"Father just wants me to be successful, that's all."

"No," he whispered harshly. "No, Molly, he doesn't. He's controlling you through negativity and fear of failure. In my book, he's manipulating your emotions, keeping your back pinned to the wall."

Stunned by Cam's intense emotional reaction, Molly whispered, "My father cares about me, Cam. It's just that he had all his hopes pinned on Scott, and now Scott's crippled for life. He has a dream—"

"Dammit, Molly! It's his dream and Scott's dream, not necessarily yours!" Cam released her hands and stood, breathing hard. "I'm sorry, I'm way out of line for saying that."

Molly continued to sit, her hands clasped in her lap. "My father cares for me," she repeated.

Cam bit back a reply. He saw the desperation in her eyes. "Controlling another person isn't expressing love, Molly," he said in a low, vibrating tone. "He's controlling you. Can't you see that?"

"No."

"Then why is he cutting you down instead of building you up?"

Molly stared up at Cam. He was angry and upset. "I don't understand," she whispered.

"From what I heard of the two wonderful family chats you just had, they were emphasizing what you *weren't* doing right—not taking a look at what you are doing correctly. Is that a fair analysis?"

Molly gave a jerky nod of her head, her throat constricting.

Cam crouched down again, this time not touching Molly for fear that he'd sweep her into his arms and hold her. He so badly wanted to give her a place of safety and protection. How had she stood four years of abusive tirades? It suddenly dawned upon Cam that Molly was desperate for love from her father, negative or not. He was all she had, and she clung to him. Sickened, Cam fought his anger.

"Anytime one person has to control another is bad news, Molly," he said softly. "It means the controlling person is insecure—afraid he's going to lose something he wants. A controlling person doesn't allow other people to live their own lives. Instead, they have to live within the parameters the controller has set up for them. It's like being a puppet on a string, your entire life a dance to someone else's steps."

"And you're saying my father's that way?" Her voice had gone off-key with tension.

Cam nodded, holding her frightened gaze. "In a healthy relationship, Molly, one partner doesn't control the other. I don't care whether it's a parent and child or a husband and wife, the same rule applies."

Almost angrily, Molly rose and circled the couch, stopping behind it, her arms crossed defensively on her chest. "You act like you know so much about this," she hurled back at him bitterly. "Why should I believe you? My father loves me! He's not doing this to hurt me."

"Listen to me, Molly," Cam rasped. "I was married to the most wonderful woman on earth and we had a son. I loved her with my life for seven years. She taught me what a healthy, loving relationship was all about. I know the difference." Cam looked away. He hadn't spoken to anyone about Jeanne or Sean since their deaths. His voice cracked. "Dammit, you've got to believe me when I tell you, a loving parent wouldn't do what your father's doing to you!" He forced himself to look at her, misery flooding him as never before. "My wife and son taught me what love was all about, Molly. They died a year ago in a plane crash, but I still carry that knowledge with me. Love doesn't control someone else. Love gives you the ability to allow the other person to be herself, not what you want her to be.''

Thunderstruck, Molly stood very still. She stared across the living room at Cam. The terrible sadness that she'd seen in his eyes from the first day was there again, but magnified. His shadowy features were twisted with grief, and it cut through to her heart as nothing else ever could. Forgetting her own pain and defensiveness, Molly took a step forward, her arms dropping to her sides.

''My God, you lost your family!'' she breathed, and her eyes welled up with tears.

Chapter Eight

Molly's cry shattered through Cam. He took in the devastation written across her face. What he saw was what she was feeling for *him*.

"I'm so sorry, Cam," Molly whispered, moving tentatively toward him. She saw the naked anguish carved in every line of his face. How could she ever have accused him of being an unfeeling machine? He'd lobbied so passionately on her behalf that he'd revealed his own wounded heart.

She saw the indecision, the utter hopelessness and ravaged feelings that losing his family had inflicted upon Cam. He stood tensely at her approach. Halting before him, Molly tilted her head to keep contact with his narrowed eyes.

"It makes my problems seem so inconsequential."

"No!" Cam rasped, snapping his head up. "It doesn't."

Hesitantly, Molly reached out with her hand, her fingers barely touching his arm. Cam was trembling. What love this man must have had for his family. As she searched the darkness in his stormy blue eyes, Molly realized how much he must care for her to relive this agony. Her fingers tightened around his arm.

"I'm going to try and understand what you're saying," Molly said, her own voice shaky.

Molly's fingers felt like fire on his arm, their warmth burning through his shirt to his flesh. Cam's heart and shredded emotions screamed at him to sweep her into his arms, but he fought the need. God, sweet God, he needed Molly! He needed the warmth and compassion she was offering him. She stood serene and strong, when he felt neither. Wildly aware of her hand on him, Cam closed his eyes and dragged in a deep, shaky breath.

"You're special, Molly. You've got the brains to do this. Don't let your father and brother continue to control you. You can't fight two wars on two different fronts at the same time. I don't know how you made it through Annapolis with them on your back like that."

"My friends, Dana and Maggie," she answered simply.

Cam swallowed hard, tears welling up within him, begging to be shed. He hadn't cried at the funeral. He'd merely felt utterly gutted and numb throughout the entire service. And tears had come only twice in the year since. Now, with Molly standing so close, Cam intuitively knew she could be strong enough for him, if he wanted to sink into her arms and sob out the grief still trapped in his heart.

"Cam?"

He winced at her low, pleading tone. In a superhuman effort, because Cam realized this was the wrong time and place for them, he pulled from her grasp. "I've got to get going, Molly," he muttered, blindly turning away.

Bereft, Molly watched him move toward the door. Cam needed her. He needed to be held so he could cry. She could see it. But why was he leaving? Hurrying to catch up with him, she met him at the door.

"Why don't you stay for a while, Cam?" she asked gently. "You're in no shape to drive right now."

"No."

Molly stood her ground. His voice had been harsh, grinding like a dog snapping a bone between powerful jaws. "Look at you. You're trembling, Cam."

Cam stared down at Molly in disbelief. She was blocking the door! Her voice was calm and reasonable when he felt anything but. Feeling not anger but desperation, he reached for the doorknob.

"No!" Molly whispered, gripping his hand and holding it. She stared up at him. "What's going on here, Cam? It's okay to help me, but you don't let anyone help you?"

"I don't know what you're talking about."

"Yes, you do. I want you to turn around and go back to the couch. Let me pour us some brandy. We both need it. We need to talk."

For an instant, panic seized Cam. He wanted to push Molly aside and escape. *Why?* a part of his brain whispered to him. Molly was offering solace, a safe place when he'd had none in the past year. Surprisingly, the softness that was Molly had transformed her into a woman who was firmly in charge. He regarded her, too caught up in his own emotional reactions to figure out what had taken place.

"Come on," Molly insisted, dragging Cam away from the door. She kept a tight grip on his hand as she led him back into the living room. Placing her hands on his shoulders, she pushed him down on the sofa. "Now, sit there. And don't you dare move while I get the brandy and snifters. Understand?"

Cam nodded, hanging his head, the anxiety gone—replaced with such a sense of loss that he felt physically weakened.

In the kitchen, Molly quickly wiped the tears from her eyes. Cam mustn't see them. He needed her strength, not her tears right now. As she brought the snifters down from the cupboard and located the apricot brandy to pour a bit into each, Molly shook her head.

"What's going on?" she muttered to herself. There was no denying it any longer, Molly thought, capping the brandy and setting it back in the cupboard. Never had a man made her feel so much or want so much.

As she carried the snifters into the living room, Molly realized she was seriously drawn to Cam. She'd had relationships before, but none had ever touched the deep chords of her heart or turned her dreams into torrid longing until now. Molly tabled that discovery, knowing she couldn't allow it to interfere with Cam's healing process. It was obvious he was still grieving—and perhaps venting it for the first time—for his lost family.

Girding herself internally, she joined Cam on the couch. Slipping the snifter into his hands, she said, "Drink it. All of it."

He twisted his head and looked at Molly with curiosity. There was nothing soft about her now. She was very much in charge. Grateful, he lifted the snifter and gulped down the small bit of brandy. His lips pulled away from his teeth, sucking air between them as the apricot brandy hit his throat and then his stomach.

"That's powerful stuff...."

Molly smiled tautly. "My grandmother's recipe. She was a real healer. I remember her telling my mother that a good dose of brandy always helped in emergencies."

Cam studied the snifter as he slowly turned it around in his hands. "Yeah, this stuff will heal any crisis."

Molly curled her legs beneath her, a foot away from Cam. She'd purposely turned off the living-room lights, intuitively understanding that darkness was preferable under the circumstances. Cam's face was harsh and alive with emotion, the interior shadows cutting cruelly across its planes, emphasizing the grief he'd allowed to surface.

"There are many ways to heal," Molly began in a low voice, watching him for reaction. "I want you to tell me about your family, Cam."

"Why?"

"Because I care enough to listen." *I care for you.* Molly bit back the real truth. "When I came to TPS and saw you for the first time, you scared the heck out of me. I'd never seen a man with such an emotionless face. I've never seen someone able to control their feelings to the degree you do. I kept wondering why you were that way. Now—" Molly sighed "—I know. You lost your family...."

"I lost everything," Cam whispered harshly, his control starting to unravel, "to that goddamn airliner crashing. The bastard of a pilot tried to land during a thunderstorm. Why didn't he take the plane around? Why didn't he have the guts to tell the tower it was too dangerous, too dicey, and have them wave him off the landing pattern? Why couldn't the son of a bitch have the brains to get rerouted to another field?"

Cam gripped the snifter hard between his hands as he stared out into the gathering darkness beyond the open windows. No longer was he in Molly's apartment, nor did he feel her next to him as he talked. He heard the pain, the anger and utter hopelessness in his own voice. He thought he sounded like a wolf baying into the night, haunted and alone.

Molly sat, unmoving, her snifter of untouched brandy resting on her thigh. Every line of Cam's body was frozen with tension, his shoulders steeled beneath the load he'd carried so long by himself. She didn't dare move or reach out to touch him, for fear of breaking the connection he'd established with his deeply suppressed feelings.

"I dropped Sean and Jeanne off at the airport. Her parents lived in Dallas, Texas, and they hadn't seen their grandson in two years. It was May, and a good time to go. I was stuck here at TPS with a new class and couldn't get leave to go with them." Bitterly, Cam rasped, "That was at three o'clock. I got off work a couple of hours later and went home. I already missed them. God, we'd been apart more than together in our seven-year marriage. I was aboard an aircraft carrier when Sean was born. Jeanne had to go through it alone. I wanted so damn badly to be there for her... to see my son born.

"I'd turned on the television because I couldn't stand the quiet in the house. It was human voices, something to break the silence. I was out in the kitchen fixing myself a can of soup for dinner when the national news came on. I heard them announce that the plane Jeanne had been on had crashed at Dallas during a thunderstorm. They said there were no survivors."

Cam hung his head, tears driving into his tightly shut eyes. His hands gripped the brandy snifter almost painfully. A sob worked its way up his throat. He clamped his lips shut and tried to fight it back.

Molly set her glass on the black lacquer coffee table in front of them. Gently she pried Cam's snifter from between his clenched fingers. Sliding her arm around his shoulders, she whispered, "Come here," and drew Cam against her, letting his head rest against her shoulder and neck.

Just the softness of Molly's voice, her excruciatingly gentle touch, ended the battle between Cam's emotions and his iron-clad control. As he leaned into her opened arms the first sob tore from him, shaking his entire body. He felt Molly's arms enclose him, holding him tightly with her woman's strength, her woman's compassion.

Molly lay back against the couch as Cam's arms reached around her, gripping her so hard that they squeezed the breath from her. It didn't matter as first one sob and then another ripped out of him. She'd never seen a man cry, and it tore savagely at her heart and soul. Cam's weeping was that of a storm having broken, wild and relentless in its fury. Her blouse was soaked with his tears. His hands opened and closed against her back as her body absorbed the painful sobs she thought would tear him physically apart.

All Molly could do was hold Cam and shakily stroke his hair, whispering words meant to comfort and heal. Molly had no idea how long they stayed locked in each other's embrace, for time had ceased to exist. She cried for Cam, for his pain, his terrible loss. Understanding what it was like to lose someone she desperately loved, it was easy to capitulate to Cam's grief and share it unselfishly with him.

Her eyes were wet with tears as she finally opened them. The storm had passed. Cam held her tightly, but his grasp had loosened somewhat. Except for the gossamer light from the kitchen, darkness surrounded them. Molly didn't move, absorbing the feel of his strong body pressed against her.

Gradually, Cam released his hold on Molly. Her once silky hair beneath his jaw and cheek was damp with his tears. Inhaling deeply, he wanted to remember her wonderfully feminine fragrance, a sweetness subtle and yet unforgettable. She wore no perfume. It was her natural scent that dizzied him, reminding him of life, not death. Opening his eyes, Cam took in Molly as a woman—soft with curves, flexible and giving. God, was she giving—in a way he'd never felt before.

Though he wanted to keep her in his arms forever, Cam knew it couldn't be. He was still healing; the past must continue to be put to rest. He lifted his head and gently broke their embrace. Looking down on her silhouetted features, he saw the paths of tears tracing down her cheeks. The fact that she'd cried for him shook him anew.

With his thumbs he wiped the remnants of tears from her pale cheeks. Her skin was velvety firm, and the newly awakened part of him, the man, wanted her. Dizzied by Molly's closeness, Cam found it impossible to sort through all the emotions he was feeling. Sitting up, he placed his elbows on his thighs and rubbed his face.

"That was a long time in coming," Molly said quietly, sliding her hand along his strong back. It felt good to caress him, to continue to give him comfort.

Her slender hand outlining the curve of his shoulders felt unbelievably healing to Cam. He was in awe of Molly's intuitive knowledge of what he needed, and he sat like a starving man, absorbing what she offered him in the form of touching. He felt shaky and raw inside, still craving physical contact to stabilize him after the harsh release of his grief.

"When my mom died," Molly went on in a low voice, "I didn't know what to do. When you're ten, the word *cancer* doesn't mean much. She had liver cancer. It hit her fast and hard. She wasn't sick for very long. I remember her coming into my bedroom one day when she didn't look very well. Pooky jumped up and lay on my bed while she talked to me. Mom picked up my favorite doll, Amanda, and held us both in her lap. She tried to explain about the disease and where it was in her. She used Amanda to show me.

"I guess I didn't have a very good grasp of heaven at that time. Mom said she'd be leaving soon for heaven. She said it would be as if someone took Miss Amanda from me and I never saw her again." Molly sniffed back the tears. "That got my attention. I could understand if Miss Amanda suddenly disappeared from my room and never came back. She was my best friend next to my mom. I started to cry when it all sank in—that someday soon, my mom wouldn't be coming back to me. We sat there all afternoon. She held me in her lap and just rocked me. I remember everything she told me even to this day. At the time, some of it didn't make sense. But it does now. I loved her so much, Cam. She was such a warm, wonderful person."

Cam roused himself, his heart feeling every nuance of emotion, both for himself and for Molly and her desperately unhappy childhood. Turning, he captured one of her hands and squeezed it between his. "You must be exactly like your mother," he told her in a raspy voice. "A very special person."

Molly avoided his burning stare, her hair acting as a curtain when she lowered her head to hide her feelings. "I'm glad I was here for you, Cam. You needed someone...anyone...to help you release your grief at losing your wonderful family."

GET 4 BOOKS

Return this card, and we'll send you 4 brand-new Silhouette Special Edition® novels, absolutely FREE! We'll even pay the postage both ways!

We're making you this offer to introduce you to the benefits of the Silhouette Reader Service™: free home delivery of brand-new romance novels, months before they're available in stores, AND at a saving of 33¢ apiece compared to the cover price!

Accepting these 4 free books places you under no obligation to buy. You may cancel at any time, even just after receiving your free shipment. If you do not cancel, every month, we'll send 6 more Silhouette Special Edition novels and bill you just $2.92* apiece—that's all!

Yes, please send me my 4 free Silhouette Special Edition novels, as explained above.

Name _____

Address _____ Apt. _____

City _____ State _____ ZIP _____

235 CIS ACJT

Get 4 Books FREE

SEE BACK OF CARD FOR DETAILS

DETACH ALONG DOTTED LINE AND MAIL TODAY! – DETACH ALONG DOTTED LINE AND MAIL TODAY! – DETACH ALONG DOTTED LINE AND MAIL TODAY! – DETACH ALONG DOTTED LINE AND MAIL TODAY!

FREE MYSTERY GIFT

We will be happy to send you a free bonus gift along with your free books! To request it, please check here and mail this reply card promptly!

Thank you!

BUSINESS REPLY CARD

FIRST CLASS MAIL   PERMIT NO. 717   BUFFALO, NY

POSTAGE WILL BE PAID BY ADDRESSEE

SILHOUETTE READER SERVICE
3010 WALDEN AVE
P O BOX 1867
BUFFALO NY 14240-9952

NO POSTAGE
NECESSARY
IF MAILED
IN THE
UNITED STATES

Cam fought the urge to raise her hand to his lips and kiss it. Instead, he released it and placed his fingers beneath her chin, forcing her to look at him. There was such beauty in her green-gold eyes, such depth of understanding. "I think you missed your calling, angel. You should have been a counselor of some kind. I've been walking around with this time bomb inside me since the funeral, and no one—not the chaplain, not my best friends, not even my mother—could dig it out of me. But you did."

Shakily Molly tried to smile, but it hurt to do so. Cam's ravaged features looked hauntingly vulnerable. She ached to lean those few inches forward and kiss him, kiss him and breathe life back into him. On some deep level, Molly knew she could eventually do that. The magic that sprang effortlessly between them when they were together could make that happen.

"It was time, Cam, that's all. If you were home right now and started talking to your mother about it, I'm sure you'd have cried with her instead."

He grazed her chin with his thumb. The ache to kiss those delicate, parted lips was almost too much for Cam. Forcing himself to take his hand away, he shook his head and held Molly's luminous gaze.

"Dodging and running again?" he taunted her gently.

Molly gave him a startled look.

Cam managed a slight smile. "Your father's control over you has made you so unsure of yourself, Molly, that you don't even realize your own strengths. You can't even take an honest compliment." To hell with it. Cam reached out and gripped her hand hard in his. "You just helped me through one of the worst times in my life. And I'm not about to let you continue to throw yourself to the wolves, Molly. I'm going to be here for you, the way you were for me.''

"I don't understand."

Grimly he said, "You will." *With my help.* Somehow, Cam knew he could show Molly what her father and brother were doing to her. He had her unequivocal trust. "Look, we've shared something rare, something good. Whatever's between us works. You've helped me. Now I'm going to help you."

Molly shrugged. "Friends always help each other." Cam was grateful, that was all. The newness of her love for him flowed through her. He didn't love her. No. He saw what she'd done as an act of mercy on his behalf. His love was still tied up with the past. It hurt to admit it, but Molly refused to lie to herself.

Friend wasn't exactly the word Cam wanted to use with Molly. Even so recently after releasing the painful grief he'd carried so long, Cam was beginning to understand what Molly really meant to him—to his newly awakened heart. "Yes," he whispered hoarsely. "Friends help each other."

Chapter Nine

"Bad news, Molly." Lee Bard handed her the weekly flight assignment as he entered the computer room. Although no one else was in the room, he kept his voice low. "You've got Martin."

With a groan, Molly took the paper and looked at it. For two months, she'd been lucky and had every pilot but Martin. She wasn't sure if it was because Cam had influence over those sorts of things or not. She'd asked him once, and he'd said only that the commandant made out the schedules.

"Looks like my luck ran out," she muttered unhappily.

"Sorry. Martin's hard on everyone."

"Yes, and at our expense, not his." Molly knew her grades were slowly climbing. Right now, she was rated sixth out of eight engineering students. In order to graduate, she had to make third or fourth. She had three more months to prove her mettle.

"Well, you've got the weekend to come up with a great flight test and the rest of the week to perfect it so Martin can't blow holes in it and blame you," Lee said, sitting down at another terminal. Friday afternoons were always quiet around the facility, as many instructors left early.

Glumly, Molly sat at her computer, feeling her stomach begin to knot in anticipation. If only she could talk to Cam about this. In the two months since Cam had wept in her arms, there had been an incredible change in him. Everyone around TPS had noticed it. He smiled occasionally, and even joked from time to time in the classes he taught.

She picked up her calculator, her enthusiasm dampened considerably by the news of being assigned to Martin. Well, Cam had been counseling her on how to become a better defender of her own turf—on her terms. At one time or another, all the pilots, with the exception of Dalton, had tried to blame their faults on her flight test instead of their own flying ability. And each time, Molly had been better able to defend herself and the test. Gradually she was getting respect from everyone.

"Jeez, what bad timing," she whispered, staring at herself in the monitor screen. But her confidence was steadily materializing. Part of it, she knew, was Cam's quiet, shadowy presence in the background. He'd never openly defend her in a debrief. Instead, he gave her the courage to try the tools he'd taught her to use. Sometimes he'd smile at her afterward as they were filing out of the debrief room. At times like that, Molly felt as if she were walking ten feet off the floor.

Rising, she packed her computer printouts, calculator and extra notebook paper into her briefcase. "I'm going home, Lee. I'll see you Monday."

He raised his head from his work. "Yeah. Get some sleep, you hear?"

With a shrug, Molly waved goodbye and left. Sleep was a privilege that got shunted aside for work. As she made her way to the parking lot, she met Cam, whose car was parked next to hers.

"You look upset," he noted.

"I am. Martin's assigned to me for next Friday's flight."

Cam sauntered over to where she stood by the open door of her station wagon. The past couple of months had been hard on Molly, he thought. She'd lost some weight, and her face was usually drawn and pale. The only time he saw color in her cheeks was when she was either embarrassed or angry. Cam wanted to reach out and touch her.

"I saw the list," he said, instead. "Sorry, but it was bound to happen sooner or later."

"Why not much later?"

He smiled, trying to give her hope. "Chin up, Molly. Better now than earlier. You've been working hard on developing some excellent assertiveness tactics with these pilots. They don't run over you anymore."

"None of them have Martin's barracuda personality, either."

With a sigh, Cam barely touched her cheek. "Hey," he told her softly, "it's not the end of the world. Go home, get a good night's sleep and start work tomorrow morning. Use your weekend to good advantage."

"Always the tactical genius. I'm sorry, Cam, you didn't deserve that shot. I'm just upset."

"No harm done," he assured her. "I wish I could do more for you, but this is your battle to fight."

"I know," she murmured tiredly. "It's just that I'm exhausted by the past two months. I thought I knew what studying and working hard was all about, but TPS is hell."

"No argument from me." Cam controlled his screaming need to help her—to hold her. Giving her a pat on the shoulder, he said, "I'll see you Monday."

Molly nodded. Right now, the way she felt, she simply wanted to walk into Cam's embrace and be held.

"I'll see you then," she responded wearily, climbing into her car. As she drove off, Molly looked ahead to Friday. The next seven days would be focused on one half-hour flight. And Martin would be gunning for her. He wasn't doing very well in class, and was marginal for making it to the top four slots by the end of the course. Chewing on her lower lip, Molly knew it was going to take everything she had to get even a halfway decent grade. Martin was going to be more than ready to blame her for any flight-plan infractions so he could lift his grade. If she got lower than an eighty percent, she'd slip back to seventh place in the ratings.

"It can't happen," she whispered tautly. "It just can't happen!" Her father was furious about her poor standings, anyway. And no matter what she did to try and explain how hard TPS was, he refused to accept it or her efforts.

Cam made the rounds in the facility Thursday night, since he had the duty and the key to lock up the building. Everyone had to be out of the building by 2100. It wasn't a surprise to find Molly in the computer room, working hard on the program she would fly tomorrow afternoon with Martin.

"Hey, time to quit," he called, entering the air-conditioned room.

Molly lifted her head. Her heart beat once to underscore the fact that it was Cam. He looked confident and alert—two things she presently was not. "Okay..."

Frowning, Cam walked over to her terminal. "Look up," he ordered.

She lifted her chin.

Cam's frown deepened. "When did you sleep last?" There were dark circles under her eyes, and she looked exhausted.

"I don't know. I think I got a couple of hours last night." Molly shut the computer off and slowly leaned down and picked up the briefcase at her feet. "I've gone over this program two complete times this week. I've run it and rerun it on the computer," she muttered. "I just want to make sure it's right."

Cam's heart twinged with concern. He compressed his lips. "You shouldn't be spending that kind of time on such a simple flight program, Molly."

"I'm flying with Martin, remember? I want this program to be perfect. Last time I flew with him he accused me of having bad math computations. He got Vic Norton to check my printout and there were errors in it. I can't understand it. I'd swear there weren't any math errors. I'm not going to let it happen again."

Cam came around the terminal, his hands on his hips as he watched her dully gather all her materials. There was such vulnerability in Molly when she was tired. "You're driving yourself into the ground," he muttered.

Molly rose, almost dizzy with exhaustion. "Cam, don't get angry. I can't handle it right now."

There was no one else in the building, so Cam gripped her by the shoulders and forced her to look at him. "Angel, I wasn't angry, just concerned." He hadn't mean to call her by his endearment for her, but Molly was so tired that she didn't seem to realize he'd said it. "Look, go home and get a good night's sleep. Will you do that for yourself?"

"Cam," she protested, "I can't!" Molly pulled from his grip. If she didn't, she thought, she would collapse into his arms and make a complete fool of herself. Learning to stand on her own two feet had been a painful lesson. She couldn't afford to give up now.

"You're going home to check this program again?" Cam asked in disbelief. She stood before him, a dazed look in her eyes.

"Yes."

"Then give it to me, Molly."

"What?"

"Dammit, you're ready to keel over. You don't know when to stop and rest."

Tears jammed into her eyes, but she fought them back. "You're not taking my program away from me so I'll rest! I'm not some little girl to be treated like—"

"Whoa. I want the program, and I'll check it for you."

"You'll what?" Her voice cracked and went off-key.

Cam smiled gently and brushed her cheek. "I admire you for making it this far without any help, Molly. You're learning to apply a lot of new things under some rough circumstances. As a friend, I'd like to help you. Let me check your test. I'll have it waiting for you on my desk tomorrow morning. Okay?"

"Why are you doing this for me?"

Taking her program from her briefcase, Cam muttered, "Because your heart's bigger than your need to survive, Molly Rutledge. Now get out of here. I don't want to see you stepping through that door until 0800 tomorrow morning. Understand?''

Molly didn't know whether to cry or to throw her arms around Cam in thanks. His voice was gruff with warmth, and she took a step back, rubbing her brow. ''Yes...I understand.''

Cam walked Molly to her car. The August evening was coming to a close and the humidity was high. It was a sultry summer night over the Chesapeake Bay area. Over the past week, Cam had watched in agony as Molly's newfound spunk had deteriorated, then deserted her on learning that she had to fly with Martin. There was such defeat in her face. He leaned down, resting his hands on the sill of the open car window on the driver's side.

''Has your father been calling you more than usual, lately?'' he demanded. Cam had discovered well over a month ago that Jason Rutledge had a nasty habit of making extra phone calls when Molly needed them the least.

Molly sat, numb. All she wanted was sleep. ''Yes, he called me last night. When he found out Martin was flying with me, he called me twice this week to make sure I'm doing the best I can on this damn program so Martin doesn't sandbag my scores.''

Clenching his teeth, Cam was silent. Then he said gently, ''Go home and sleep, Molly. Take the phone off the hook.'' He reached out, squeezing her shoulder. ''You'll do fine tomorrow with Martin. I know you will.''

Battling back tears, Molly nodded and quickly drove off. Cam was the only one who had any faith in her ability to be a winner, not a loser. Exhaustion lapped at her, and just the drive home left her feeling like a zombie. Friday morning would come soon enough.

* * *

Cam was waiting for Molly the next morning. He had the 0600 duty to open the building, and got there a little early. Molly arrived in a freshly pressed flight suit exactly at 0600 and made a beeline for his office. He smiled at her as she appeared at the open door.

"Good morning," he said, gesturing for her to come in and sit down. On his desk, within her reach, was a cup of steaming hot coffee he'd just made and a McDonald's sack containing breakfast.

Molly sat down in the leather chair and positioned her briefcase next to it. "Good morning. What's this?" she asked, noticing a second McDonald's bag and another cup of coffee.

Cam grinned and got to his feet. He came around the desk and quietly shut the door. If some of the students came in early, he didn't want them to see Molly and him sharing breakfast. It was taking a huge risk, Cam knew, but he had to do something to help her—even in small, supportive ways.

"Breakfast on the run. Go on, one sack's yours."

Molly stared at Cam as he sat down opposite her. "You didn't have to do this."

"Sure, I did. My damsel was in distress." He shoved a sack toward her. "Eat," he ordered more sternly.

His damsel. Molly felt heat climbing up her neck into her face. She reached for the bag. "How did you know I wouldn't get myself breakfast at home this morning?"

"Because," Cam drawled, leaning back in his chair and opening his sack, "you went home last night, took a bath, dragged yourself to bed and then forgot to set your alarm and overslept."

The food tasted delicious, and after having had little appetite for the past week, Molly discovered she was hungry. Cam looked darkly handsome, as always. She never ceased to be amazed at discovering some small, wonderful nuance about him. Today he was jovial and incredibly sensitive. It lifted her spirits.

"It's disconcerting for someone to know me that well."

"Don't worry, your secrets are safe with me."

Molly held his smiling eyes. "I've always known that," she told him seriously. "What about my test?"

"It's fine. Perfect." Cam grinned. "It's certainly going to put Martin through his flying-skill paces, but it's a sound program. Congratulations. Vic will be pleased with the complexity of it."

Molly sat back, relief sheeting through her. "Thank goodness!"

"Eat! You're too skinny, Molly. I should have paid more attention to you the past two months. You've been dropping weight, slow but sure."

"I'll be okay," she assured him, finishing off the breakfast sandwich and picking up the raspberry Danish. "This was so nice of you. You thought of everything. Even dessert."

How like Molly to always acknowledge what others did for her, Cam reflected. "It's a little thing," he said.

"An important little thing. I wouldn't have wanted to fly on an empty stomach this morning."

Lately, Cam had found himself wanting to do much more for Molly. "A little thing for a special lady." He wanted to do more than meet her once a week at the beach, where they walked slowly down the sandy expanse with Miracle at their side. He'd discovered much about her that way. Now Cam was hungry to explore her on other, more intimate levels. He sighed. It was impossible. The school would frown on it. Molly's focus shouldn't be diverted from her training, either. God knew, she had her hands full waging battles on two different fronts: one with TPS, the other with that rabid, overfocused family of hers.

Molly finished off the breakfast and sat back to enjoy her coffee. "Are my dark circles still showing this morning?" she asked with a laugh.

Cam shook his head. "Yes, but not as badly. Everyone gets them the last three months at TPS."

"I think everyone ought to get a Purple Heart just for surviving the six months," Molly groused good-naturedly, sipping the strong, black coffee.

Cam nodded. "No argument from me. When I went through it four years ago, I thought the same thing. After graduating, I tested jets for a year. Then they assigned me to instruct." He grimaced. "I'd rather have tested, but the head honchos said they needed my brilliant instructing services."

"You're a wonderful teacher," Molly said fervently. "Look what you've taught me about standing up for myself."

With a smile, Cam eased forward and tossed his sack into the wastebasket. "You've been a joy to work with, Molly. And to be honest, sooner or later you'd have done the very same things I've taught you."

"I don't think so."

"I do." She looked exquisite with her blond hair wrapped in a neat chignon at the top of her head, wispy tendrils framing her temples, her thick bangs brushing her brows. "Pygmalion and Galatea we're not."

"Well," Molly insisted stubbornly, "whatever we share is good and positive."

Cam nodded, thinking how much more he wanted to share with Molly. He glanced at his watch. It was 0630. "As much as I'd like to continue our breakfast chat, I think we ought to get to work.'' He handed her the flight-program printout and she placed it in her briefcase.

''Right,'' Molly said, understanding exactly what Cam meant. If students or other instructors saw them together like this, it could mean problems. She rose and picked up her briefcase. Cam went to the door with her.

''Thanks again,'' she whispered, meaning it.

Fighting the urge to lean over and kiss her lovely lips, Cam nodded. ''I always was a sucker for a damsel in distress.''

She smiled warmly. ''It's nice to be called a damsel. Maggie would hate it. Dana would turn up her nose and wrinkle it, but I'm glad someone in this hard climate of steel and machines sees me as a woman, not a computer on two legs.''

With a laugh, Cam opened the door. ''Any man who doesn't see you as a woman is crazy.''

As she walked out into the empty, quiet hall, Molly commented, ''There are a lot of crazy men at TPS, then. I'll see you later.'' Heading for the computer room, where all the flight engineers would meet to discuss their programs with their instructors before flying, Molly felt buoyed. What would she have done without Cam's help? Still, her hands were damp from nervousness. Martin was going to be offensive and aggressive—the two things she disliked most in men. The debriefs would take place this afternoon. What would happen?

Cam was still in his G-suit, with no time to change before the debrief session. He'd just finished flying chase plane to Dalton's spin-test flight. Hurrying down the hall, he carried the duffel bag containing his helmet and oxygen mask in his left hand. How had Molly done? Anytime a student flew the spin-test flight, a chase plane was needed. Part of the student's grade hinged on his observation.

Dalton caught up with him. The Missourian grinned broadly. "Hell of a test, Captain."

"You did well," Cam praised. He liked Dalton. The man had a good sense of balance with an aircraft. Lee Bard, the flight engineer who had flown with him, followed a few steps behind. Cam looked over at his shoulder at the short engineer.

"How are you doing?"

Bard grimaced. "Dalton called them on the money, but my stomach's still rolling up there with those spins."

All three men laughed as they walked through the open door to debrief. Cam's gaze immediately went to the other end of the table where Molly sat. Martin sat as far away from her as he could, at the opposite end of the long, oval table. Neither of them looked very happy.

"Sorry we're late," Cam apologized to his fellow instructors. He sat down and got out his notebook and pen. Glancing over at Vic Norton, who sat to his right, Cam nodded.

"Go ahead, Vic, I'll catch up."

Cam had to wait two hours before Molly and Martin's flight came up for examination, the last one of the day. He watched Martin tense, his face tight with anger.

"Molly, what do you have for us?" Vic asked, getting ready to make notes on his evaluation sheet.

She sat up and opened her knee board with all the flight tests on it. "We were to do a series of inside loops, flying the F-14 upside down at exactly fifteen thousand feet for one-half mile and then—"

"Everyone here knows you don't fly an F-14 upside down for that long," Martin growled.

Cam tensed. Martin had no right to butt in on Molly's debrief. His glance moved to Vic, who had shifted his attention to Martin.

"Lieutenant Martin, if you don't mind, I'd like to finish my evaluation," Molly said. "Now, Mr. Norton, as I was saying..."

Inwardly Cam smiled, silently cheering Molly on. She'd quickly and firmly taken back control of the situation. Martin glared at her, his fist clenched on the table. Vic's attention moved back to her.

"By flight parameters, the F-14 cannot go on indefinitely in an upside-down flight position because gravity interferes with flow of fuel from the wings to the engines. If the F-14 isn't brought out of the position in time, one or both engines could stall."

"No kidding," Martin said tightly. He jabbed a finger at Molly. "You deliberately took the worst flight characteristic of the F-14!"

Coolly, Molly stared Martin down. Her heart was beating hard in her chest, her hands wet with sweat. Trying to keep her voice unruffled, she continued, "Nevertheless, the F-14, during times of war, will have to fly upside down occasionally, if for no other reason than to defend itself." She returned her attention to Vic. "Mr. Norton, I did set up a test to put the F-14 at the edge of its flight envelope. But every time we went into that position, Mr. Martin would *not* hold it as long as I asked."

"That's because we were nearing a stall!" Martin shouted.

Cam scowled. "Mr. Martin, we're all adults in here. Shouting's not necessary."

Martin tightened his mouth and sat back, a pout on his lips.

"Molly, how long did you want him to hold the position?" Vic asked, pen poised.

"Fifteen, twenty and twenty-five seconds. He did fine on the fifteen-second test. But on the other two, he refused to meet the criteria."

Nostrils flaring, Martin rounded on Vic Norton. "I can't believe you'd approve an idiotic test like this! I've been flying Tomcats for longer than she's been in the Navy, and my flight record is impeccable! I've never had an accident or even a near miss! This is picky stuff. I consider her test invalid! She's asking the impossible of the plane and the pilot. Have you ever flown upside down in that jet for that amount of time, Mr. Norton?"

"Er, no."

"You ought to try it!" Martin raged. "Dammit, I'm sweating out the stall-warning buzzer screaming in my ears while she's back there coolly counting off the seconds. There's no way I'm gonna keep that jet on its back for that amount of time!" Martin jabbed his finger at Norton's evaluation form. "She ought to get a low score for setting up this kind of lousy test. It proves nothing! Nothing!"

"I want the video reviewed," Molly said tightly, getting Norton's attention.

"It isn't going to show a thing!" Martin retorted.

"Mr. Norton, I want the video viewed," Molly repeated stubbornly. To her chagrin, Martin seemed to be persuading Vic Norton to his side of the argument. How could she get him to understand that her test *was* valid?

"Okay," Vic consented, doubt in his voice. "But I don't think it will show much."

With a sinking feeling, Molly went and slipped the videotape into the machine. The television set was at the correct angle for everyone in the room to view it. Her heart dropped when Vic didn't even bother to get up and come closer. Doggedly, Molly read off the parameters of the test. Martin had been right: the video wasn't going to confirm anything conclusive.

Vic shrugged after the video was completed.

"The air was real rough up there, too," Martin griped. "She chose an altitude with a lot of turbulence. It was hell keeping that plane on a steady altitude."

"It wasn't that rough, Mr. Martin," Molly shot back as she sat back down. She saw the indecision on Vic's face. If he gave her a poor grade... Desperation wound in her with real fear.

"Well, it sounds like a combination of factors up there today," Vic said finally, scribbling out a grade. He handed it to Molly.

Her throat constricted: a seventy-eight percent. Anger, hot and galvanizing, moved through her. She glared at Martin, who sat back with a sated look on his face. As she signed her name and handed the notebook back to Vic, a sense of helplessness overwhelmed her. She'd fought back intelligently. Her flight program had been good. Why hadn't she been able to convince Vic of its merits?

As debrief broke up and everyone headed for home, Molly was one of the first to leave. She knew Cam had seen her grade because he'd been sitting next to Vic. Angry and frustrated, she hurried out of the building and drove home—home to wait for the dreaded phone call from her father and brother.

Chapter Ten

Molly had been home exactly five minutes when her doorbell rang. In the bedroom, ready to change out of her flight suit, she hesitated. Who could it be? Too filled with misery to venture a guess, Molly hurried into the hallway and crossed the living room. She opened the door.

"Father!"

Jason frowned. He stood with a briefcase in hand. "May I come in?"

Openmouthed, Molly stepped aside. "Sure..." Her mind spun. "What are you doing here?"

Moving into the living room and dropping his luggage beside the sofa, Jason turned to his daughter. "I felt it was time we talked, Molly. Come in and sit down. You look like hell. What's going on?"

Stunned by her father's unexpected appearance, Molly took precious seconds to respond to his command. She saw the flat, gray look in his eyes. Never had her heart beat harder. In anguish, she slowly entered the living room.

"I'm just tired, that's all," Molly whispered. "May I get you some dinner?"

"No. I've got a reservation at a hotel nearby, and I'll eat there. Come, sit down."

Numbly, Molly sat in the overstuffed chair opposite the sofa, the black Oriental coffee table between them. "Is Scott all right?" Fear for her brother, whose health had been fragile since the accident, rose in her.

"Scott's fine," her father said. "It's you I'm worried about."

Molly tensed. "Is that why you flew down here?"

"Yes." Jason drilled her with a probing look. "I can see our phone calls and letters haven't been doing the job, Molly. Your grades aren't good enough. You're failing."

Molly sat up, trying to control her uneven breathing. "Father, I'm doing the very best I can, here at TPS. You were right, it's the toughest school in the world. And contrary to your opinion, I am *not* failing."

"Trying isn't good enough, and you know it. You're number six in the standings. We both know you need to be fourth or third in order to graduate."

"I have three months to reach that position, Father." The words ground out of her. When she realized she was clenching her teeth, Molly was horrified.

"What was your test score today?"

Sweat popped out on her upper lip. Molly forced herself to hold his stare. "I received a seventy-eight." There, it was out. She tensed, watching his face turn pale.

"A seventy-eight! My God, that's ridiculous!" Jason jumped to his feet. "That will put you in seventh! What the hell are you doing over there? Screwing around? Going on dates instead of studying?''

Before Molly could answer, the doorbell rang. Nonplussed, she froze. Her father glared at the door and then at her.

''I suppose that's your date coming to pick you up for a Friday-night dinner?'' he snarled.

Shakily, Molly got to her feet. ''Father, you're way out of line. I don't know who's at the door. I don't have a boyfriend, nor do I have a date!''

Molly moved to the door, numb with misery and trembling with anger. She jerked the door open. Her eyes widened. ''Cam!''

Cam stood in civilian clothes—a plain white shortsleeved shirt and jeans. His hands were crammed into his pockets. ''Hi . . . I thought you could use some company after what happened this afternoon.'' Cam saw how intensely pale Molly was. When she turned and looked over her shoulder, he realized she was literally shaking. ''Molly? What's wrong?'' He pulled his hands out of his pockets and took a step forward, his hand resting against the door.

''I . . . uh . . . my father just flew in to see me,'' she stammered, stepping aside to allow Cam to enter.

''No date?'' Jason demanded coldly, moving to the foyer.

Cam scowled, instinctively moving between Molly and the older man. It didn't take much to realize they'd been fighting. Grimly, Cam faced Jason Rutledge. ''You must be Molly's father. I'm Captain Cameron Sinclair, a flight instructor at the Patuxent River test-pilot school.''

Rutledge stared at the hand he was offered. ''No doubt Molly's date for tonight,'' he growled, taking a step back and refusing to shake hands.

"Father, that's—"

"Hold it, Molly," Cam whispered, keeping her behind him. "Mr. Rutledge, you're obviously upset about something, but I came over here to speak to your daughter about her flight test today. She flew a good program and defended it in debrief. Unfortunately, her instructor chose to be swayed by one of my students who flew the test with her. I'm not here as her date. I'm here to tell her that the pilot got a sixty-five-percent grade for his antics in that debrief. He failed. She didn't."

The absolute chill of Cam's voice sent shivers down Molly's spine. For the first time in her life she felt protected. She stood behind Cam, who faced her father as if it were the easiest thing in the world to do. Molly looked from one man to the other. Her father's face grew red with fury.

"It's awfully good of you to tell me that, Captain. But she got a seventy-eight."

"So?" Cam challenged darkly.

"So it will drag her down to seventh place."

"No, it won't. It doesn't alter her standing."

"Captain Sinclair, you're well known to me. You've helped Molly before. And judging from her performance, your interest in her isn't to help her grades!"

"Father!" Molly cried, moving between them. "That's enough! Cam *has* helped me get better grades!"

Jason glared at both of them. "Molly, you always were naive.... You'd better look in this young man's eyes again. What I see in them isn't an instructor's concern for you—it's a man protecting his woman."

Cam saw Molly's face crumple with such injury at the cruel words that he could no longer remain silent. Gently he pulled Molly away from her father.

"Mr. Rutledge, you've pushed beyond the envelope on this issue," he rasped in a low, controlled voice. "Molly has studied twelve to sixteen hours a day, nonstop, since she's been here. She has no boyfriend, she has no social life, and all she gets for her hard work and care is a bunch of sniping, bitching and destructive phone calls from you and your son. If you want to help Molly, you'll build her up instead of continuing to tear her down."

Jason's eyes narrowed in fury. "Just who the hell do you think you are, telling me how to handle my own daughter?"

"Molly isn't a little girl anymore. She's a woman! You don't 'handle' a woman, Mr. Rutledge. She's an adult and deserves to be treated as such. I believe in her, Mr. Rutledge. I've watched Molly battle her way from last on the roster to sixth place. My money's on her to make the grade." Cam stepped forward, threatening. "But if you keep lunging at her, tearing her apart, upsetting her with those lousy phone calls and letters, she won't make it. I really think you want her to fail, not succeed."

Rattled, Jason took a step back. "I've always been on Molly's side! You young whelp, you have no idea of the pressures on me to make something successful out of Molly!"

"Molly isn't to be 'made' into anything! I don't give a flying damn about your problems, Rutledge. Don't you care what happens to her?" Cam's lips drew away from his teeth as the words hissed between them. "I'm not convinced you want Molly to win. The way you talk to her, cutting her down every chance you get, is that positive? Any football coach will tell you he gets more out of a kid by being supportive than by pointing out the negatives. Are you one of those men who's been trained to believe that only a man can succeed—that woman are weak and useless?''

Molly sobbed and grabbed Cam by the arm. ''Stop it! Both of you, stop it! I won't have you fighting. I can't stand it!''

Cam gripped Molly by the shoulder, keeping her well away from her infuriated father. ''I'm sorry, Molly, but this has been a long time in coming. Rutledge, leave your daughter alone. If you can't help her feel good about herself, whether she fails or succeeds, then leave her alone.''

With a curse, Jason turned on his heel and stalked back to the living room.

''Father!'' Molly ran after him. She pulled him to a stop just as he leaned down to pick up his briefcase. ''Please, don't go. Let's talk this out. I know we can—''

He jerked his arm away from her. ''Get away from me, Molly. It's obvious to me whose side you're on. You're just like your mother used to be. She was just as hard-headed and stubborn as you are, refusing to listen to me. All right, if you want to be left alone, we'll leave you alone! From here on out, I'm cutting off your allow-ance. There won't be any more phone calls. I'll order Scott to stop writing to you.'' He stood in the foyer, his head held high, looking at Molly and Cam imperiously.

''Don't cut me off from Scott,'' Molly begged, chok-ing back the tears. ''Cam's right. If you could just be more supportive of me, see what I've done well in the week, instead of what I've failed to do, it would help. Please, try to understand.''

Cam stood aside, opening the door. He was proud of Molly for standing up to her father. He saw anguish in Molly's face, the tears reflecting hurt in her beautiful green eyes. It took everything in him not to reach out and grab Rutledge by the collar and shake some sense into him. He knew exactly what her father was doing to Molly, manipulating her vulnerable emotions.

"There's nothing to understand," Jason told Molly in a rasp, heading for the open door.

"Don't go!" Molly cried. "Please, Father, let's talk—"

Rutledge jerked his head over his shoulder and hesitated at the door. "I'm disowning you, Molly. I'm writing you out of my will. No daughter of mine would behave as you have. I'm ashamed of you."

"Get the hell out of here," Cam said.

"With pleasure."

"No!" Molly sobbed. "No..."

Cam caught her before she could go after her father. He shut the door with his foot and drew her deep into his arms. Sweet God, but she was shaking like a leaf. "It's okay, angel. He doesn't mean it." Cam stroked her tangled hair and felt Molly sink against him, her sobs muffled against his chest.

Damn Rutledge! Molly's weeping was tearing him apart. In one motion, Cam picked her up. He carried her into the living room and deposited her on the sofa next to him, then drew her back into his arms. The evening light filled the room, as did Molly's pain, expressed in the sound of inconsolable weeping. Her tears soaked Cam's shirtfront.

Cam shut his eyes tightly, holding Molly against him, rocking her and whispering words he hoped would take away the pain her father had inflicted on her. She'd had a rotten week and a worse day. To have Rutledge here tearing her apart was more than any human being could expect to stand.

"Shh, angel, it's going to be all right. I'm here. I'll take care of you. Just cry and get it out of your system...." How good it felt to have someone he loved in his arms again! How good it felt to be needed! Opening his eyes, Cam realized he'd just admitted to himself that he loved Molly. With a groan, he laid his head back on the couch, absently stroking Molly's back and shoulders to soothe her. When had it happened? How?

Ever since he'd met Molly, he'd been powerfully attracted to her. And she invited his protection not by acting weak or playing coy, but by exposing a vulnerability that few people had the courage to wear outwardly.

Without thinking, Cam pressed a kiss to her fragrant hair. The silky texture beneath his lips goaded him to kiss her again. This time, his lips touched her wet cheek, and he became lost in the feel of her velvet firmness, of her slender warmth pressed against him. Sliding his fingers up along her clean jawline, he eased Molly back into his arms and tilted her chin upward until his mouth fitted perfectly against hers. He felt her tremble once, tense, and then, as he moved his mouth slowly across the wet surface of her lips, she sank into his offered embrace.

The world of pain and anguish Molly was experiencing was soothed by Cam's mouth fitting gently against her own. The sob caught in her throat turned into a moan of pleasure, not of pain. Her hand had moved away from his chest when he'd first touched her lips. Now her fingers flexed, relaxed and then flowed around Cam's shoulder, buried in the thick hair at the base of his neck. She tasted the salt of her tears and tasted the strength and gentleness of Cam—as a man, an equal.

Gradually, ever so gradually, he eased his mouth from her lips. Molly lifted her tear-beaded lashes. Cam's eyes burned with a fever that sent her blood flowing hot with need of him. Her emotions were on overload, and all she could do was stare up at him. Molly remembered her father's blistering words that Cam was more than just an instructor, that he wanted her for his own. The turbulence in his stormy blue eyes confirmed that observation, and more. In that moment, Molly realized just how much Cam had hidden from her until now.

Cam saw Molly's eyes, once dazed with pleasure, turn anxious. He cursed himself for letting down his guard and allowing the situation to force his hand, showing his real feelings for her. It was the wrong place and time. He managed a slight smile and asked, "Where do you keep the Kleenex?"

Molly sniffed. Cam's shirt was blotched with her tears, and so was her blouse. "I'll go get some," she whispered.

"No, stay put," he ordered. "For once, let someone take care of you."

Molly hung her head, tears welling up in her eyes once again. "There's a box in the kitchen," she croaked.

Cam got up and located it. He also found a bottle of brandy and poured her some. When he came back he found Molly sitting hunched over, her face buried in her hands. Sitting down next to her, he put a couple of tissues in one of her hands and the shot of brandy in the other.

"A very beautiful and compassionate young lady once gave me some brandy when I was having a rotten night. Go on, drink it. She told me her grandma always said it helped in a crisis."

Molly lifted her chin and looked at Cam through her tears. "Did anybody ever tell you you've a pretty good shoulder to cry on, too?"

His mouth curved gently. Cam reached over and drew her hair aside and placed it behind her ear. "I've had some experience down that road once or twice. Go on. Drink the brandy, angel." Cam cringed inwardly. How easy it was to call her "angel," because she was one in his eyes. A battered angel in need of a little care and love.

Just the tenderness in Cam's voice and touch healed some of the pain Molly was undergoing. She gulped down the brandy, then choked and coughed. Cam took the glass out of her hand and patted her on the back.

"Your granny made some powerful stuff," Cam said, grinning.

When she'd finished coughing, Molly managed a short laugh. She blew her nose and wiped her eyes free of the tears. Sitting in the silence, she whispered, "Thanks for staying. You didn't have to." Swallowing hard, she added, "And thanks for coming to my rescue. I've tried standing up to Father before, but I always let myself get beaten down."

"That's because you love him," Cam explained. "It's hard to stand up to a parent who doesn't respect you."

Pain flowed through Molly, and she touched the region of her heart with her fingertips. "I couldn't believe what you said to him."

"It was all true, Molly. Since you've started sharing the phone calls and Scott's letters with me, it's been easy to put together what he's doing to you."

Cam rubbed her slumped shoulder. "I owe you an apology, Molly. I didn't mean to step in and take on your father, but dammit, he was chewing you up. I couldn't allow it to happen. You did nothing to deserve it. I figured you'd told him about your grade. I was hoping that when he found out that I failed Martin on the test and you hadn't lost your standing, he'd cool down, but he didn't. Your father wasn't really interested in the truth."

Molly nodded, gripping the Kleenex between her hands. "If Maggie were here, she'd be cheering you on or jumping in with both feet to help. She's never liked my father."

"I can see why."

"Dana didn't, either."

"Your friends were good barometers of the situation," Cam said quietly. "They love you and didn't want to see you get hurt. Neither do I." *Because I love you, too.*

"Why did he do that, Cam? Why did Father disown me?" Molly kept picking at the tissue until it was in shreds in her fingers. Her voice grew strained. "I try so hard to please him, to please Scott. God, the last thing I expected was to see him here tonight. Father's never done this before. I was so shaken up at seeing him at the front door."

With a sigh, Cam took the shredded tissue from her hands and gave her a new one. "Your father has abused the privilege of your love for him, Molly. Look, he's got a lot of guilt driving him."

Miserable, she looked over at him. "What do you mean?"

"He probably in some way feels responsible for Scott's accident. I'll bet he favored Scott over you growing up, didn't he?"

"Well ... yes. But don't all fathers favor a son over a daughter?"

Cam shook his head. "No. Listen to me, Molly, you're going to have to separate what is your responsibility from what he wants you to be responsible for in your family situation. You have every right to live your life for you, not him. He acts like he owns you. He tries to run your life for you."

Molly nodded. "I guess I've been coming to that conclusion for a while. It's just so hard to accept, Cam. My mother—God, I miss her so much. She was wonderful."

"She was the buffer between you and your father," Cam guessed grimly. "When she died early, you were left unprotected, Molly. There were no arms you could run into to feel safe for a little while, were there?"

"No, I guess not." The brandy was beginning to ease her fear and roiling emotions. "I never did have a safe place, except my room."

Whether Cam wanted to or not, he knew he had to leave. If he didn't, he'd stay the night. Molly didn't need that on top of everything else she was struggling with. "You have me, Molly. I'll be your safe place when you need one. Deal?"

She gave Cam a warm, grateful look. "I felt so protected when you challenged my father."

"I'll always be there for you, Molly," Cam said, slowly getting to his feet. "Take this weekend and heal. Just rest." He reached over barely grazing the skin beneath her eyes. "Get rid of those dark circles. Sleep a lot. Don't work on any programs until Monday."

It was sound advice and Molly knew it. She caught his hand in her own. "Thank you, Cam."

The urge to sweep Molly back into his arms was becoming an excruciating torture. Cam gently squeezed her fingers. "Anytime," he promised thickly. "Because you're worth fighting for, Molly. Don't ever forget that. Look at what you did right today and tonight. I'm proud as hell of you. You stood up to Martin and Norton."

"And my father."

A pained smile shadowed Cam's mouth. "Especially your father. Once he gets over his anger, he'll call you. This disowning thing is nothing more than a manipulation on his part. I don't think he even realizes why he did it. You didn't fall for it, so he's going to have to regroup and learn to treat you in a different way. All this thing needs is time, and you've got that."

With a slight laugh, Molly said, "Maybe I'll do better without the weekly phone calls." And then she sobered. "But I'll miss talking to Scott."

"Well," Cam remarked grimly, "if that brother of yours isn't completely under your father's thumb, he'll call you anyway. I'll see you Monday?"

Although she still hurt, Molly felt as if weight had been taken off her shoulders. "Count on it."

Cam squelched the desire to lean down and touch her wonderfully soft, sensitive mouth. "Good night."

Afterward, Molly sat in the semidarkness of her apartment. So much had happened that it took hours to sort it all out. Later, she got up, took a bath and changed into a pale lavender bathrobe. Near ten o'clock, Molly went to bed and slept deeply. In her dreams, Cam was kissing her, and making slow, beautiful love to her.

Chapter Eleven

"Listen, you be careful up there," Cam warned Molly. He'd caught her just outside the women's locker room. They stood alone in the hall. She wore a body-hugging G-suit, just as he did.

Molly forced a grimace. "With one more month to go, holding on to fourth place in overall standings, don't think I won't be."

Cam walked along the hall with her. It was Friday afternoon, and hers was the last flight of the day before debrief. Unfortunately, the critical spin-test flight was with Chuck Martin. At the stairs they separated, Cam taking the exit door and Molly the stairs.

Molly clenched the knee board that held her flight test tightly in her left hand. On the first floor, students in flight suits were coming and going. Breaking out in a sweat, she went out a back door to meet the van that

would take her, Martin, Cam and Norton to their waiting F-14 Tomcats at the nearby hangar.

The weather was bright and dry, a perfect October day
on the bay. The breeze coming off the water had a bite to
it, but Molly was sweating too profusely to be chilled. As
she walked to the van, she saw Martin in the back, a
scowl on his face. Cam sat up front with the driver. Vic
Norton offered his hand and she took it, climbing
aboard. The door slid shut, and they rode off down the
landing apron toward the hangars.

On this flight, Vic would fly chase with Cam. Molly
felt better that the two of them would be along for the
ride. Her and Martin's conversation and actual tests
would be monitored by both instructors, as well as
videotaped. Nothing like two sets of eyeballs, as far as
Molly was concerned. Confidence was something she'd
built, brick by brick, since the crisis with her father.

Molly tried to remain focused on the spin test to come,
but as always, her father rose in her thoughts in off moments. The phone calls had ceased completely, and she
found her life free of pressure. Scott had found the
courage to call her sporadically, obvious strain in his
voice each time he took the risk. They didn't talk about
her career. He was distraught, and so was she.

Molly's gaze drifted to Cam's back and broad set of
shoulders. Warmth flowed through her, a balm to her
nervousness over the upcoming test. Through everything, Cam had remained unobtrusively in the background. He never told her what to do, but he supported
any decision she made. The past two months had been
sweet torture as far as Molly was concerned.

Never again had Cam reached out to hold her or kiss
her, but Molly couldn't forget that tender kiss the night
her world had shattered. And the longing she saw in

Cam's eyes wasn't her imagination. She felt it, absorbed it and hungered for more. Much more. But always, the harsh demands of school and her drive to succeed on her own, took precedence. They had to, for her own sense of well-being.

The van drew to a halt and everyone climbed out. The sunlight was bright, and Molly put on her aviator's sunglasses. She hauled her helmet bag to the second ladder hooked to the side of the sleek F-14 fuselage. The urge to turn and say goodbye to Cam was there, but she fought it. No one knew of their relationship, and it had to stay that way.

Molly climbed into the radar information officer's cockpit seat, directly behind the pilot's, and the crew chief helped her strap in. A firewall separated the two cockpits. Molly removed the firing pins from the ejection seat she sat on and stowed them. Fitting the helmet on her head, she gave a thumbs-up and thanked the young crewman. He saluted her and removed the ladder.

If she weren't flying with Martin, now ranked fifth in the standings, Molly would have enjoyed the outing. She loved to fly. Making sure her knee board was secured around her left thigh and all the plastic-coated pages were in proper order for the test sequence, she glanced over at the Tomcat containing Vic and Cam.

Her heart nearly burst with fierce pride for Cam. It was a privilege to see him working in the cockpit, his profile clean and his mouth set with the responsibilities of his job. Her feelings toward him grew daily. Whatever had occurred between them that fateful night when he'd held her and kissed her, had unlocked hidden doors in her heart.

"Ready?" Martin demanded.

"Yes," Molly said, positioning the oxygen mask against her face and strapping it closed on the side of her helmet. The huge canopy slowly descended and locked into place. Setting aside her feelings for Cam, Molly got to work. After takeoff, they would meet the chase plane at thirty thousand feet above the Chesapeake Bay in the restricted airspace where tests took place. Cam would fly his plane approximately half a mile from theirs as Martin put the F-14 through a series of spins. They would fall from thirty thousand and, at Cam's order, come out of the spin at eighteen thousand feet.

Molly automatically tightened the array of harnesses that kept her against her ejection seat as the F-14 trundled toward the end of the runway, its twin engines whining around them. Sunlight glared through the canopy, heating the inside of the cockpit. Molly adjusted the air-conditioning to make it more comfortable.

The two fighters took off together, a few yards separating their wings. Molly allowed herself to enjoy the powerful thrust that pushed her deep into the seat, thrilling to the incredible surge of power that made the F-14 one of the premier fighters in the world. Martin set the nose of the aircraft straight up, afterburners on. The fighter growled like a hurtling beast lunging toward the edge of the azure sky, thousands of feet unwinding in seconds.

The G-forces were terrific, and Molly concentrated on breathing properly during the swift acceleration of the agile fighter. The sky turned cobalt in color as they neared the thirty-thousand-foot level. The Chesapeake looked small below them, the land on either side of it a mass of orange, yellow and red fall colors.

"Let's get this over with," Martin growled.

Molly knew his snappish order would come, and was prepared for him. "Roger, Lieutenant. Our first test is a spin from thirty thousand to eighteen thousand feet." From prior training, Molly knew that if Martin wasn't able to get the jet out of the spin at the correct altitude, he had three thousand feet to spare to get the plane under control. It was Cam's responsibility to order them to bail out if they slipped below the fifteen-thousand-foot mark.

Spins were the most dangerous and most intricate of all the flying demands on plane and pilot—a deadly dance in the sky. Molly had flown a series of spins with Dalton last month. She knew what to expect and made sure there was nothing in her cockpit that could fly around and injure her when the spin started. As an aeronautical engineer, Molly knew that if the F-14—or indeed, any type of plane—went from a spiral spin into a flat spin, it could be dangerous. Pilots were usually unable to bring a plane out of a flat spin, forcing them to bail out.

"I'll need four complete revolutions of the plane before you straighten it out at eighteen thousand," Molly reminded Martin. Four wasn't a lot. Her other two tests were designed for tighter, harder spins, consisting of five and six revolutions within the same altitude requirement.

"Roger," Martin responded.

Molly was glad they were separated. Martin's voice was always antagonistic, but this time, it sounded as if he wanted to rip her head off. "Anytime you're ready, Mr. Martin."

Molly had no more than gotten the words out of her mouth when he slammed the F-14 into the series of spins. The G-forces built suddenly, pressing like powerful, unrelenting hands against her chest. She gripped the arms of her seat with her gloved hands and tried to keep her head from slamming back and forth as the fighter fell and tumbled, seemingly out of control.

"Twenty-five thousand," came Cam's calm voice over her headphones.

Molly knew he'd read off the altitude for Martin. Right now, Martin had his hands full just keeping the jet under his command. Blue sky and brown earth rapidly changed positions in front of her eyes. The fall was breathtaking, her body pounded by the brutal G-forces.

"Twenty-two thousand. Start pulling her out, Martin."

"Twenty thousand."

"Nineteen thousand."

Molly gasped as the F-14 suddenly straightened out from the spin. Martin had cranked the aircraft into level flight right on the money at eighteen thousand feet. She saw Cam come along side and Norton began to check the undercarriage of their fighter for any hydraulic leaks. After the inspection was completed and they were pronounced "clean and dry," she heard Cam give Martin the order to climb to thirty thousand again.

In the second spin test, Molly counted four-and-a-half revolutions, not five. As they were being checked for leaks, she brought it to Martin's attention.

"That wasn't five spins, Mr. Martin."

"Like hell it wasn't!"

Molly's mouth flexed. "It was four and a half."

"You can't even count. Captain Sinclair, didn't you count five?"

Molly was barely hanging on to her building anger. Martin wasn't supposed to ask Cam anything. Her assessment was all that was needed.

"You completed four-and-a-half spins, Mr. Martin. Next time, I suggest you listen to Ms. Rutledge. She's your flight engineer on this test. Out."

Cursing on the cockpit intercom, Martin snarled, "Now you've got him twisted around your little finger, Rutledge."

Molly wondered if Martin had turned off outside communications. He must have, to be saying things so brazenly.

"You're upset because you didn't make the mandatory five spins, Mr. Martin."

"I'll tell you what, Rutledge—I'm not going to allow you to drag my grades down again. Last time I flew with you, Sinclair flunked me. Never again."

She heard the shaking hatred in his voice. "You failed yourself, Martin. I had nothing to do with it. Now let's get to thirty thousand and complete the last test. I want six spins."

"Don't worry, you'll get them," he grated.

Cam frowned. He could see Martin talking and gesturing in the cockpit. What was being said? The pilot had switched to IC, intercabin communications, and Cam had no way of knowing what went on. When Martin switched back, he sounded furious.

"I'm ready, Captain Sinclair. Let's get this final test out of the way."

"You're clean and dry. Let's go to thirty thousand," Cam ordered.

"Martin sounds upset," Vic said on IC.

"Yeah, I don't like it."

"He's a hothead when he doesn't get his way."

Cam nodded, easing his fighter upward, the nose pointed toward the cobalt sky above them. Worry ate at him. "Martin was sloppy on that last spin series."

"Roger that."

If Martin couldn't make five spins, what made him so sure he'd complete six? A good pilot could, and Cam knew it. Martin had his weaknesses, just as any pilot did. When Cam had taken him up for spins before Martin was accepted as a student at TPS, he'd done average on that maneuver, but they weren't his forte.

As the fighters flew together in a rectangular flight pattern within the restricted airspace, Cam took a look at Molly. With her helmet on and the dark visor and oxygen mask across her face, he couldn't tell if she was a man or woman. Still, something nagged him. He didn't like the edge in Martin's voice. Pressing the intercom button on the stick, he made contact with Martin.

"Are you all right, Martin?"

"Sure, I am."

"Are you ready for this last test?"

"Of course."

Cam knew that Martin would have to play the F-14 at the very edge of its envelope to make those six spins in regulation altitude requirements. Part of Cam wanted to stop the test; part of him didn't.

"Permission to start the spin, Captain Sinclair?" Martin demanded. "There's turbulence at twenty thousand, and I want to get this done before it gets any worse. *That's* what caused me to abort that fifth spin."

Cam had felt no turbulence at twenty thousand, but he was flying a half-mile circle around the spin aircraft. It was possible Martin had hit a nasty air pocket and had to abort the fifth spin. He'd have to check with Molly. Both would have felt it. "Permission granted. Ms. Rutledge, start your countdown," Cam ordered.

Molly called off the numbers. When she called out "Ten," Martin kicked hard left rudder and sent the F-14 into a tight, spiraling turn. Slammed against the seat, she mentally began to count the spins. One...two... three...four...

"Twenty-two thousand."

She forced herself to breathe in. Martin was too low to make the six spins!

"Twenty-one thousand. Begin to pull out," Cam ordered.

Five spins! Molly felt the G-forces building, causing pain in every part of her body. She grunted, forcing the air into her lungs.

"Nineteen thousand. Martin!" Cam snapped. "Pull it out! Pull it out!"

A gasp tore from Molly. Suddenly, the F-14 lurched violently, slamming her head against the cockpit canopy.

"Flat...spin!" Martin croaked.

"Eighteen thousand!"

Molly's eyes bulged. Brown earth and blue sky and green water all started blurring together before her. Out of control! her mind screamed. The plane's out of control! The G's made it feel as if invisible hands were forcing her eyes out of her head.

"Seventeen thousand!" Cam yelled tautly. "Get that bird out of the flat spin, Martin! Now!"

Oh, God! Molly thought, her fingers clenching the arms of her ejection seat. If Martin doesn't get the bird under control at fifteen thousand, we'll have to bail out! Something had gone wrong. The fifth spin had turned into a flat spin. The F-14 tumbled wildly out of the sky, the G's brutally crushing at her body.

"Sixteen thousand! Martin!" Cam screamed. "Recover! Recover!"

"Bail out!" Martin cried. "Now, Rutledge! Now!"

"Fifteen thousand!" Cam cried. "Bail out!"

Panic struck Molly. From hours and months of training, she managed to hit the button. The canopy blew off, the wind slugging into her like pulverizing fists. Wind tore at her as she fumbled to find the levers beneath each arm of her seat. She couldn't breathe. She couldn't think. Eyes shut tightly, she heard Cam's and Martin's voices screaming in her ears. Locking the back of her arms against the seat, shoving her helmeted head tightly against it, she jerked the levers upward.

Seconds shattered into a nightmare sequence. The rockets fired, lifting her seat out of the fighter. Pain and pressure exploded along Molly's spine as the ejection seat cleared the twin tail of the careening fighter. Everything became slow motion in front of her opened, widening eyes. The earth and sky blurred together, black dots dancing in front of her. Just like the fighter somewhere below her, she was tumbling end over end.

Suddenly, the chair separated, and at ten thousand feet in the icy air, her parachute pack opened. The nylon sang out, snaking above her. Molly tried to prepare for the jolt, but couldn't really. The straps bit deeply into her thighs and shoulders as the chute billowed and opened fully above her. Gasping in shock, she tried to clear her head. To her right, she saw Martin's F-14 suddenly come out of the flat spin.

To her left, she saw Cam's aircraft slowly circling around her. Below her was Chesapeake Bay. It was going to be a water landing! Breathing hard, Molly held on to the chute lines, dangling in the silence of the sky. Her mind raced with what had to be done to make a safe water landing. Oh, God, it was going to be dangerous! Molly drifted closer and closer to the choppy water. The bay was a turgid green, white caps grasping upward like greedy fingers. As she floated closer, the wind became erratic, a real danger to her landing.

Jerking her head up, Molly looked above her at Cam's aircraft. A cry broke from her.

Cam cursed softly, quickly switching his radio to the Coast Guard Search and Rescue channel. Vic was working the other radio in his cockpit, notifying the station of what had happened. He saw Molly drifting closer and closer to the water. The winds were erratic at five thousand feet, the F-14 bucking beneath his hands. If Molly landed downwind into the water, the chute strings could fall across her and tangle in her equipment and helmet, possibly dragging her down and drowning her.

"She's in trouble!" Vic cried. "That wind's terrific. She's got to turn around and face the wind!"

Helplessly, Cam watched the unfolding scenario. Already, the Coast Guard Dolphin helicopter was on its way. It would be at least half an hour before they could effect Molly's rescue. His hand tightened around the stick of his fighter.

"Turn, Molly!" he whispered tensely. "God, turn into the wind!" Cam didn't care if his voice went out to the whole world. Molly *was* his world. He flew three thousand feet above her, watching her battle a new foe, the air currents. His anger and concern congealed into terror as he realized Molly wasn't going to be able to turn into the wind in time. Was she injured? A broken shoulder or arm? That would explain why she couldn't use the shrouds to turn the chute around. His heart lunged into his throat as he saw her hit the bay with a terrific splash, the water spewing upward twenty feet into the air where she hit.

"God, that'll knock her out!" Vic rasped.

Water funneled up into Molly's nose and down the back of her throat. She coughed wildly, jerkily clawing to keep her head above water. Parachute lines crisscrossed her like webs woven by a spider that had captured her. The silk of the chute lay like a white snake in the water, quickly absorbing the liquid and starting to sink beneath the surface.

The heavy flight boots, the G-suit and harness were rapidly taking on water. Molly yanked the helmet off her head, and it sank like a rock. Gasping, spitting up water, she tried to push off the strings that surrounded her and get to her Mae West vest. She only had a minute, perhaps less, before the chute would submerge and drag her into a watery grave, vest inflated or not.

Molly didn't want to drown! Clawing for her survival knife, her hand shook so badly that she couldn't open the sheath. The lines began to tighten around her. She felt the first tug from the chute. With a cry, water washing across her face, Molly fumbled again for the knife. She had to cut the lines or she'd die!

There! Her fingers closed around the butt. The Nomex gloves she wore were slippery on the handle. Grabbing the first bunch of lines across her face, Molly arced the knife upward, slicing through them! Frantically, she worked to capture the other lines that had balled like yarn around her body. Even a few lines could drag her under and kill her. Sobbing for breath, kicking with her feet to tread water, she hunted for the last of the slippery lines.

A few lines remained tangled around her lower left leg and flight boot. Molly felt the powerful pull of the chute as it sank beneath the water. Too tired to pull her leg upward to get at them, she couldn't reach the lines. If she was going to survive, she would have to dive under the surface to locate them.

Taking a gulp of air, Molly knew she had to find them on her first search or she was dead. Eyes open, she could see the lines as she dived. The weight of the equipment she wore was pulling her down. She was sinking quickly! Her fingers outstretched toward her left boot, Molly hauled her leg up. There! Yes! Wrapping the last of the chute strings around her hand, she sliced downward with the knife. Free! She was free! She released the knife.

Twisting around and looking up, Molly realized she was at least twenty feet below the surface. She fumbled for and found the strings to inflate her vest. Yanking them simultaneously, she prayed they'd work. Instantly, her life vest inflated. Her lungs were on fire. She had to breathe! She was going to drown!

Shutting her eyes, kicking violently toward the surface, Molly felt her strength evaporate. Oh, God, she was going to die! *No, no, not now! Cam! Cam, I love you!* As her lungs seemed to burst, Molly cried out silently, the last of the oxygen escaping her mouth in a sheet of bubbles. She'd never get to tell Cam she loved him. Never know the beauty of loving him, or of being loved by him in return. Her vision started to gray, and Molly felt her arms begin to free-float.

Bursting to the surface, Molly gasped. Air! She floundered, throwing her head back, coughing. The inflated vest kept her head and shoulders out of the water even though the heavy flight suit and boots continually wanted to pull her under. Never had air felt so good. Molly vomited out the water she'd swallowed. Her hair was a wet mass about her face and shoulders. But she was alive! Alive!

Cam circled dangerously close to the bay's surface. An involuntary cry had torn from him when he'd seen Molly dragged under by the tangled chute strings. He thought he'd lost her when it was nearly three minutes before she surfaced again. But when he saw her weakly lift her arm, he knew she'd survived.

"Let's get back to base," Vic said, his voice shaky. "She's going to be okay, Cam. Search and Rescue will be on scene in another twenty minutes."

"No, we're staying on station until they arrive," he croaked, his voice undisguised with feeling. "I'm not leaving her out here alone."

"She almost bought the farm," Vic whispered.

Cam tried to separate his emotions from his responsibilities. Molly floated below them, out of danger. Had she been injured by the ejection sequence? Any internal bleeding? She could be hurt and they wouldn't know anything until the Coast Guard got her to the nearest hospital for examination.

"Vic, call the Coast Guard. Ask them which hospital they'll take Molly to."

"You bet."

Shakily, Cam pushed the dark visor off his face and wiped the sweat from his furrowed brow. To the left of him, at a much higher altitude and disappearing, was Martin's F-14. Cam had ordered him back to Patuxent River. He tried to separate his anguish from his suspicions. Had Martin deliberately put that F-14 into a flat spin to get rid of Molly? At ten thousand, Martin had gotten the bird out of the spin and stabilized.

Scowling, Cam continued to cruise the F-14 just this side of stall speed, flying long, lazy circles at three thousand above where Molly floated. If only he could talk to her, find out her condition! God, he loved her. Loved her! If that bastard Martin had deliberately planned this and nearly cost Molly her life, Cam would have his wings. First things first. The Coast Guard had to pick up Molly. Then, and only then, would Cam fly back to base.

"Cam, they're going to take her to Crisfield Hospital at Crisfield, Maryland. That's a long way from Patuxent. A good five-hour drive."

"It doesn't matter," he whispered, his voice shaking. "I'm going to drive there today and make sure she's okay."

"Someone will have to be sent to investigate the ejection," Vic said. "Why shouldn't it be you?"

The weekend was coming up. Cam had the time off. He fought to stay unemotional, but it was impossible. "Vic, when I get back to TPS, I'm going to get permission to drive to Crisfield immediately. We'll delay the student debrief until Monday for everyone. Is that all right with you?"

"Sure, no problem."

Cam could hear the unasked question in Vic's voice. Why was he going to such lengths to see Molly? Normally, only the investigation team would go see her. "Thanks," he said, aware of his shredded emotions, his life in a turmoil he'd never expected.

Chapter Twelve

The windshield wipers flicked back and forth with a monotony that made Cam want to scream. The blackness of the night, the headlights of oncoming cars blurring against the rain-splattered windshield—all contributed to his exhaustion. Crisfield, Maryland, sat at the very end of the landmass, five hours away from Patuxent.

Wiping his eyes tiredly, Cam didn't even try to hide from the fact that his hand trembled. It wasn't from physical exhaustion; it was from worry about Molly. After landing at Patuxent River, he'd gone directly to Operations, where he had to fill out a report on the incident.

Frustrated by the hour it took to fill out the forms, Cam had called the Crisfield Hospital twice before leaving the station for the long drive. Yes, Molly had been admitted to the emergency room and no, they didn't know her condition.

Fortunately, the commandant had agreed to Cam being the investigator on the incident and ordered him to drive to Crisfield with Molly's personnel file. Her father had been notified by someone else at Ops, and Cam had left.

How was she? My God, she'd nearly drowned in the parachute lines. Cam swallowed hard, tears burning in his eyes. He loved her. God, how he loved her! His raw emotions were boiling through him, and he could barely think, much less stay focused on driving.

Still wearing his flight suit, Cam got soaked by the driving autumn thunderstorm as he ran from the visitors' parking lot to the hospital's emergency-room doors. Taking off his garrison cap inside, Cam gripped Molly's file under his left arm. He zeroed in on two nurses standing behind the admissions desk.

"Excuse me, I'm Captain Sinclair from the Patuxent River naval air station. Do you have Ensign Molly Rutledge here?"

The red-haired nurse, the older one, smiled. "Yes, sir, we do." She leaned over the computer monitor. "Dr. Paul Winklemann is her doctor. You'll find him on the third floor. He can discuss her case with you, Captain."

His throat constricted, Cam asked, "How is she? What's her status?"

"Good condition, Captain."

Relief shattered through Cam, and all he could do was stand there, his eyes closed as the mountain of fear that had cascaded through him evaporated. "Thank God," he whispered, opening his eyes. Both nurses were giving him curious looks, but he didn't care.

"The elevator is right down this hall and to the left," the nurse provided more softly. "I'm sure Ensign Rutledge will be glad somebody cares enough to check on her and make sure she's alive."

Cam frowned. "Her relatives were notified. Haven't they phoned?"

"No, sir. No calls have been taken. She's all alone."

Alone. Spinning on his heel, Cam took long strides down the white hall toward the bank of elevators. The smell of antiseptic always made him wince. He didn't like hospitals or doctors, but knew they were necessary evils upon occasion. As he restlessly waited for the elevator doors to open, Cam wondered what Molly thought of hospitals. In a few minutes, if he was lucky, he'd get to see her.

In the elevator, his mood spiraled from euphoria back to sheer terror. He loved Molly; it was that simple. The bailout had forced him to confront his feelings. But did Molly love him? Or did she still see him as merely a friend? Cam had never felt so tenuous in his entire life as when he stepped off the elevator and onto the third floor. Could he hide his love for her? Cloak his need to take her in his arms, hold her and kiss the hell out of her?

The nurses' station was busy, so Cam walked up to a man in a white smock who was signing off a patient medical record on the far side of the U-shaped counter. The man glanced up.

"I'm looking for Doctor Winklemann."

"You've got him." He smiled. "You must be the investigating officer from the naval air station we heard was coming to speak with Ms. Rutledge?"

"That's right. I'm Captain Sinclair." Cam shook the doctor's hand. "How's Molly?"

Winklemann's smile deepened. "Except for being black-and-blue all over, and some spinal compression, she's in excellent shape."

Cam took a deep breath. "Great news."

Winklemann placed the chart on the counter. "Yes, it is. When they brought her into emergency five hours ago, she looked like a drowned rat. We gave her a tranquilizer for the shock, checked her over thoroughly and put her to bed. Rest is what she needs right now."

"Is she asleep?" Cam tried to keep the desperation out of his voice.

Winklemann looked up at the clock. "It's past visiting hours, Captain, and frankly, I don't think she's up to being grilled right now."

Cam glanced at the file he held. "No...I just want to see her, that's all. She needs to know someone cares enough to be here for her. I'll take her report tomorrow morning. There's plenty of time for that."

"In that case, go on down to room 304. It's a double room, but she's the only one in there. I've given the nurses standing orders that any snoopy journalists from local newspapers are to be denied access."

"Good," Cam said. Molly didn't need reporters hounding her.

"Come on. I'll walk you down. I've got a patient in the next room I've got to check in on," Winklemann invited, coming around the counter.

As they walked shoulder to shoulder down the hall, Cam asked, "Has Molly received any phone calls?"

"Other than from reporters, none. Why?"

"Her father in New York City was notified by us five hours ago. I was just wondering if he'd called her yet."

"No."

"I see." Damn the man! Cam fumed inwardly. The bastard was so filled with his selfishness that he couldn't even stoop to call his only daughter when she needed him the most. What had it been like for Molly to come into a strange emergency room where she knew no one? To be in shock, needing to reach out and be held? Bitterness coated Cam's mouth. He'd felt all those things after the shocking news of his own family's death. Fortunately, the wives of other pilots had come to his rescue. His pilot friends had been supportive, too. In times of crisis, military families were tight-knit, a lifeline to the one in trouble. Molly had had no one. He wanted to cry for her.

Winklemann gestured to the door and Cam halted. His hands were sweaty, his heart beating so hard in his chest it felt like a drum inside him. Trying to gather his shredded emotions as best he could, Cam pushed the door open. There were two beds in the room. One was empty. The one next to the window was where Molly lay.

Walking quietly across the tile floor, Cam thought she was asleep. Only a night-light above the bed was on. Her blond hair, which had been washed and brushed until it shone, formed a golden halo about her features. They must have bathed her earlier to remove the brine from the bay. He searched her serene features anxiously, soaking the sight of her into his heart, his soul. A bruise colored her right temple, and a red mark stretched across the bridge of her nose. The oxygen mask fitted there, and Cam knew the force of ejection had probably imprinted the mask on her flesh.

She wore a light blue cotton gown, and the sheets surrounding her emphasized her paleness. An IV hung above her bed, and was taped to her left arm. How slender and beautiful were her fingers clasped across her chest. Cam halted at the foot of the bed, torn. He didn't want to waken her. Her pale lashes swept like small fans across her cheeks. The word *fragile* struck Cam. Everything about Molly—her small, clean limbs, her long, graceful fingers and fine eyelashes—was a sign of her delicate nature.

Molly moved slightly and Cam's breathing suspended. Her lashes slowly lifted, her green-gold eyes sleepily coming to rest on him. He managed a small shrug.

"I'm sorry, I didn't mean to wake you," he said hoarsely, frozen to the spot.

"Cam?" Molly blinked, disbelief in her scratchy voice.

"Yeah—" he smiled uncertainly "—it's me."

Molly slowly sat up, pushing her hair away from her face. "How long have you been here?"

Molly looked heartrendingly vulnerable. Cam walked over to the side of her bed and placed the file on a nearby table. "I just got here."

Rubbing her eyes, she murmured, "You flew here?"

He ached to reach out and thread his fingers through the soft blond hair lying across her shoulders. "No, I drove."

"You drove? That's a long way."

"You were worth it."

Molly sat very still, searching his features. Cam needed a shave; the darkness of his beard accentuated the planes of his face and how exhausted he was. His eyes were bloodshot and anxious. "I'm glad you came," she choked out.

"I wouldn't want it any other way, Molly." His voice cracking, Cam reached out and cradled her cheek. "I'm sorry you were alone when this happened. I was scared to death for you. I thought you were going to drown out there."

Just the touch of his large hand cupping her cheek drove tears into Molly's eyes. She sniffed. "I—I'm not feeling very strong emotionally right now, Cam. The bailout left me kind of shaky."

With his thumb, he gently stroked her smooth, soft flesh. "No apologies needed, angel. It's common after a bailout. Believe me."

"Really?"

Sweet God! How Cam wanted to lean down and kiss her trembling lower lip. "You're still in shock. It'll take a couple of days." He saw the terrible darkness in her eyes and groaned. "Come here, Molly...."

With a little cry, she opened her arms. After being alone and nearly dying, Molly needed to be held. She felt Cam's arms slide around her and press her tightly against him. She gave a tremulous sigh.

"Everything's going to be okay now," Cam rasped, rubbing his cheek against her silky hair. "You're safe now. You're safe and you're needed." His heart was bursting with such powerful emotions that Cam could only hold Molly as tightly as he dared and absorb her slight, willowy form against his harder one.

Burying her face in the folds of his flight suit, Molly clung to him. "I was so scared," she said, her voice muffled against his chest. "I thought I was going to die, Cam. I—I never felt so helpless. I didn't want to die. All I could think of was you. I felt cheated. I felt angry and scared, all at the same time. When the parachute dragged me down into the water, I wanted to scream at the unfairness of it all." Her fingers opened and closed against Cam's strong back. Tears trailed down her cheeks and soaked into his flight suit.

Cam kissed her hair and gently ran his hand slowly up and down her gowned shoulders and back. Her admission was all he needed to know, and he struggled to hold himself in tight check for her sake. Right now, Molly was in shock. Often, Cam knew from personal experience, the truth came out in such times of stress. Molly cared for him—perhaps even loved him as he did her. Her words were sweet music to his ears and his heart.

"I flew above you," Cam rasped, "wanting to bail out just to try to help you. I saw the chute lines fall over you. I knew what might happen." He shut his eyes tightly, tears leaking out from beneath his lashes. "I've never felt so helpless, Molly. You've been alone—trying to make it on your own since you were ten years old. You were alone down there in that water."

"I nearly lost you," Molly sobbed, the horror of the past six hours finally surfacing. All she really needed, she thought, was someone who genuinely cared about her. "I was just reacting to the situation, not thinking. I thought they called those nylon lines shroud lines. I was wondering if those shroud lines would be my funeral."

Cam trembled violently, gripping Molly hard. "Jesus, don't say that! I couldn't stand it. I couldn't stand losing someone I needed again," he whispered hoarsely.

His cry serrated Molly, and she pulled away just enough to look up into his tormented face. Cam's eyes were wet with tears. With trembling hands, she framed his face, and his beard prickled her palms. Leaning upward, she pressed her lips to the tortured line of his mouth.

Groaning, Cam hungrily drank in her offered gift. Her lips were pliant and soft beneath his hot, hungry exploration. Their breathing grew ragged as they absorbed each other into their souls. She tasted sweet, her lips yielding, telling him she needed him as much as he did her. Fire met and mingled with fire as he memorized every detail and nuance of her mouth beneath his. There was such urgency as they tasted each other. Slowly, so slowly, urgency turned to gentleness, then tenderness. Cam framed Molly's face, wildly aware of her dampened skin, the velvet promise of her mouth beneath his and the love he held fiercely for her alone.

Their breathing joined and became one, gradually changing from a ragged symphony to an even one. He couldn't get enough of Molly, of her special texture and taste. The fragrance of her hair between his fingers increased the ache in his lower body. He was struck by their slow, mutual exploration, as if each of them were imprinting on the other for forever.

Finally Cam eased from her mouth, leaving her lips glistening and well kissed. He held her gaze, golden and dazed in the aftermath. With trembling hands, he awkwardly smoothed the hair framing her face.

"This is real," Molly breathed.

"We're real."

"Cam..."

He drowned in the beauty of the joy and care in the depths of her eyes. How could what he saw in Molly not be love? Cam wasn't certain. Ever since his life had been destroyed by his family's death, he'd taken nothing for granted. "When I first saw you coming up the steps of TPS, I called you an angel," he told her in a low, thick voice. "You looked so clean and sweet compared to the life I was living. Hard men in a hard, unforgiving world of metal, computers and mathematics. Everything had edges to it, Molly. I was living in a numb place where I couldn't feel.

"When I saw you, I felt for the first time in a year," he continued. "I didn't know what to do. The way you walked, your utter femininity, was the complete opposite of the world I'd hidden away in. You had gold hair—" he touched it reverently "—and it reminded me of sunlight." His gaze moved to her eyes. "I thought your eyes were the color of green summer leaves on a tree with sunlight striking them." He brushed her lower lip with his thumb. "And your mouth—your mouth reminded me of a sculpted red rose, as corny as it sounds. You reminded me of summer, growth and light. Your mouth promised me that laughter, that feeling good, wasn't dead inside me, after all." Cam bowed his head and gently took her into his arms. "Molly, you brought me life when I was swimming in a pool of darkness. Just being around you gradually brought me out of that black hell enough to see the light at the end of that tunnel I'd been trapped in for so long."

Molly eased away, her hands on Cam's shoulders, and she held his tear-filled gaze. "No one's ever said anything so beautiful to me before," she whispered.

"It's the truth, angel, and don't you ever forget it." Cam stroked her head, following the natural curve of her hair down to her shoulders. He held the gossamer strands in his long fingers. "The last five months have been hell on you, and even though I recognized what was wrong, I also knew you had to pull yourself up by your own bootstraps." His gaze moved and held hers. "Dammit, Molly, I wanted to protect you. I wanted so much to stand between you and everything in life that had you by the throat."

She shook her head. "You couldn't help me. Maggie told me a long time ago that if I was to get strong, I had to do it on my terms and time. When she said that, it scared me. But in some deep level of myself I knew she was right."

"And you've done it," Cam added gently. "These past five months I've watched you grow and blossom despite your damned family and people like Martin aiming for you."

With a little laugh, Molly gave a shrug, then grimaced with the pain of her bruised muscles. "I've tried, Cam."

"You're a winner, Molly, no matter what anyone says. I'm proud as hell of you. Do you know that?"

She gave a single shake of her head, lost in the smoky blue of his eyes that promised her so much that was yet unsaid. "I've got to tell you, it's nice to have someone in my corner. You were there all along, Cam. You never deserted me."

His throat tightening, Cam touched her temple. "I never will, Molly, and that's a promise I intend to keep."

"I was so afraid of you when I met you that second time in the library. You looked so fierce and unforgiving in the hall when Martin cornered me." She looked away. "I felt like such a klutz up there in the library, dropping my books, almost upsetting the desk that I—"

Gently, Cam forced her to look at him, his hand resting beneath her trembling chin. "That's when I made that promise to you, angel. That's when I began to realize how hard and callous I'd become because of my family's death. Your vulnerability, your ability to be a human being, faults and all, touched me like nothing else could. Do you understand that?"

"I think so...." Molly smiled lamely. "When you helped me pick up my books and spoke to me in that tone you're using right now, I lost my fear of you. I saw the man underneath that cold mask you wore, Cam."

He pressed a slow, tender kiss on her waiting lips, glorying in her warm, melting response. Easing away, he whispered, "Just know I'm at your side, Molly, through everything. Your eyes are dark. You're exhausted. I want you to get some sleep. Tomorrow morning I'll come over and we'll have breakfast together. How's that sound?'' What Cam really wanted was to take her to bed and hold her through the night, to give Molly the support she so richly deserved. It took everything in him not to say *I love you. I want to spend the rest of my life with you.* But he couldn't. Not yet.

Never having felt so loved or cared for in her life, Molly acquiesced to Cam's reasoning. A huge part of her craved his continued nearness. Swallowing her disappointment, she nodded. ''You're right. I feel so tired.''

Cam waited until she'd lain back down, and he helped her arrange the blankets. Molly's cheeks were flushed a bright red, her lips slightly swollen from their torrid, hungry kisses, her hair a golden halo about her head. Reluctantly he picked up the folder.

''I'll be at a nearby motel. I'll call the nurse at the desk and leave a phone number and room where I'm staying. If you need anything, anything at all tonight, you call. Understand?''

Barely able to keep her eyes open, Molly nodded. ''Just knowing you're here is enough,'' she slurred softly.

Cam smiled gently and stood in the gathering silence, watching Molly fall asleep. He reached out, lacing his fingers through hers. Despite her fragile appearance, Molly was a lot stronger than she realized. And it was her own courage that had created that backbone of steel she'd need for life's unexpected hardships.

Frowning, Cam realized Molly had felt abandoned by her own family during her crisis. He was sure the topic would come up tomorrow morning. Slipping his fingers from hers, Cam stepped forward and lightly kissed her cheek.

"Good night, angel. Sleep the sleep of an angel, because you are one," he whispered.

Cam showed up at Molly's hospital room at exactly 0800. Dressed in comfortable civilian clothes—brown slacks, a beige polo shirt and a dark brown corduroy sport coat—he tracked down Dr. Winklemann before going in to see Molly. Now, as he knocked lightly on Molly's door and entered, happiness thrummed through Cam.

"Hi," Molly greeted. She was sitting on the side of her bed, her bare feet dangling inches above the floor.

"You'll catch your death of cold that way," Cam warned, smiling. This morning, Molly looked wonderful. Except for the bruise on her temple, no one would guess at her harrowing escape from death yesterday afternoon.

"You caught me before I could get into some slippers." She held up her left arm. "Look, Dr. Winklemann said I was healthy as a horse and could get rid of the IV."

The urge to kiss Molly's smiling lips was pure torture to Cam. There was such dancing light in her green eyes—the eyes of a thrilled and joyous child. It made him feel the same way. If decorum didn't have to be observed, Cam would have followed his wild urge to pick Molly up and twirl her around and around in his arms until they both fell laughing to the floor.

"I've just got done talking to him. They'll release you this afternoon if you want."

"Great! I'm ready to go. I *hate* hospitals!" Molly got up, holding on to the sidebar of the bed. Cam went to the nurses' station and got her some slippers and a robe.

"I thought we'd go down to their cafeteria and eat breakfast," she suggested. "I don't like staying tied up in a bed."

Cam placed the slippers before her, watching as she daintily slid her slender feet into them. "Are you sure you're up to all that?"

"Now you're being overprotective," Molly teased.

Cam held out the robe and she slipped into it. The dark blue robe was many sizes too big for her, and he thought Molly looked like a bedraggled ragamuffin, endearing and very desirable. "Probably am," he groused good-naturedly. "How are you feeling?"

"My back's a little sore and I'm not as limber as I'd like to be, but the doctor said that should go away in a week or so." Molly pointed to her rear. "Can you believe, I'm black-and-blue right across my butt and hips?"

With a laugh, Cam placed his hands on his hips. "I'd like to see that."

"Cam Sinclair, how dare you!"

His grin broadened. "You're a fighter at heart, angel. And don't slap my hand for thinking such things. Just slap it when I try them."

Flushing hotly, Molly avoided Cam's hooded stare, molten with promise and invitation. "This is a new side of you," she said with a smile and walked toward the door.

"No, it's always been there," Cam reassured her amiably, opening the door for her. "You just bring out the best in me, I guess."

Molly's happiness increased as they walked down the hall toward the elevator. Cam came alongside her and slipped his hand across her shoulders, bringing her gently beside him. On awakening this morning, Molly had wondered if all those fevered, starving kisses they'd shared had been nothing more than dreams created out of her shock and trauma.

"Cam?"

"Yes?" They moved into the elevator and the doors whooshed closed. Molly was suddenly nervous, chewing on her lower lip, unable to meet his eyes. "Last night…"

With a sigh, Cam drew Molly into the shelter of his embrace. "It really happened. It was real."

She pressed her cheek against his chest and heard the solid, slow beat of his heart beneath her ear. "I thought I'd dreamed it," she whispered, relieved.

Cam's laugh was soft. "I woke up this morning wondering the same thing, angel. I was hoping I hadn't, but I've had dreams before that were so real, I could have sworn they'd happened." Cam searched her upturned face, thinking the purity of honesty ran through every fiber in Molly's sweet body. "When I saw the welcome in your eyes this morning, I knew I hadn't dreamed it."

The doors opened and Molly eased from his embrace but remained close to him. Cam slipped his hand into hers and led her down the hall toward the cafeteria. The small gesture meant everything to Molly. Her world was in a tailspin. First, her father disowning her, then the bailout, and now a heated awareness of Cam's undeniable interest in her. Molly was grateful that he seemed to sense she needed space, not pressure from him. Her battered emotions couldn't stand much more.

After seating Molly at one of the tables in the far corner of the cafeteria, Cam got them breakfast, coming back with a tray laden with food. As he approached, Molly wondered what it would be like to wake up and share breakfast with him every morning. The idea was startling. Evocative.

"You've got to be starved," Cam confided, sitting down at her elbow after setting the tray on an empty table.

Molly grinned. "Cam, there's enough food here for five people!"

"Shock makes you hungry," he told her, digging into a plate filled with scrambled eggs, bacon and biscuits.

"Your shock or mine?" she returned wryly, picking up her fork.

They fell to the task of eating, sharing a warm silence. It was Saturday, and few people were in the cafeteria. Molly had spotted the file Cam had brought with him and realized she'd have to give him a debriefing report on the incident. Her stomach knotted automatically, the fear coming back strongly. She stopped eating.

"What's wrong?"

Amazed at his sensitivity to her mood change, Molly glanced over at Cam. "A replay of the ejection sequence."

"Flashback," Cam assured her gently. "It'll happen a lot at first. With time, they get less intense and more sporadic. Finally, they'll go away."

"You've ejected before?"

"Yeah, once."

Molly cringed. "How awful."

"Not something one wants to do every day of the week," Cam agreed. "Come on, try to eat a little more. You've barely touched your food." He watched Molly rally. How little encouragement she needed in order to pick herself up and try again. Cam felt humbled by her spirit.

After breakfast, Cam cleared away the dishes. Over coffee, he worked on the investigation report. Writing everything in neat, printed letters, it took an hour to fill out all the forms. Molly dawdled over her second cup of coffee, trying to be precise in her description of the experience.

"By the way," Cam asked, "did you note turbulence at twenty thousand feet, as Martin reported?"

"What turbulence?"

"He reported it on the second spin test. Said there was turbulence at twenty thousand and that's why he didn't get the five spins in."

Molly snorted. "There was no turbulence, Cam."

"Maybe an air pocket? Sometimes hitting one of those unexpectedly can bauble a test."

"No. Absolutely not."

Grimly, Cam put the information into his report, a gnawing feeling in his gut. "Was there any turbulence on the third test when Martin lost control of the bird and it went into the flat spin?"

Molly leaned forward on her elbows and held his probing look. "Cam, there was *no* turbulence encountered at *any* altitude, at *any* time during our test sequences."

"You're absolutely positive, Molly?"

Frustration laced her tone. "Of course I am."

Cam shook his head. "Dammit."

"What?"

He glanced over at her. Should he tell Molly what his instincts were screaming at him? Or should he protect her?

"I heard Martin tell you on the second test that we encountered turbulence," Molly grumped. "I was going to speak up, but it didn't seem important at the time."

"The meteorology report said there was no clear air turbulence over the bay. It was calm winds except at five thousand and below."

"It was calm," Molly stated quietly. She compressed her lips. "Cam, what's going on? I can see that look in your eyes. You suspect something, don't you? That Martin lied? That he deliberately set the Tomcat into a flat spin to get rid of me or in some way make me look bad? Or—" she sighed heavily "—to create an incident that would force both instructors to overlook his lousy flight performance and concentrate on something more important, like a flight engineer bailing out?"

Cam sat very quietly, having thought of all the scenarios she calmly laid out before him. Molly was astute as well as intelligent. "I don't like to think any pilot would go to this length."

"Fortunately, not all pilots are as desperate as Martin," Molly put in drolly.

Cam shook his head. "None of this can be proved, Molly. Do you realize that? It's your word against his about the turbulence. We can't record it on instruments or video in this case. Nothing will show up."

"And no one can prove that Martin deliberately kicked the fighter into a flat one, either," Molly added. With a sigh, she asked, "Are you going to grade him on the flight?"

"No, I can't due to the in-flight emergency."

"Then Martin got exactly what he wanted. He got rid of me, blew the test and gets to start over clean and dry for a second try."

"Well," Cam replied grimly, "if this is what really happened, then Martin's never going to get a chance at you again. I'll make damn sure of that."

"He still has to complete the spin tests in order to graduate, Cam. Who will he pick on next? The next test-flight engineer might not be as lucky as I was."

Clenching his fist on the table, Cam said, "I just don't want to believe that Martin is capable of such a thing."

"I don't, either. That's the worst-case scenario. I think the fighter got away from him on that third spin test, Cam. Compared to Dalton, Martin's skill in the spin department is weak, in my personal estimation."

Cam's gut continued to scream at him. He tried to shake the sensation, the gut instinct that had never led him wrong before—even in combat. Well, this wasn't actual combat, but it was another, subtler form of it. What Molly didn't realize in her tendency to see only the best in others was that some jet jocks would do damn near anything to come out on top, to win or appear to be the best. There were a few bad apples in the pilot barrel of every service. Cam knew Martin might have lied and deceived them. And the one who'd nearly paid with her life had been Molly. Chilling anger snaked through Cam. If he could ever prove Martin had done these things on purpose, he'd probably kill him or come close to it. No one put Molly's life in jeopardy. *No one.*

Chapter Thirteen

"Free at last!" Molly said, getting into Cam's sports car. Her flight suit had been washed by the hospital and it was all she had to wear for the five-hour drive home, but she didn't care. By regulation, she was to wear her shoulder-length hair above her collar, but she allowed it to swing free. No one would see it.

Cam smiled and waited until she'd buckled up before starting the Corvette. If not for Molly's slow, careful maneuvering into his car, no one would know that she'd bailed out twenty-four hours earlier. "You're ready to go home. I can tell," he observed, driving out of the hospital parking lot.

Leaning back, Molly closed her eyes, the autumn sun warm through the dark-tinted window. "Am I ever." She sighed.

"Tired?"

"I shouldn't be."

"But you are." Cam reached over, gripping her hand momentarily. "Go to sleep, Molly. You're still coming out of shock."

Drowsily she turned her head to look over at Cam. His profile was clean and rugged. "Sure?"

"Positive."

His hand felt good on hers, and she smiled slightly. "Thanks for understanding. I wouldn't make a very good copilot right now, anyway."

There was so much Cam wanted to tell her, share with her, but he withheld it. Molly had another month of school left, and somehow he had to control his need for her. She was so close to succeeding on her own merits, on her own strength and courage. He didn't want to interfere in this process that was crucial to Molly's well-being. Reluctantly, Cam removed his hand.

"Sleep, angel," he whispered. Cam doubted Molly even heard him. Her eyes were already closed, her lips softly parted. Even now, darkness still shadowed the pale skin beneath her golden lashes.

His mind revolved forward to Martin and to the possibility the pilot had gone into a flat spin on purpose to blow the test and make Molly look bad. Martin wasn't good at spins. Or was he? Cam shook his head. Fifty percent of the time when a pilot got into a flat spin, it was impossible to pull the aircraft out of it, and a crash resulted. Martin had to be *very* good to purposely put a jet into one and then get it out again.

His emotions seesawed between brutal anger toward Martin if that was so, and a grim determination to protect Molly. Dammit, he loved her. He'd lost one woman he'd loved to events completely out of his control. This time he could control or at least influence the outcome.

Wiping his damp brow, Cam glanced over at Molly. Her head was tipped to one side, and she was sleeping deeply. An ache spread through his heart—an ache so intense and filled with hope that it drove tears into his eyes. His future sat next to him, sleeping the sleep of an innocent. *Sweet God,* Cam thought, *she's so good and pure.* Despite the punishing military system, Molly had kept her vulnerability and idealism intact. That in itself showed her inherent strength, her ability to survive on her own terms.

The discoveries he was making about Molly were like seeing the light at the end of a seemingly endless tunnel he'd walked by himself for so very long. Each nuance she revealed to him was exhilarating, humbling. A fierce love for her swept through Cam, as startling as it was potent. The future seemed alive with promise, alive with such hope that he wanted to stop the car, drag Molly into his arms and love her.

Cam shook his head, forcing himself to concentrate on the two-lane road. Bright autumn-colored trees and rolling green hills surrounded him. The day was a mirror reflecting the promise and hope that dwelled in his hammering heart. Never had the sky seemed bluer, the clouds whiter or the sun brighter—the color of Molly's hair.

Scratching his head ruefully, Cam wondered what had happened to him. He was turning into a dreamer, seeing the world from a completely different perspective. How could that be? Cam knew what love—real love—was. He'd felt it, shared it with Jeanne and Sean. Glancing over at Molly, he experienced new sensations, wonderful feelings that sprang from an unknown chamber of his heart that he hadn't realized existed, until this moment with her.

Relief, sweet and splintering, flowed through Cam, and a huge, nameless weight was lifted from his shoulders. Miraculously, he felt lighter, more free. As he drove on, mile after mile through the countryside that paralleled the bay, he gradually understood what had happened. He'd finally released his family—and it had been Molly's love that had made it possible.

Cam savored the realization, the hours flowing around him in a cocoon of memories and good feelings. He'd never forget his family. No. They owned a piece of his heart and his memory. He knew that Molly would never feel threatened by that, and that he'd always hold Jeanne and Sean close in a good and positive way.

By the time they reached the bridge that spanned the Chesapeake Bay and would guide them by Annapolis, Molly stirred. Cam divided his attention between driving and watching her slowly awaken. How badly he wanted to see her wake up in his arms some morning after making slow, beautiful love all night. Each of her movements was graceful and unhurried as she stretched and yawned.

"I was dreaming," Molly said in a sleepy voice, her eyes half open. The spans of the bridge crisscrossed like shadows on the windshield of the car.

"Happy dreams?"

"No..."

"Tell me about it."

Molly dragged in a deep breath. "They were about my father." She studied her hands. Several of her fingernails had broken during the ejection. That was how she felt inside presently: broken up. Glancing over at Cam, she saw the softening of his mouth, the tenderness in his blue gaze when it held hers briefly.

"I know his not contacting you hurt," Cam ventured.

"Do you really think he loves me?" Molly grimaced. "What a stupid thing to ask. I know he loves me. That sounds silly."

"No, not silly at all."

"I feel abandoned, Cam."

"I know. But—" he smiled gently "—you've got me, plus your friends Dana and Maggie. You aren't alone."

Molly reached out, sliding her hand across Cam's. It was such a natural response. His long, strong fingers wrapped around her hand, and some of the pain fled from her heart. "Friends are so important to me. I don't know what I'd have done without all of you through the past five years."

"Your father loves you, Molly. He just doesn't realize it yet."

She couldn't keep the hurt out of her voice. "I'm so angry at him, Cam. I nearly died out there yesterday. He could've called. He would've flown down to see me if I was really important to him." Her eyes mirrored her anguish as she looked out the window, not seeing the beauty of Maryland. "He's got Scott so wrapped around his finger that he didn't call, either."

"It's a messy, complex situation," Cam agreed quietly. "I think the only thing that will help will be time and keeping the lines of communication open, Molly."

"Oh, sure. Once I get back to my apartment, I'll call him and say, 'I'm okay, Father. I almost died out there, but I'm fine now.'"

"Your father has too much pride. It's a very expendable emotion, Molly. Don't wear it like he does. Do whatever it takes to let him know you love him and Scott. I know it's hard, but it's the only option you've got unless you want to close up the way he has. That could last years. I've seen it happen in other families. Is that what you want?''

"No," she muttered. Rubbing her temple, she said, "I don't want to talk to him. I'm too emotional right now. I'll write a letter instead."

Cam nodded. "Letters are fine. I'm proud of you, Molly. I really am."

She managed a slight smile. "Nobody said living was supposed to be easy, did they?"

"Sometimes it's more a can of pits than a bowl of cherries."

Laughing, Molly wanted to throw her arms around Cam's shoulders and kiss him. There was such care and love in his eyes as he glanced over at her. Her heart beat painfully hard beneath her ribs. Yes, she loved Cam. Nearly losing her life had forced Molly to rip away the blinders and admit the truth. Did he really love her? A part of her thought so. Another part didn't know. Time, she cautioned herself. They had to have time.

"I'm going to take you over to your apartment and then go over to TPS for a while," Cam told her. In another hour and a half, they'd be home. *Home.* What would it be like to have Molly at his house? It would be a home then—not the empty shell it was now.

"You've got work to do?" Molly asked in disbelief.

"Well," Cam hedged, "I have to get this accident report filed and on the commandant's desk by Monday. Now, don't go looking scared, Molly. You're in the clear on this. No grades will be given to either student. I'm sure the commandant will want the test repeated."

"By Martin and me?" she demanded, her eyes widening.

"Not if I can help it," Cam answered grimly. No way in hell was he going to let Martin get at her again. On Monday, Cam would learn the commandant's decision.

"It appears to be a fluke in the test," Captain Rawlins told Cam and Vic, who stood at parade rest in front of his desk. He placed the file in front of them. "Schedule Martin and Rutledge to fly on Wednesday. They'll also have to fly again on Friday with different students. I expect Rutledge to have her next test-flight program ready for Friday, Vic."

"Yes, sir."

"Captain," Cam said tensely, "I'm going to step out of line and say that I don't feel it's in Martin's or Rutledge's best interests to have them fly together again."

Rawlins looked up. "Oh?"

Cam squirmed. He couldn't prove Martin had done anything wrong on that flight. To stand here and accuse him of such would be stupid and foolhardy. Rawlins would want proof, and he had none. "Sir, there's a real personality conflict between them. Vic will validate that—"

"Yes, sir, there is," Vic chimed in.

Scowling, Rawlins sat back in his leather chair, scrutinizing them. "That won't wash, Cam, and you know it. If you want, check Martin out on spin tests before you send them up if you're worried about his performance. If he screws them up, let's reassess his capabilities." He jabbed a finger at him. "But that's the only scenario where I'll reassign Rutledge to another pilot so she can complete the necessary spin-test requirement for graduation. Understand?"

Disheartened, Cam nodded. "Yes, sir. I'll go up with him this afternoon."

"Good. Dismissed, gentlemen."

Out in the hall, Vic walked at his shoulder. "You're worried about something, Cam. What is it?"

"Nothing," Cam muttered, keeping his personal feelings tightly controlled. Rawlins had given him a way out. He'd take Martin up in an F-14 this afternoon and make him do spins until he was airsick, if necessary. But if Martin passed the examination, Cam was helpless to stop the test from being reflown.

Martin walked cockily across the apron from the hangar, helmet and duffel bag in hand. He grinned over at Cam.

"You look a little green, Captain Sinclair. Did my spins get to you?"

Cam shook his head. Darkness was coming over the air station as they walked to the waiting van that would take them back to Ops. "Your spins were acceptable, Mr. Martin."

His smile widened. "So I go up with Rutledge on Wednesday. Is that it?"

Climbing into the van, Cam nodded. "That's right." After he got back to TPS and changed into civilian clothes, Cam was going over to visit Molly. He felt sick inside, helpless to protect her when his gut was telling him Martin was up to something. But what?

Molly smiled and stepped aside to allow Cam into her apartment. He had Miracle with him, and she leaned over, hugging the dog affectionately.

"This is a surprise," she said, closing the door. Cam wore a pair of ivory corduroy slacks and a cranberry flannel shirt with the sleeves rolled up to his elbows. The shadow she saw in his eyes lessened her smile. "What's wrong, Cam?"

There was no sense in scaring Molly or making her worry about his unproved suspicions. "Nothing." He forced a smile. "You look pretty." Molly wore a dark blue turtleneck and a plaid wool skirt that grazed her ankles. She looked old-fashioned, beautiful and incredibly delicate as she stood before him. Cam tried to separate his feelings from his reason for coming over. It was almost impossible. Molly's blond hair lay in mussed abandon around her shoulders, her green-and-gold eyes alight with such happiness that Cam wanted to crush her in his arms and hold her forever.

"Thank you. Come in. I was just making some lemon tea from my grandmother's old recipe."

"I like your grandmother. I'm just sorry I never got to meet her," Cam said, following Molly in the kitchen. Everywhere he looked the decor was Oriental. Instead of stainless-steel bowls, Molly had copper ones that hung from various hooks around the modern kitchen stove in the center of the room.

"She'd have loved you," Molly told him, meaning it. Pouring the tea into two delicate china cups, she handed one to Cam. "It's been quite a day. Everyone with the exception of Martin was really glad to see me at school. I got pats on the back, handshakes and congratulations." Molly laughed and moved to the living room and sat down on the couch. Cam sat on the overstuffed chair nearby.

"Anybody who survives an ejection is looked upon with respect," Cam informed her.

"Heck of a way to earn respect." Molly laughed, curling her feet beneath her, and smoothed out the wrinkles in the plaid skirt.

"You've changed those guys," Cam said seriously, sipping the fragrant, tart tea.

"At first they thought I was a joke because I was a woman invading their strictly male territory."

"Yes. But after five months, with hard work, savvy and your own brand of statesmanship, you've changed their minds."

Molly grinned and watched Miracle come and lie down between them, resting her head on her paws. "My womanly diplomacy, you mean."

"Exactly. TPS is better off because of your presence here. A gentler spirit has made the men realize there's more than one way to approach and solve problems."

"You mean," Molly suggested, "I've taught them you don't need to bang heads, curse and outshout the other person to get your point across."

Cam nodded.

"What's bothering you?"

He moved uncomfortably. "You have to fly with Martin on Wednesday."

Molly frowned and compressed her lips. She held the cup between her slender fingers. "I guess I knew that in my heart. There's no reason why the commandant wouldn't order us to repeat it, is there?"

"No...." And then Cam told her about retesting Martin on spins earlier that day. He saw some of the worry leave Molly's eyes.

"Want to take a look at my Friday test? It's a really good one." Molly got up and went to her office and got the printout. She spread it across the coffee table, and they knelt beside each other, checking her test. Cam devoted his attention to her mathematical figures, and the complexity involved in it.

"Looks good," Cam congratulated.

"At least I won't have to fly it with Martin. I hope I get Dalton. He's really a top pilot."

Cam smiled. "See? You're already behaving like a test-flight engineer. You've got your favorite pilots picked out."

Gathering up the printout, Molly smiled. "*You're* my favorite pilot, but I've never flown with you."

Sitting down on the sofa, Cam smiled. "I trust your assessment is strictly an emotional and personal opinion, Ms. Rutledge?"

Molly nodded and sat down next to him, curling into her favorite position. "I like what we have, Cam," she admitted hesitantly. "Maybe this is the wrong time and place to talk about us, but after Saturday, something happened."

Cam held the teacup gently in his hands, slowly turning it and studying the flowers painted on its sides. "I like what we're becoming to each other, Molly," he admitted quietly. He turned his head and held her lustrous green gaze. "Dammit, I'm having one hell of a time keeping my hands off you, keeping my feelings to myself and giving you the room you need in order to focus on TPS."

His admission flowed through her like a warm wind after an icy, chilling storm. "Saturday ripped away a lot of things," she whispered.

"Saturday was hell," Cam said flatly. "Hell."

"Is this why you're so worried about me flying with Martin? Because you..." She hesitated, hating to put words in Cam's mouth. "You care for me?"

Placing the teacup on the coffee table, Cam moved toward her and picked up her free hand. "I care very much, Molly." His voice vibrated with barely leashed feelings. "Everything I said to you in the hospital when we kissed and I held you, I meant. Nothing's changed. It's just that . . . well, dammit, it's the wrong time for you.''

"Me?"

"You've got a month of school left. You need to focus on that, not on us.''

Her mouth curved faintly. "Cameron Sinclair, you've been a part of my focus from the day I met you in the hall staring blackly at me." Molly realized she might have said too much and hastily added, "But you're right, it's only a month.''

"It's important that you graduate for yourself, Molly. If I walked into your life, like I want to, I'd end up destroying your focus. I know that.''

She grinned recklessly. "Pretty sure of yourself, aren't you?"

"Marines know they're number one, angel.''

With a laugh, Molly clapped her hands. "I never realized you had this playful, teasing side to you. I like it!''

Her laughter went straight through him like blazing, heady sunlight. There was so much Cam wanted to share. His smile dissolved and he held her delighted gaze. "One month," he promised her thickly, "just one more month, and then, Molly Rutledge, you're fair game—so watch out.''

She thrilled to the dangerous undertone in Cam's dark voice. The need to love him, to share her dreams, her hopes with him, spiraled hotly to the surface. Stilling those needs, Molly nodded. "Okay, one month.''

With a groan, Cam stood. "I want you to know it's hell being around you. But it's the sweetest kind of hell I've ever experienced.'' There was something to say about taking his time with Molly. Cam found himself enjoying nuances he'd never discovered about any woman.

Getting to her feet, Molly said, "I've got a favor to ask of you."

"Sure."

"You have the duty at the station tomorrow night?"

"Yes, I'm station-duty officer. Why?"

"I want to make one last computer run of my flight test before I print out the one I'll give to Vic. I'd like to do it tomorrow night over at TPS. Since you've got the duty, you've got the key to let me in after hours."

Cam nodded and slowly walked to the door with Miracle at his side. He didn't want to go home. He wanted to stay here tonight, with Molly. "No problem. How about if we both go out and eat and I'll take you over to TPS after that?"

"Great idea."

"Our first, unofficial dinner date," Cam teased, opening the door. If he didn't leave now, he'd stay. God, how he wanted to stay. Molly looked lovely standing there, her hands clasped in front of her.

"Make it 2100? That's when you close up the school. We can run over to the base restaurant, grab a bite and then go back. It will only take me an hour to run my program."

Groaning, Cam nodded. "Some date."

"You'll survive, Sinclair. I'll see you tomorrow." She leaned up on tiptoe, placing a chaste kiss on his cheek. "Good night."

"See you in my dreams," Cam whispered, kissing her lightly on the lips, but wanting to capture her and hungrily make love with her.

They were sitting at the restaurant on base when Cam's beeper went off. As duty officer, he carried one for the entire twenty-four hour shift. Molly frowned and sipped her coffee. Any problems that arose, he had the responsibility to handle them. When he came back from making the phone call to the duty office, he looked unhappy.

"There's been a break-in at the exchange," he told her. "I called Shore Patrol and they have a key for the school. I told them you have permission to go there." He glanced at his watch. "It will probably take me an hour to check this exchange problem out."

Molly rose and slipped the strap of her purse over her left shoulder. As always, they were in flight suits while on the base. "Fine, I'll be kept busy, believe me."

"I wanted another half hour here with you," Cam complained, walking her out the door after paying for their meals.

Molly smiled as she stood outside the restaurant. A Shore Patrol truck would pick her up and take her to TPS. "See you later."

Cam waved and walked toward the parking lot at the rear of the building. The crisp November night was frosty, his breath white. The hour he'd planned on savoring with Molly was gone. With a sour smile, Cam got into his Corvette and shut the door. Well, he would just have to be patient and stop trying to plan odd moments alone with her like this. Being on SDO duty meant expecting the unexpected.

The Shore Patrol driver opened the rear door to the darkened facility for Molly. She thanked him and he nodded. Once the door was closed, the young sailor locked it again. Locating the switch, Molly flicked on the hall lights. The place was deadly quiet as she turned and climbed up to the second floor via the emergency exit stairs.

Noticing a dim light in the computer room down at the end of the hall, Molly frowned. She hadn't seen it from outside the building because the room was windowless, as most mainframe computer rooms tended to be. Perhaps Cam had forgotten to turn it off during his last tour of the facility before locking up for the night.

Her garrison cap in one hand and her briefcase in the other, Molly pushed open the door to the facility. There were four rows of computer terminals, three monitors at each station. Her frown increased. She always worked at terminal two, monitor three, and that's where the light was on. Moving down the long room, Molly turned and halted. She saw that her flight test was on the screen of the monitor. Not only that, but as she moved closer to inspect, she noted that the printout was of her forthcoming Friday test.

Placing her purse and garrison cap nearby, Molly sat down. Several numbers on the printout were circled in red ink. Cross-checking them against those on the monitor, Molly realized they had been changed. Her heart started a slow pound. Someone was deliberately changing the numbers on her flight test! Who? Molly looked around, but the computer room was silent except for the hum of the equipment.

Whoever it was had a key to get in. An instructor? Stymied, Molly sat looking around. Was the person still in the building? Or had he fled the scene when the Shore Patrol let her into the building? Getting up, Molly walked to the other end of the room where a phone was located. She would call the SDO office and ask them to send Cam over immediately.

Picking up the phone with a trembling hand, Molly turned so she had an unobstructed view of the rows of terminals and the door at the opposite end of the room.

The phone rang four times on the other end before someone answered.

"Yes, this is Ensign Rutledge over at the TPS building. Get ahold of Captain Sinclair, SDO. There's been a break-in here, and the person may still be in the building." Her voice shook slightly, and Molly hoped the sailor didn't notice it. Just as she opened her mouth to speak, the door to the computer room was violently jerked open. Molly quickly put the receiver back into the cradle and stood anchored with fear.

Chapter Fourteen

Molly swallowed against a dry throat as Chuck Martin stepped into the computer room. His gaze flicked to where she stood at the rear of the room. His eyes narrowed in anger.

"What the hell are you doing here?"

It was now or never. Molly knew to appear weak would invite Martin's attack. Gathering all her strength and resolve, she lifted her chin and hardened her voice. "I should ask you the same thing," she hurled back. Forcing herself to move, she went over to her station. "Just what are you doing with *my* printout sheet for Friday's flight?"

Martin placed a mug of fresh coffee down on the table. "I always check out the flight engineer's program before I fly it with *him*," he grated back. He doubled his fists and placed them on his narrow hips. "You still have to answer my question—what are you doing here?"

Molly saw the dangerous glint in Martin's narrowed eyes and sensed the tension in his body as he stood menacingly over her. Her mind whirled with questions and options. Martin was upset. What would he do? She remembered Cam telling her that she saw only the best in people, but that it could be dangerous if carried to an extreme. Martin was just such a person not to underestimate.

"No," Molly rasped, jabbing her finger down at the printout. "You tell me how *you* got in here, Martin. I got permission from the SDO and Shore Patrol to let me in. I'm on the office log as being here. Are you?" She saw Martin's eyes widen in surprise over her attack.

"I got permission."

"From who?" Molly shot back, standing her ground, her heart starting a low, hard beat.

"It doesn't matter."

"Yes, it does." She turned and looked at her printout and then back at Martin. "No one has the computer access code to bring this printout up except me and my instructor, Lieutenant Norton. Just how did you get ahold of it, Martin?"

Martin grinned. "None of your business, honey."

"Don't call me honey!"

"Maybe *bitch* is a better word," Martin snarled.

Molly's mouth dropped open. Fury shot through her. Before she realized what she was doing, she stepped forward and slapped Martin across the face. The pilot reacted instantly, taking a step back, his hand going to his reddening cheek.

"How dare you!" Molly cried fiercely. "I haven't done anything to you, Martin! I will not have you call me names or show disrespect!"

Rubbing his cheek tenderly, Martin sized her up. "Why, you little—"

"Don't you *dare* call me anything more! You're in a lot more trouble than you realize." Molly grabbed the printout with the red-circled changes on it.

"Hey! What are you doing?" Martin lunged forward.

With a cry, Molly leaped back, the printout under her left arm. She saw the pilot's face twist in hatred, and knew he was going to take the evidence away from her. That couldn't happen! Whirling around, Molly raced around the end of the station, heading toward the door to escape.

"Come back here!" Martin roared, sprinting after her, his hand outstretched.

Molly's fingers wrapped around the handle. Jerking open the door, she lunged through it. Just then, Martin's fingers dug into her shoulder, slipped off, but caught the fabric of her flight suit instead. Crying out, Molly was pulled off balance. She half twisted around, falling out the door.

Martin landed heavily upon her. The wind was knocked out of her. The printout went sliding down the polished tile floor just out of her reach. Lashing out, Molly used her fingernails, which were blunt and short, to strike out at Martin's face.

"Oww! You bitch!" Four red scratches appeared on his left cheek.

Dodging his fist, Molly pushed Martin off her. Just as she scrambled to her knees, Martin threw his arms around her legs. With a scream, Molly fell to the floor. She was being dragged backward! Fighting wildly, she loosened one of her booted feet and took aim at Martin's face. He wasn't going to get her printout! If he got it, he'd destroy the evidence, and then there'd be no way Molly could prove he'd altered her flight program.

Teeth clenched, she put as much strength as possible into kicking Martin. Her boot grazed his jaw and solidly struck his shoulder. It only infuriated him. Breathing hard, her breath coming in gasps, Molly freed herself.

"No way!" Martin roared at her as she staggered to her feet.

Molly was barely standing again when Martin hit her full force from behind. She slammed onto the floor, her head striking the tile first. The air was forced out of her, and she lay stunned, unable to move.

"Hold it!"

Molly blinked, realizing it was Cam's voice. With the last of her strength, Molly looked up. Her eyes widened. Cam stood poised at the other end of the hall, his face etched with fury.

Martin hesitated only fractionally, then leaned down, scooping up the printout.

"Stop him!" Molly cried, trying to get to her feet.

Cam snarled a curse as he ran down the length of the hall after Martin. He saw Molly sitting on the floor, disheveled and bruised, with blood dribbling from the corner of her mouth and nose. He knew Martin had done it, and hatred more driving and savage than he'd ever experienced exploded through him.

Recovering her breath, Molly realized Martin would scramble for the stairs to escape. Every bone in her body hurt from the jarring fall, but she ignored the pain and thrust out her foot to trip Martin as he started to run past her.

The pilot hadn't expected Molly to do anything but cower in a heap on the floor. When she stuck her leg out in his path, he tripped and fell forward. The printout flew through the air, arcing over Molly's head and striking the glass door to the computer room.

Cam lunged just as Martin got to his knees. Where the hell was Shore Patrol? His fingers dug deeply into Martin's shoulders and he jerked the pilot to a stop.

Hissing a curse, Martin doubled his fist.

Cam was prepared. Just the sight of Molly bleeding was enough to make him want to kill Martin. He took great satisfaction in striking the pilot in the face. Bone crunched and broke beneath the force of his well-aimed blow. Martin cried out and crumpled to the floor, covering his face with both his hands.

"My nose! You broke my nose!" Martin shrieked.

Breathing hard, Cam hunkered over him, his fist wrapped in the pilot's flight suit. "You son of a bitch! I'll break more than your nose. Don't move!"

Sobbing for breath, Martin kept his hand over his head. "I won't, I won't! Don't hit me again!"

Molly heard several men running up the rear exit stairs. Three sailors with Shore Patrol badges on their left arms appeared at the other end of the hall and hurried toward them. Once they arrived, Cam released Martin to their custody and straightened.

"Arrest Lieutenant Martin for trespassing without authorization, and for assault," he snarled.

Still sitting on the floor, Molly breathed a sigh of relief. She saw anxiety replace Cam's unadulterated anger as he came over to kneel beside her.

"Johnson," he snapped at one of the Shore patrol men, "call an ambulance."

"Yes, sir!" The petty officer went into the computer room to use the phone to call the dispensary.

"No," Molly protested. "I'm okay. Really, I am."

Cam's hands shook badly as he framed her face. "Like hell you are. You're a mess. You're bleeding from your nose and mouth, Molly." He carefully touched her brow where it was turning black-and-blue.

"I am?" She reached up and touched her upper lip. "Oh, dear..."

Cam kept his hand on her shoulder as she paled considerably after that discovery. Was Molly going to faint on him? He wouldn't blame her. "Hold on," he pleaded with her. "I'll get you over to sick bay in a few minutes."

Darkness kept edging her vision. Molly remembered what Dana had told her about how to stop fainting, and lowered her head between her knees so the blood would flow back into her skull. Cam's hand felt comforting on her shoulder.

The Shore Patrol took Martin away, and she and Cam were alone in the hall. Molly kept her head bowed for at least three minutes until the black dots in front of her eyes disappeared. Slowly she lifted her head and looked up into Cam's grim features.

"I found my printout on the table and the flight program on the monitor, Cam. Somehow, Martin got my access code and retrieved the information." She pointed to the printout sheets scattered nearby. "He changed some of the numbers, Cam. They're circled in red. When I tried to take the evidence, he stopped me."

Cam shook his head. "He could have killed you, Molly." God, how courageous she'd been. He saw anger and stubbornness in her green-and-gold eyes.

"I wasn't about to let him foul up my flight plan again, Cam! I figured it out. He changed my other flight plan, too, and made me look bad. I got a poor grade on that test flight."

"Yes. And he was the one who brought up the fact to Vic that he should recheck your math figures on the printout," Cam muttered. "It all makes sense. That bastard!"

Pressing her fingers to the bridge of her nose to stop the bleeding, Molly started to feel giddy and happy. "That's why I had to keep that printout as evidence. I tried to get out the door, but Martin jumped me from behind." With a grimace, Molly added, "I'm afraid I'm not much of a fighter. I'm sure Dana or Maggie would have beat Martin at his own game. All I did was scratch, claw and scream."

Cam slid his arm around her shoulders. His voice was low with feeling. "Angel, you could have been killed. I don't know if Martin would have gone to that length, but it wasn't worth the risk. I need you alive. God, I was so scared when I came up here and saw you sitting there bleeding."

Molly whispered his name and threw her arms around Cam's shoulders. Reality was starting to impinge on her state of shock. She clung to him, her head nestled against his shoulder. Just the smell of Cam was like a perfume to her heightened senses. "Cam, just take me home. Stay with me tonight. I don't want to be alone. Please?"

His voice was gravelly with emotion. "I wish I could, but I've got the duty, angel." God, how Cam wanted to be with her, hold her and care for her! Right now, Molly needed him. Gripping her by the shoulders, he stared down into her traumatized features. "What I'll do is have Johnson drive you home after the doctor's seen you." His voice deepened. "I'm sure he's going to tell you to stay home and rest tomorrow. You can fly that spin test next week sometime. I'm sorry I can't be with you tonight, Molly. I want to be. . . . God, how I want that for both of us."

She tucked away her disappointment, realizing Cam was right. An SDO couldn't go off base for the night and return in the morning. No. Cam had responsibility for everything that happened on base for a twenty-four-hour period. He couldn't be with her, no matter how badly they both desired it. "I'm sorry. I should've remembered," she whispered unsteadily, her head beginning to ache in earnest.

Cam heard several men coming up the stairs. It had to be the medics that Johnson had allowed to enter the facility. "Can I take a rain check?" he asked. "Friday evening I'll come over. We need to talk, Molly, about a lot of things."

She nodded. "If you came over tonight, I don't think I'd be of much use to anyone. I feel awful, Cam."

He tenderly kissed her hair. "I know, angel. You took a lot of punishment from Martin. Here come the medics. They'll take you out on a gurney."

Molly started to protest. But, when she struggled to rise, Cam clamped his large hand on her shoulder and forced her to remain sitting. Used to taking care of herself all her life, Molly realized she'd forgotten what it was like to be cared for. Acquiescing, she allowed the medics to check her over and place her on the gurney. Once she lay down, Molly felt exhausted. It was as if the physical confrontation with Martin was the last straw. There was no more fight left in her.

Cam nervously fingered the huge bouquet of autumn flowers in his hands as he waited for Molly to answer the door to her apartment. The November wind cut through him, although he wore a leather bomber jacket with a white wool scarf around his neck. The door opened. Cam's heart thudded once to underscore how very much he needed to see Molly. She stood there smiling at him, dressed in an ivory crewneck sweater and a pair of pink cord slacks. His heart went out to her when he realized she was just as nervous, perhaps more so, than he was.

"Come in," Molly invited.

Cam inhaled. "You must have cooked me dinner." He grinned as he gave her the bouquet after she shut the door.

"I did. The flowers are just gorgeous! You didn't have to do this." Molly sniffed at the flowers' individual scents, loving Cam for his thoughtfulness.

Shrugging out of his jacket and scarf, Cam hung them up in the hall closet. He noticed a black-and-blue goose egg on Molly's forehead. Otherwise, she looked incredibly well. "You deserve a Purple Heart, not flowers," Cam teased, shutting the door and coming to join her. Nervously he put his hands in his pockets. "How are you feeling?"

"Like new." Molly reached up, slid her arm around his shoulder and pressed a kiss to his mouth. "Thank you." It had taken everything on her part to initiate the kiss that was begging to be shared between them. Before she could move away, Cam's hands came out of his pockets and captured her. The flowers were between them.

"Do you know how much you've changed?" Cam asked, holding her startled but pleased gaze. His body cried out to consummate the love he knew had grown and blossomed between them.

Molly relaxed in his embrace. "No. I feel the same old Molly."

He smiled and pushed back her blond bangs so he could inspect her goose egg more closely. "I wonder if, five months ago, you'd have fought back—or fought at all—for what was yours? Not that I condone you going after Martin." Cam frowned. "He confessed to everything today, Molly. Not only did he change figures on two of your flight programs, but he did it to another engineering student, too."

Cam's touch was fleeting, and Molly savored his closeness and care. "Not to mention the assault on me."

"He's up on charges for that, too." Cam allowed his fingers to drop away from her hairline and he tilted her chin. "How are the nose and mouth?"

"When I hit the floor I just jarred my whole head. My nose is fine, and I have a small cut inside the corner of my mouth. That's all."

"At first I thought you might have broken your nose or lost some teeth," Cam admitted. With the huge bouquet of flowers still between them, he knew it was useless to embrace her. Which was exactly what he wanted to do. Reluctantly, he released Molly and walked with her into the kitchen.

With a laugh, Molly placed the flowers on the drain board and hunted up a vase to place them in. "I've got a hard head, Cam, so no real damage was done. This will end Martin's career, won't it?"

Sitting down at the table, which was set with Oriental-designed plates rimmed in gold, and gold-colored flatware, he nodded. "He'll get court-martialed for this," he promised grimly.

Molly cut the stems of the bouquet of flowers one by one and placed them in a cobalt-blue vase. "I can't believe any pilot would do what he did. Doesn't say much for competitiveness, does it?"

"Martin went overboard." Cam watched Molly arrange the flowers, her every movement graceful and lovely to watch. "Did you call your father and tell him what happened?" he asked her finally.

"No." Molly put the vase at one end of the table, pleased with her artistry. "Why should I? He didn't care that I almost drowned in the Chesapeake after ejecting. Why would he care if I got into a brawl with a male pilot?"

Cam said nothing, but he saw the hurt in Molly's eyes. She poured them each a glass of white wine and placed a shrimp salad before him. She sat down at his elbow.

"You didn't have to make me dinner, you know," Cam said, enjoying each forkful of the tangy salad.

"I wanted to. It's so much fun watching you enjoy every bite. I've never met a man who loved his food as much as you do."

"It comes from seven years of being spoiled," Cam told her.

The reference to his past caused a twinge in Molly's heart. She kept her head bent and continued to eat.

Cam had seen her eyes grow dark. He placed his fork beside the emptied salad bowl. "What are your plans after you graduate? You know you have two weeks' leave coming after that, don't you?"

"First, I have to graduate, Cam. I've got another month to go."

"You're number four in the standings."

"That doesn't promise anything."

"I'm sure that once the commandant reviews your case and the fact that Martin altered your flight software figures, he'll probably reassess your grades upward."

"Do you really think so, Cam?" Molly felt a thread of hope. She saw him smile. It was a tender smile for her alone, and it made her feel wonderful.

"I'd put money on it. If he does, that'll cinch the number-three position for you. Then all you have to do is maintain your average this last month and you're home free."

Sitting back in the chair, Molly whispered, "Wouldn't that be wonderful?"

"You're going to graduate," Cam repeated. "What are you going to do with that two weeks' leave?"

"I hadn't thought about it," she admitted ruefully, getting up and taking the salad bowls back to the drain board. Pulling baked chicken with long-grain rice from the oven, she put it on a huge platter. "I've been living one day at a time, Cam, ever since I got to TPS."

"Look ahead. What will you do with it?"

Molly set the platter before him on the table. She brought the gently steamed broccoli over in another bowl and sat down again. "Why are you pushing me on this?"

Cam carved up the chicken and dished some onto her waiting plate. "Because I want to spend a week of it up in the Smoky Mountains hiking with you, that's why."

Molly stared at him.

"Okay?" Cam put chicken on his plate and spooned out some rice beside it. He glanced up at her, his heart beating hard in his chest. Would she turn him down? There was a look of surprise in her eyes. "Well?"

"I..."

"You don't want to?"

"No! I mean—no, it's not that," Molly said hastily, joy cascading through her along with confusion. "Tell me more about this week I'd be spending with you."

"I know a nice rustic resort up in the Smoky Mountains. You can rent a cabin by the day or week, and hike the Appalachian Trail. I thought it might give us the time we need to know each other better."

"Better?"

"Yeah, you know."

"No, I don't."

With a grimace, Cam put down his flatware and then picked up one of Molly's hands. "I feel we deserve the time to get to know each other, Molly, without the stresses of school. Ever since I met you, I've wanted to pursue a more serious relationship with you. Going to the cabin with me has no strings attached, no pressure and nothing expected from either one of us. I just want the time alone with you." *Because I love you, and I want to find out if you love me, too.* Cam searched her serious features.

Curling her fingers around his larger hand, Molly smiled shyly. "I'd like that, Cam."

"Yeah?"

"Yes."

"How much?"

She smiled. "A lot."

"What about the other week?"

With a sigh, she said, "I think it's time I faced my father and brother. If I graduate, I don't expect them to come down. But I want to go home and try to patch up things."

"Want company?"

Molly held his tender gaze. "Are you serious? You'd come with me?"

"I'll come if you want me to, angel."

Molly smiled uncertainly. "I'd like that. Although I'm not sure Father will be happy to see you."

"That's his problem." Cam released her hand, and suddenly his appetite returned with a vengeance. He dug hungrily into the food, asking, "What'd you make for dessert?"

With a shake of her head, Molly said, "Baked apples with vanilla sauce."

"God, I'm in heaven with an angel for a cook."

"And you're such a pushover, Cam Sinclair." Throughout the meal, Molly could barely think, only feel. A week with Cam alone! The thought was like lightning striking through her, filled with promise, with hope. If only she would graduate. If only...

Chapter Fifteen

"Moll, you look great!" Dana, who was also in a dark blue naval winter uniform, came over and hugged her. The graduation ceremony had just ended in the large auditorium on station and Molly, diploma in hand, had rejoined her friends. "Congratulations!" Dana said warmly.

"Thanks," Molly whispered, hugging her friend. Beside Dana was her fiancé, Lieutenant Griff Turcotte, who grinned and thrust out his hand.

"Whiting's loss was Patuxent's gain, Molly. Graduating number two in your class isn't bad."

Molly thanked him. It was obvious that Dana and Griff were very much in love. On Dana's left hand a beautiful diamond engagement ring sparkled. They had set their wedding date for Christmas Day—less than three weeks away.

The room rang with festivities all around. At least a hundred people, mostly relatives and friends of the students, had come to the graduation of the eight who had made it through the toughest school in the world. Molly tried to hide her disappointment that her father and brother weren't among the revelers. She had sent them an official invitation, but it had remained unanswered.

"I got great video of you!" Maggie called as she threaded her way through the packed crowd. "You looked awesome in your dress uniform taking that diploma, Molly."

As usual, Maggie's presence turned heads, and Molly smiled, loving her red-haired friend dearly. "Thanks for doing the honors," she said. She hugged Maggie, who had opted to show up in civilian clothes—a winter-white wool suit and green silk blouse—instead of wearing her uniform. With her red hair, Molly thought she looked like a beautiful Christmas gift. A number of single officers were eyeing Maggie, checking her out and obviously liking what they saw. Maggie, on the other hand, seemed completely oblivious to their interest and inspection.

Molly's attention was drawn to Cam, who, unlike Maggie, moved with the quiet of a cat, disturbing and disrupting no one. In Molly's eyes, Cam was devastatingly handsome in his dark blue dress uniform, with each brass button polished, the rows of ribbons on the left side of his chest colorful and the medals proudly displayed beneath them.

"That guy's a hunk," Maggie told her in a conspiratorial tone. "Is he Sinclair?"

"Yes," Molly breathed, wondering if Cam was going to remain at arm's length after graduation. Before, it had been necessary. Now formality, to a degree, could be dropped.

"Niiiice," Maggie purred. "Very nice. You've outdone yourself, Molly."

"Maggie! You never change, do you?"

Grinning impishly, Maggie shrugged. "Going into fighter-pilot training with an F-14 strapped to my you-know-what has only made me worse. Those jocks at Miramar are the worst caveman types I've ever run into. If I'm not in combat in the air with my jet, I'm in combat on the ground with them at the O club afterward. Talk about pitched battles... Whew!"

"You love it," Molly responded with a laugh. But her eyes and her heart were centered on Cam as he approached. To her surprise, Cam knew Griff Turcotte. They shook hands, warmth and camaraderie evident between them. It was a small world in naval aviation, Molly realized and it made her happy that Dana's husband-to-be knew Cam.

Cam shifted his attention to the women officers, shaking their hands in turn. Finally, he stood at Molly's side and smiled down at her.

"It's common for the family of each graduate to give them a graduation gift," he told all of them. Cam looked around at the small, tight group of Molly's friends. "And since your real family couldn't be here, I thought this gift would speak for all of us who are part of your extended family." Cam pulled a small box wrapped in gold foil and red ribbon out of his jacket pocket. He placed it in Molly's hand. "For you, angel," he whispered, holding her tear-filled gaze.

"Ahhh, Molly, you aren't gonna cry, are you?" Maggie teased, digging into her pocket for a tissue.

"Of course, she is," Dana said, already holding a tissue ready for Molly to use.

Sniffing, Molly smiled and wiped away her tears. Cam drew close, his arm around her waist, sensing that she needed his touch. "Thank you, Cam."

"Open it," he urged, lifting his head and smiling at the curious group. His heart pounded with nervousness and hope. Would Molly like his gift?

Opening the box, Molly discovered a pendant that had been fashioned into a small set of gold wings. At the center of it was a square-cut emerald. She looked up at Cam as she lovingly touched it with her fingertips.

"Cam," she breathed, "this is beautiful!"

He smiled down into her lustrous eyes. "It's the set of wings you deserve. The green and gold together remind me of the color of your eyes. When we're testing or flying, we can't wear any jewelry, but I thought they might let you get away with wearing this around your neck."

"It's beautiful," Dana said. "Exquisite, just like you, Moll."

Maggie craned her neck to get a look. "Check this out! Hey, your own set of wings, Molly. This pair's even prettier than the ones we got at Whiting."

Touched beyond words, Molly could only stare down at the special gift. "They look exactly like the pilot's wings you wear," she agreed softly.

"A smaller version," Cam said. "But no less important." He ached to take her into his arms and kiss her breathless. "Maybe you can wear this when we leave for the Smokies," he suggested.

Molly caught Maggie's flash of a knowing grin and she promptly blushed. Dana's smile told her she approved of the idea. It felt good to have her friends' support and understanding. Reaching out, Molly hugged each of them. "I'm just so lucky to have all of you," she sniffed. "Thanks for coming, for being here...." Even if her family had refused to come.

A light snow was falling silently in the blue-hazed Smoky Mountains when Molly and Cam arrived at their cabin. Long, thin gray branches of thousands of trees surrounded the secluded house. A stream gurgled nearby, a thin bit of ice coating its banks. Molly got out of the car, immersed in the sights, sounds and colors that surrounded them.

Cam smiled and began to unpack the car and take their luggage into the cabin while Molly stood like a child, mesmerized by the beauty of the setting. The air was crisp, but Cam didn't feel the chill. Instead, there was such a warmth bubbling within him that he doubted he'd be aware of much else. Darkness would fall in another hour.

Eventually Molly came and joined him inside the cabin. While he started a fire in the large stone fireplace, she busied herself with getting them dinner. A small kitchenette at the other end supplied the modern necessities for roughing it in style. The rest of the main room was furnished with antique maple and oak pieces, and huge, braided throw rugs decorated the polished cedar hardwood floor.

Sighing contentedly as she completed dinner preparations and stepped out of the kitchen area, Molly felt a peace she'd never known. Reflected firelight danced off the shiny floor. The rug in front of the hearth was a tanned sheepskin, the ivory wool beautiful against the reds and golds of the cedarwood surrounding it.

Cam came out of the bedroom. He'd changed into a pair of jeans, red chamois shirt and hiking boots. Molly stood in the center of the living room and watched him approach. There was a smoldering look in his blue eyes, a heat that made her wildly aware that she was a woman.

"You look like a woodland nymph," Cam teased, settling his hands on her shoulders. The wool sweater she wore, a floral crewneck with a delicate scrolled design and dusty-colored roses around the yoke, gave her a decidedly feminine look. The burgundy cord slacks enhanced her slender figure. He stroked her loose blond hair, glinting like spun gold in the firelight.

"I feel different," Molly admitted, resting her hands on his arms as he drew her against him. Their hips met and lightly touched.

"Different?"

"A good kind of different." Molly gazed around the quiet cabin, the only sound that of wood popping and spitting in the blazing hearth. "This is such a dichotomy. For six months I'm in a pressurized military atmosphere and then, suddenly, here I am in a lovely cabin miles away from everything and surrounded with such beauty that I feel as if I'm in a dream." She smiled and touched the pendant that rested against her throat. Since receiving the gift from Cam yesterday, Molly had refused to take it off.

"We are," Cam whispered. "Angels only appear in dreams, didn't you know that?" He didn't want to hurry Molly, or assume that she wanted what he wanted. Her eyes, however, mirrored his desire to kiss her. Cam obliged.

Molly sighed as Cam pulled her close. This was what she wanted, needed—him as a man and human being. Parting her lips, she wasn't disappointed, feeling the controlled strength and power of his mouth upon hers. It was such a tender, exploratory kiss. Molly felt the tension in Cam, and knew that he was keeping himself carefully controlled where she was concerned.

Cam had opened a bottle of champagne earlier and filled the two fluted glasses that sat on the pine coffee table near the couch. Now he led her over and handed her a glass. Touching the rim of his glass to hers, he said, "To a lady with real courage."

Molly smiled uncertainly, sipping the champagne but not really tasting it. The banked coals of yearning in Cam's eyes telegraphed his need of her, and she felt her body responding effortlessly. "And to the man who had the courage to help her get in touch with her own strengths and abilities."

Cam set his glass aside and gathered Molly's hands into his. "It was there all along, Molly. You just weren't aware of it."

"Cam, my strength didn't come out at Whiting."

"That's because I wasn't there."

Grinning, she leaned forward on impulse and kissed him. The words *I love you* were begging to be said to him. But did Cam really love her? Or was she simply a part of his healing journey from the past? Molly wasn't sure at all. It made each moment spent with Cam an exquisite torture, a sweet torment.

Startled by her unexpected kiss, Cam studied her in the gathering silence. His hands tightened around her slender ones. "We're good for each other," he admitted hoarsely.

"I know you're good for me," Molly whispered. "I can't see that I've done much for you except serve you some decent food."

A reckless grin shadowed Cam's mouth. "Guilty as charged, angel. You are a great cook—but you're important to me in so many other ways."

She lay back against the couch, facing him, her hands resting in his. "Tell me how, Cam, because I really don't realize what I do for you."

Cam looked at Molly, narrowing his eyes, then decided she meant what she said. She had slipped off her shoes and tucked her legs beneath her body in a typical Molly gesture. He held her worried gaze. Why was she anxious?

"When you first arrived at TPS, my heart started to feel again," he told her in a low voice. "As the months went by, I became aware that I was ready to start living again instead of living in a numb cocoon of grief, Molly." He hung his head, studying her slender fingers, thinking how delicate and yet how strong she really was. "You helped me work through that grief in your own way and helped me put the past behind me." Lifting his head, Cam studied her compassionate features. "I'll never forget my family. But now, I hold them in my heart as a wonderful memory. I don't wear them like a ball and chain anymore." He lifted her hand and kissed the back of it gently. "The past couple of months, I've been ready to live again.

"I was trapped, Molly. When I realized after that fight with your father that I loved you, it became a living hell to keep my real feelings to myself." He saw her eyes widen. There was such relief in her features when he admitted his love for her. "You were on a tightrope, trying to balance your new confidence against loss of your family support. If I'd admitted it to you then, you might not have fought to carve out life the way you needed it to be—on your own terms."

Cam managed a slight smile and gently cradled her cheek against his palm. "I had to stay in the background and let you fall, pick you up and keep on striving. Every time you fell, I ached for you. I wanted to take you into my arms and hold you, love you. I wanted to protect you...."

"If you had," Molly said in a scratchy voice, "I wouldn't have believed in myself."

"That's right, angel. It's easy to lean on someone and let them do part of your work."

"I'm glad you didn't let me."

"Molly, I love you too much to do that. But you needed to understand that I'd be there whether you were a success or a failure." He framed her face, holding her green and gold gaze. "Honey, what you needed to understand was that as long as you gave it your best shot, you couldn't fail. Even if you hadn't graduated from TPS, you still wouldn't have failed in my eyes. Do you understand that?"

She nodded. "I learned that from you, Cam. When you were there for me no matter how bad or how good it got, it sank in. I finally understood what you were trying to tell me."

Cam drew her forward. "By standing on your own, Molly, you've gained confidence. Anything life throws at you from now on won't be any easier, but you'll have new ways of coping." He brushed her waiting lips, a groan tearing from deep within him. Her lips were eager, hungrily kissing him in return. When Molly placed her hands on his shoulders and leaned into the circle of his arms, Cam felt complete.

"I love you," Molly quavered, sliding her hand up across his beard-roughened cheek. "I think I did from the day I met you."

Cam held her close, contentment flowing through him. "I know I fell head over heels for you, angel. Time's been on our side."

There was something wonderful about having waited, letting the anticipation build like a sweet, hot fire within her. Molly nodded. "I was so afraid you didn't love me. I thought I might be a part of your healing process, that's all."

Cam shook his head, cradling her against him and threading his fingers through her beautiful gold hair. "You healed me. But I don't love you out of gratefulness. I love you because of yourself. You."

His words shattered the last of Molly's fears. With a soft cry, she threw her arms around Cam's broad shoulders. "I want to love you so badly, Cam. Please?"

The dinner could wait. Cam kissed her cheek, her lips, and then her cheek again. "You never have to ask, Molly. You and I," he whispered, lifting her off the couch and into his arms, "are equals."

As Cam carried her toward the bedroom, Molly sighed. Darkness had fallen throughout the cabin. The night surrounded them. The flames in the fireplace created yellow, orange and red tongues of dancing light. Cam's arms felt strong and protective around Molly, and she rested her head against his neck and shoulder, content as never before. A fire more hungry and powerful than she'd ever known, burned deep within her.

Cam lowered her onto the thick goose-down comforter that lay across the brass bed, firelight from the living room flickering through the darkness, then lay down beside her. Molly reached up, beginning to unbutton his shirt. There was such adoration and need for her in his eyes that her fingers trembled with anticipation.

"I've never wanted anything more than I have you," she admitted. Cam's smile was very male and very sensual.

"You're my life, angel...."

Molly lay within the embrace of Cam's arms. They sat on the sheepskin rug in front of the fireplace, sipping hot mulled wine spiced with cinnamon and nutmeg. It was near midnight, and she was pleasantly tired. She wore a floor-length pale pink flannel gown, its neck and cuffs interlaced with ivory-colored satin ribbon. Cam sat behind her in a dark blue terry-cloth robe.

"This is heaven," Molly admitted, her eyes half-closed as she languished in the haven of his arms.

Leaning down, Cam kissed her mussed hair. "No. You are."

She smiled softly, her fingers around the ceramic mug, the tangy scent of the wine surrounding them. Outside, huge snowflakes fell lazily against the window. "Everything's perfect, darling."

Cam nodded, resting his jaw against her hair. Just holding her sweet, giving form made him acutely aware of how precious life was.

"What would you think about moving into my house with Miracle and me?" he asked her.

"I'd like that."

Cam roused himself and fitted Molly against his left shoulder so he could gaze down into her serene features. "First, you'd have to agree to marry me, though."

Molly sat up and put her mug to one side. "Are you serious?"

"I guess I'm kind of old-fashioned," Cam admitted, a slow smile stealing across his mouth. "The lady that

shares my bed, my home, should be my wife. What do
you think?''

Molly gasped, clasping her hands against her breast.
"Cam...I just didn't expect this.... I mean, this
soon...maybe never!"

He absorbed her childlike response and reveled in the
happiness he saw in her eyes. Reaching into the pocket of
his robe, he drew out a jeweler's box and opened it.
"Here, this is for you, angel."

Molly held the red satin box in her hands, staring down
at the sparkling row of diamonds set in a channel design
so the facets wouldn't catch on anything. "Ohhhh,
Cam..."

"Do you like it? It's a wedding ring. In our business,
jewelry isn't encouraged. But with the diamonds flush
with the surface of the ring, it will—"

With a cry, Molly threw her arms around Cam. "I love
it! I love you!" she sobbed. "It's beautiful, so beautiful!"

Laughing, Cam was thrown off balance as she flung
her arms about him. Taking her weight, he slowly eased
her down on top of him. "I love you, Molly Rutledge,"
he whispered fiercely. "Will you marry me?"

Molly felt hot tears and blinked them away. His
laughter-filled eyes were tender with love for her alone.
"How could I not marry you?"

"Got me. I'm a pretty good catch when I think about
it," he teased. "I pick up my socks and put them in the
clothes hamper. I'm responsible for doing dishes and
stuff like that. I'm prettily easily trained."

With a laugh, Molly hugged Cam fiercely. "I love you.
And more than anything, I want to be Mrs. Molly Rutledge Sinclair."

"You got a deal, honey," Cam said, and swept her into his arms, sealing their love with a hot, melting kiss that made the smoldering flames in the fireplace pale by comparison.

Breathless afterward, Molly suddenly became still. "What about my family, Cam?"

He sighed and kept her next to him, his arm a pillow for her head. "We were going to see them anyway. We'll break the news to them then. Okay?"

Chewing on her lower lip, Molly nodded. "What if Father doesn't want to see us?"

Grazing her flushed cheek with one finger, Cam replied, "I think he will, angel. Let's take it one step at a time. We've got a week here at the cabin alone. We'll fly into New York City and confront him after that."

Scott gave a cry of welcome when they came through the front door. Forgetting her fear and anxiety, Molly stepped around the butler and ran down the hall toward her brother. How much Scott had changed! Molly thought as she leaned over, embracing him. His hair was longer and he was growing a beard. A beard!

"It's so good to see you," Scott quavered, gripping her arms. "I've really missed you, Sis."

Molly sniffed and touched Scott's bearded cheek. "I love you so much, Scott. The last few months have been awful. Look at you!"

He grinned, leaning around Molly to see a man approaching in civilian clothes. "Wait till I tell you all that's happened. Who's this?"

Molly placed her hand on her brother's shoulder and turned. "This is my fiancé. Cam, I'd like you to meet my brother, Scott."

"Fiancé?" Scott crowed, thrusting out his hand. "Hey, nice to meet you, Cam. Are you the captain Father was talking about in such derogatory terms a few months ago?"

Cam smiled and shook Scott's long, thin hand. How much he looked like Molly. Both children obviously took after their deceased mother. "One and the same, Scott. Glad to finally meet you. Molly's told me a lot about you over the past six months. Looks like you're going hippie on us," he teased.

Molly stood aside, a fierce love for both men in her heart. Scott looked so much stronger and seemed to have some of his old confidence back. She was astounded by the change in him.

Scott ruefully touched his beard. "Yeah, I guess to a military man, anyone with a beard looks like a hippie."

"I like your beard," Molly remarked, looking down the hall. Was her father home? They'd called ahead to announce when they would arrive.

Scott gripped her hand. "Let me tell you the best news. I've got a job at a newspaper. I'm learning to be a reporter. It's a small newspaper, but at least I'm earning a paycheck."

"Wonderful! Why didn't you tell me about this venture?"

Flushing, Scott hung his head. "I was afraid of failing, Sis. I didn't want to get your hopes up and then screw it up."

Molly exchanged glances with Cam. The familiar failure theme that her father had hung over her head was also branded on Scott. She leaned down, catching his gaze. "I'm so proud of you. You did this on your own, didn't you?"

"Yeah . . . kind of. After Father disowned you and ordered me not to call you anymore, it turned my world upside down, Molly." Scott's eyes grew sad. "I began to realize what I'd done. I was living my life through you. I had no identity of my own. That first month was a living hell for me, Sis. Father was in a constant state of anger and I withdrew. Well, actually, I got out more on my own. I found a newspaper that hired handicapped people. My strong point has always been English, so I started as a proofreader for the paper. A month ago, the editor made me a junior reporter because of my writing skills."

"Something good did come out of all of this, then," Molly quavered. She felt Cam's hand come to rest on her shoulder. "I'm glad for you, Scott. So glad."

He smiled up at his sister. "The best is yet to come— I've just rented a small apartment in Greenwich Village and I'll be moving in there next week. I'm really on my own now, and it feels good, Molly. Really good."

Her pride in Scott's turnaround made it worth coming home, Molly thought. She felt Cam's arm go around her, and she leaned against him, grateful for his support. It was as if he understood how emotionally chaotic she felt at this moment.

"Is Father home?" she choked out.

Scott nodded. "Yeah, he's in his study, but he's not in a very good mood, Sis. Actually—" Scott laughed weakly "—Father's been in a foul humor since he disowned you."

"Let's go see him," Cam urged gently, realizing Molly needed to get the confrontation over with as soon as possible. She'd been a mass of nerves in anticipation of seeing her father as the days at the cabin drew to a close.

Cam had no desire to see her tortured any longer than necessary.

Scott turned around in his wheelchair. "Look, Sis, even if Father is stupid enough to have disowned you, I haven't."

She leaned down, kissing Scott's cheek. "I love you so much for saying that. Thank you."

"When's the big day? The wedding?"

"March twenty-first, on the spring solstice. I wanted it then because spring symbolizes new starts, seeds and growth. You'll come, won't you?"

"I'll be there with bells on, Sis."

Her courage soared with Scott's support. Patting his shoulder, Molly whispered, "Cam and I have to see Father."

"Go get 'em, tiger."

As Molly walked down the foyer toward the den at the other end, she was struck by the fact that there were no Christmas decorations up as was usual for this time of year. In the past, Molly had always come home for this special holiday. Peeking into the living room, she saw no tree or gifts. Cam's arm around her waist stabilized her anxiety as they approached the study.

Molly had always disliked the den because of its dark walnut-paneled walls. The huge room seemed gloomy and depressing, with its sparse light provided by a green lamp on the maple desk. The pungent smell of leather-bound books struck her nostrils as they approached the open door.

Halting at the entrance, Molly saw her father seated in a wing chair, legs crossed, book in hand. As usual, he wore an impeccably tailored suit. She suddenly wished she'd worn her uniform, but shook off the regret. Her cotton denim dress of pale pink with floral embroidery along its front placket and collar gave her a feminine appearance—certainly not a military look.

"Father?" Her voice quavered, and Molly cringed inwardly, knowing he'd take it as a sign of weakness. She and Cam halted at the desk, which separated them from the wing chair where he sat.

Jason looked up from his book. "Why is he here, Molly?"

She tensed at the sharpness in her father's voice. Alarmed at how gray and tired he looked, she cleared her throat and said, "Father, Cam's here because he's my fiancé. He asked me to marry him a week ago, and I've agreed. We plan to wed next March." She gave a little shrug. "We're both here because we want to be. It's been such a long time since I heard from you...and you weren't there when I graduated...."

Jason scowled and looked down at the book. "You made it perfectly clear that you no longer wanted me in your life, Molly. That's why I didn't attend your graduation."

Her heart hurt. Molly glanced at Cam, whose face was grim. She realized how much he was struggling to remain silent. This was her battle, not his. "I'm not going to throw blame, Father. I can only speak for my feelings...for me. I didn't disown *you*. I've always loved you and I wanted you at my graduation. Did you know I was second in the class, with an eighty-eight percent?"

Jason shook his head and refused to look up from the book that remained open in his hands. It was a volume of Tolstoy. "At least you didn't fail again."

Cam took a step forward, his fists clenched, but stopped when he saw Molly's desperate, pleading look. Damn the man! He was playing on Molly's olive branch and attacking her again, too. The callous bastard.

Gripping Cam's arm momentarily, Molly shook her head. She refocused her attention on her father. "I want us to be a family again, Father. But not at a cost to me."

His head snapping up, Jason looked at her steadily. "What are you talking about, Molly?"

"Father, you're going to have to accept me as I am, not as what you wish me to be or need me to be. These past six months I've gotten in touch with who I really am." She managed a slight smile. "How can I apologize for that? I know I haven't met your expectations, but can't you love me anyway? Before Mom died, I remember how you used to hug and kiss Scott and me. After she died, you retreated. I felt so alone and deserted. I still do. With Cam and I getting married, we want to have a family. I'd like to share our children with you, with Scott. I want our children to have a grandfather and an uncle. Don't you?"

Rutledge slammed the book shut and rose. He glared over at Cam and then at her. "Now you're blaming me for everything! Well, let me tell you something, young lady. When your mother died, I died! No, I didn't feel like loving you or Scott after her death. How could I?" he demanded hoarsely, striking his chest. "I loved her! And she was gone. Gone! She was my life! But you don't understand that, do you, Molly? You're so wrapped up in your own selfish needs, you never saw what I went through after her death, dammit!"

"Rutledge," Cam snarled, coming around the desk and halting a foot away from him, "you're way out of line."

"Like hell I am! Now, you get out of here! It's your fault Molly's the way she's become! The first time I saw you, I knew you were after her."

Nostrils flaring, Cam jabbed his finger into Rutledge's chest. "Shut up, Rutledge. Shut up and listen to me," he rasped savagely in his face. "Don't stand there whining about what it's like to lose someone you love. I lost my wife, who I loved with my life, in an airline crash. Not only that, I lost my five-year-old son on that same flight. Don't stand there playing 'Poor me!' with Molly when I *know* what it's like to lose. Sure, you hurt after your wife died. So did I! I was married to Jeanne for seven of the most wonderful years of my life. It hurt like hell when she and my son were torn from me.

"Don't make Molly feel guilty for saying she needed your love, your touch, after your wife died. She was only ten years old, for God's sake! She lost her mother, in case you forgot. I know how easy it is to crawl inside a hole and shut the world away when you're in pain. But unlike you, I didn't feel sorry for myself, and I sure as hell didn't blame others for my misfortune, my loss. You aren't going to make Molly take the responsibility for this one. Quit feeling sorry for yourself!''

Molly stood there, thunderstruck. Cam's voice was low and off-key with such emotion that tears drove into her eyes. Her father winced visibly as each word hurled at him by Cam landed with unrelenting impact. He paled, and Molly saw tears in her father's eyes.

Breathing hard, Cam took a step away. "Now, we came here in hopes of healing past wounds. I don't give a damn what you think about me, but she's your daughter!" he rasped. "If you don't want to get out of that feeling-sorry-for-yourself mode, if you want to stay in it for the rest of your life and miss the happiness that Molly and Scott can give you, then that's your choice. And if you don't want to be a grandparent, if you don't want to hold your grandchildren in your arms, that's your choice, too. Molly and I love each other. We're happy, and we know we can make this marriage work. We came here today to share our happiness with you. But if you don't want it, that's fine with me."

Shakily, Rutledge touched his perspiring brow. He glanced uncertainly toward Molly. "You never told me..."

Her voice strained, Molly asked softly, "What, Father? What didn't I tell you?"

"About him," he said, meaning Cam.

Helplessly, Molly stood there in the thickening silence. Cam's face was tight with fury and emotion. Her father looked wan and stressed. "Well, I wanted to, but you refused to answer my calls, Father."

Jason ventured a look over at Cam. "I didn't know.... I'm sorry."

Cam shook his head. "I didn't tell you about my losses to make you apologize, Mr. Rutledge. I just wanted you to understand that there is life after losing someone you love that much. I never thought I'd love again, or at least, not as deeply as before, but I do." Cam's gaze went to Molly and his voice grew raspy. "Your daughter is something else, Mr. Rutledge. She taught me that there was light at the end of that god-awful tunnel I was walking through alone. She gave me her care, her compassion and understanding without one thought of receiving anything in return. I began to understand how special Molly was, then. I fell in love with her goodness, her courage to be herself no matter how bad things around her got. She taught me to live again, and I love her more than life itself."

Molly slowly moved round the desk and slipped her arms around her father's waist. She laid her head on his chest. "I love you, Father. I'm sorry, I didn't realize how much you missed Mom." Her eyes blurred with tears as she felt his arms go around her. "I miss her, too, even now...."

The first sob escaped Jason. He buried his head against his daughter's hair, holding her tightly. "I—I'm sorry, Molly. So sorry... God, all these years, how we've all suffered...." And his words dissolved into sounds of weeping.

Cam quietly left the den and shut the door. Daughter and father needed to be left alone, left to help heal each other's terrible wounds. Cam stood outside the heavy walnut door, a strong feeling of hope moving through him. Thanks to Molly's forgiving heart, she'd be able to help her father heal from the past. Cam loved her fiercely—and would forever.

Epilogue

Two years later
USNAS Miramar, San Diego, California

Molly dusted off her hands. Around her were the unopened boxes that had been delivered earlier in the day by the moving van. Their new apartment in Poway, California, would be close to Naval Air Station Miramar, home of Fightertown, U.S.A., and the Top Gun training-program facility. Cam had just been ordered on board a carrier based out of San Diego. He was going back into an F-14 Tomcat fighter squadron for the next two years. She stood in the sunny living room, wearing a pair of well-worn jeans and a loose cotton top, surveying the mess.

Cam appeared at the screen door dressed in his tan summer uniform. He walked in and smiled. "Looks like a tornado hit."

Molly smiled wearily in return and wiped her brow with the back of her hand. After two years of marriage,

Cam still looked as handsome as ever, she thought. "It did. I didn't realize how many boxes we had. I don't know how they're all going to fit into this apartment, Cam."

Hearing the lament in his wife's voice, Cam threaded his way through the boxes to her side. He leaned down, placing a long, welcoming kiss upon her lips. "I love you," he whispered, holding her against him, rocking her gently back and forth in his arms. "How do you feel?"

"Sick as a dog. Nobody said pregnancy was fun, Sinclair."

"Do you regret it?"

Molly looked up into his concerned blue eyes. "How could I? This baby was made out of the love we have for each other. I'll suffer grandly in silence."

Cam smiled gently and pushed several strands of her blond hair away from her damp, flushed cheek. "I hate having to leave you here alone, angel."

She shrugged. "Duty calls, doesn't it? The Navy sends you out on Far East carrier duty and me here to Miramar to work with the Top Guns."

The unhappiness in her voice tore at Cam. Molly was four months pregnant, and he was going on a cruise that would last five months. According to the Navy, the carrier wouldn't be pulling back into port until two weeks after the baby was due. "I wish I could be here when she's born," he whispered thickly. "God, how I wish."

Molly held Cam tightly, burying her face in his shirtfront. Cam hadn't been there when his son, Sean, had been born. In fact, having been stuck on carrier duty in the Mediterranean, he hadn't even gotten to hold Sean for four months. "We've exhausted all means of trying to persuade the Navy to release you from duty a month early to come home," she said, her voice muffled.

"Sometimes," Cam gritted out, kissing her hair, "I hate the military. This is one of those times. I don't want you alone here, having our baby."

Molly smiled gently and eased away from him enough to meet his worried gaze. "Darling, Maggie and Dana are stationed at Miramar. At least my best friends will be with me. They're as excited as I am. We're a sisterhood. We'll take my pregnancy and the birth in stride." She touched his cheek. "At least Griff Turcotte will be with you. You'll be in the same fighter squadron."

"Yeah," Cam griped unhappily. "Misery loves company."

With a laugh, Molly agreed. "You two can sit out there on the carrier thinking about the wives back here who love you."

He sighed, genuinely worried. Since she had gotten pregnant, Molly had turned fragile, her skin translucent and her health more delicate. "Damn the Navy!" he whispered.

"You mean," Molly teased, wanting to pull him out of his worry for her, "you love me more than you love that lady you fly?"

He grinned and released her. "I love you a hell of a lot more than that Tomcat I'm flying." Catching her before she walked away, Cam sat down on one of the boxes and guided Molly to his lap. She wrapped her arm around his shoulders and leaned against him. He steadied her with an arm around her waist, his other hand resting against her now swelling abdomen. "Can you feel her kick yet?"

Molly shook her head. "The doctor said in about three more weeks, I'll start to feel her move." She covered his hand on her belly. "I can hardly wait, Cam. I'm so excited." Molly pressed a kiss to his brow. "So happy."

Cam murmured her name and simply held her, enjoying the few minutes of quiet. He felt better knowing that both Maggie and Dana would be here to support and help her. A year ago Dana had gone from instructing at Pensacola into a new program where women were being taught to be combat fighter pilots. A year before that, Maggie Donovan had already paved the way for the initial trial program, becoming a full-fledged fighter pilot at Miramar. She now trained Top Gun candidates and was making quite a name for herself as a skilled pilot.

"I got a call from Father this morning," Molly said, sliding her hand across Cam's chest, loving the feel of his muscles tensing beneath her fingertips.

"Oh?"

"He knows I've got to work at Miramar, but he's going to take two weeks off and come out after you leave for duty—just to make sure I'm okay." She laughed gently.

Cam smiled, hugging her and running his hand gently across her belly. "He's made a real turnaround. Now he's the doting grandfather-to-be. I think Jason's worse than I am in the worry department."

Chuckling, Molly hugged Cam fiercely and placed a hot, longing kiss on his strong, male mouth. "You're the worrywart, Cameron Sinclair. I swear you've turned into one since you found out I was pregnant." Lovingly, Molly caressed his cheek. "But I know why, and I understand. Don't worry. I want your focus, your attention on those cat shots and landings on the carrier. If anything, I should be worried about you *more!*"

Carrier duty was always dangerous, and Molly knew it as well as every other Navy-pilot wife. "All I want you to do," Cam told her, "is stay on the ground, work with the instructors at Top Gun and get plenty of rest. No flying for you. No late nights. No worrying about me. That's an order, Lieutenant. Understand?''

Molly gave him a mock salute and laughed. "Yes, sir, Lieutenant Commander Sinclair. Over and out." She slipped off his lap. "Come on, I've got to get supper on or you'll starve to death."

Cam nodded and followed her to the kitchen. Here, most of the boxes were gone and there was a semblance of order. Molly never ceased to amaze him. She'd been happy with her work as a flight-test engineer for two years at Patuxent River. And when she got transferred to Miramar for ground duty as an instructor at Top Gun, she was very pleased. As he sat down at the table after pouring himself a cup of coffee, a fierce love for her welled up in him. "Which do you like more? Having a career or being a wife and mother-to-be?" he asked.

Molly smiled and put the pot roast into a large pan. "Now, if you asked Maggie that, she'd rip your head off and accuse you of being a male chauvinist."

"But you aren't Maggie."

"No." Molly blew a few strands of hair out of her eyes. "I like both."

"What about Dana?"

Smiling, Molly said, "I think she's beginning to really enjoy being domesticated. At least she's turning into a decent cook. As I've told you, when we went through Annapolis together, she couldn't even boil water."

Cam sipped the coffee, his gaze lingering on Molly's slightly curved belly. How he wished he could be here to watch her belly grow large with their daughter. Ultrasound last month had confirmed it was a girl, and Cam couldn't be happier. "I think," he murmured, "that after little Rachel Anne Sinclair is born, you'll take to motherhood like a fish to water."

Cutting up the potatoes and placing them around the roast, Molly laughed. "Of the three of us, I'm by far the most domestic."

Cam knew that Molly had to finish out her six-year obligation to the Navy, children or not. She had four years to go, and he worried that her need to be with her daughter would be stronger than the call of her career. Then he caught himself and laughed. God, he worried a lot about unnecessary things.

"What's so funny?" Molly asked, placing the roast in the oven. She dried her hands on a towel and came around behind his chair. Placing her arms around Cam's shoulders, she rested her head against his.

Cam sat back, relishing Molly's easy ability to share her love with him. He wrapped his hands around her slender arms and sank against her. "Just laughing at my 'worrywartitis.'"

She kissed his neck. "It's justified. You lost your last family. Old feelings of fear of losing us have got to be bothering you, Cam."

As always, Cam was amazed at Molly's perceptiveness. "Yeah," he admitted thickly. "That's it."

"We'll both be here in the pink of health when you sail into San Diego Bay five months from now, darling. That's a promise."

With a sigh, Cam nodded. "I love you so damn much, Molly. And Rachel... God, I want to see her face. I want to hold her already. I don't even mind the late nights and early-morning feedings. I'm looking forward to all of those things. You two mean the world to me."

Pain for Cam's fears touched Molly deeply. She kissed his cheek this time. "We'll be here when you get back, jet jock. That's a promise."

Cam's hands tightened around her arms. Molly was strong in emotional ways that he never could be. As she nuzzled him, her lips searching for and finding his mouth, Cam brought her around the chair and into his lap. The afternoon was hot, the sunlight streaming brightly through the kitchen window. Outside, he could hear the jets taking off from nearby Miramar. All those sounds impinged very little on his heightened senses as Molly kissed him deeply, erasing his worries. Her love, Cam realized dimly as he hungrily returned her need of him, was strong enough for both of them. And always would be.

*　*　*　*　*

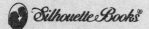

presents

SONNY'S GIRLS

by Emilie Richards, Celeste Hamilton
and Erica Spindler

They had been Sonny's girls, irresistibly drawn to the charismatic high school football hero. Ten years later, none could forget the night that changed their lives forever.

In July—
ALL THOSE YEARS AGO by Emilie Richards (SSE #684)
Meredith Robbins had left town in shame. Could she ever banish the past and reach for love again?

In August—
DON'T LOOK BACK by Celeste Hamilton (SSE #690)
Cyndi Saint was Sonny's steady. Ten years later, she remembered only his hurtful parting words....

In September—
LONGER THAN... by Erica Spindler (SSE #696)
Bubbly Jennifer Joyce was everybody's friend. But nobody knew the secret longings she felt for bad boy Ryder Hayes....

SSESG-1

Silhouette Books®

**SILHOUETTE BOOKS ARE NOW
AVAILABLE IN STORES AT THESE
CONVENIENT TIMES EACH MONTH***

Silhouette Desire and Silhouette Romance

> May titles: April 10
> June titles: May 8
> July titles: June 5
> August titles: July 10

*Silhouette Intimate Moments and Silhouette
Special Edition*

> May titles: April 24
> June titles: May 22
> July titles: June 19
> August titles: July 24

We hope this new schedule is convenient for you.
With only two trips each month to your local
bookseller, you will always be sure not to miss any
of your favorite authors!

Happy reading!

Please note: There may be slight variations in on-sale
dates in your area due to differences in shipping and
handling.

Take 4 bestselling love stories FREE

Plus get a FREE surprise gift!

Special Limited-time Offer

Mail to
Silhouette Reader Service™
3010 Walden Avenue
P.O. Box 1867
Buffalo, N.Y. 14269-1867

YES! Please send me 4 free Silhouette Special Edition™ novels and my free surprise gift. Then send me 6 brand-new novels every month, which I will receive months before they appear in bookstores. Bill me at the low price of $2.92 each—a savings of 33¢ apiece off cover prices. There are no shipping, handling or other hidden costs. I understand that accepting the books and gift places me under no obligation ever to buy any books. I can always return a shipment and cancel at any time. Even if I never buy another book from Silhouette, the 4 free books and the surprise gift are mine to keep forever.

235 BPA AC7Q

Name	(PLEASE PRINT)	
Address		Apt. No.
City	State	Zip

This offer is limited to one order per household and not valid to present Silhouette Special Edition® subscribers. Terms and prices are subject to change. Sales tax applicable in N.Y.

SPED-BPA2DR   © 1990 Harlequin Enterprises Limited

Silhouette Special Edition

proudly hails

WOMEN OF GLORY

from Lindsay McKenna

Soar with Dana Coulter, Molly Rutledge and Maggie Donovan—
Lindsay McKenna's WOMEN OF GLORY. On land, sea or air, these
three Annapolis grads challenge danger head-on, risking life and limb
for the glory of their country—and for the men they love!

May: NO QUARTER GIVEN (SE #667) Dana Coulter is on the brink
of achieving her lifelong dream of flying—and of meeting the man who
would love to take her to new heights!

June: THE GAUNTLET (SE #673) Molly Rutledge is determined
to excel on her own merit, but Captain Cameron Sinclair is equally
determined to take gentle Molly under his wing....

July: UNDER FIRE (SE #679) Indomitable Maggie never thought
her career—or her heart—would come under fire. But all that changes
when she teams up with Lieutenant Wes Bishop!